The
Dead
and the
Beautiful

Books by Cheryl Crane

THE BAD ALWAYS DIE TWICE

IMITATION OF DEATH

THE DEAD AND THE BEAUTIFUL

Published by Kensington Publishing Corporation

The Dead and the Beautiful

CHERYL CRANE

KENSINGTON BOOKS
http://www.kensingtonbooks.com

KENSINGTON BOOKS are published by

Kensington Publishing Corp.
119 West 40th Street
New York, NY 10018

All Kensington titles, imprints and distributed lines are available at special quantity discounts for bulk purchases for sales promotion, premiums, fund-raising, educational or institutional use.

Special book excerpts or customized printings can also be created to fit specific needs. For details, write or phone the office of the Kensington Special Sales Manager, Attn.: Special Sales Department, Kensington Publishing Corp., 119 West 40th Street, New York, NY 10018. Phone: 1-800-221-2647.

Kensington and the K logo Reg. U.S. Pat. & TM Off.

Library of Congress Card Catalogue Number: 2013940648

ISBN-13: 978-0-7582-5890-8
ISBN-10: 0-7582-5890-9
First Kensington Hardcover Edition: September 2013

eISBN-13: 978-0-7582-9146-2
eISBN-10: 0-7582-9146-9
First Kensington Electronic Edition: September 2013

10 9 8 7 6 5 4 3 2 1

Printed in the United States of America

To JLR

"Can't take my eyes off of you, you're just too good to be true"

Chapter 1

"I swear on my great-grandfather Geronimo's soul," Marshall Thunder, voted Sexiest Man Alive by *People* magazine, vowed. He held his hand up in some sort of Boy Scouts' honor gesture.

Nikki chuckled as she approached the gaggle of women who surrounded the blockbuster movie star under one of the large white tents on the Beverly Hills lawn. He was wearing a black Louis Vuitton tux. Victoria Bordeaux's fall garden party, in her backyard on Roxbury Drive, was *not* a casual affair.

Garden party. It was a deceiving misnomer, as far as Nikki was concerned. A person ought to be able to wear shorts and a cute tank top to a *garden party.* Instead, Marshall was wearing a tux and she was in a vintage floor-length Jacques Tiffeau silver-metallic gown.

"Don't listen to a word he says," Nikki said as she caught Marshall's twinkling eye. "He's the biggest gossip I know and you can't trust his sources."

He only got better looking with age; he was a six-foot-two Native American with hunky muscles and a face so handsome he could make women swoon. He *did* make women swoon. And a number of men.

"Geronimo was Apache," Nikki continued. "Marshall is full-blooded Iroquois."

Instead of defending himself, or disputing the facts, Marshall just laughed and raised his crystal Baccarat champagne flute to her. "One of our gorgeous hostesses and my BFF, ladies. Does everyone know Nikki Harper?"

The young women who surrounded him, all gorgeous blondes, greeted her.

Nikki smiled *the smile,* the one ingrained in her since childhood. "Mother's so pleased you could all come," she said through *the smile.* It wasn't fake, just . . . well rehearsed. Victoria, who had been a silver-screen star for four decades before her retirement from film, had always insisted on perfect manners from her children and her staff. Even at forty-one, Nikki felt as if she was still, sometimes, under her mother's thumb, particularly in situations like this. She was not an A-list party kind of girl and never felt quite in her element at these kinds of gatherings, even though she'd been attending them since she was a toddler.

But a girl did what a girl had to do. For her mother. And for her livelihood. Nikki was in the business of selling multimillion-dollar mansions in Beverly Hills. And to do so successfully, she needed wealthy clients, both buyers and sellers. So here she was, mingling, smiling, and *making contacts,* while at the same time trying to make certain all of her mother's guests were made to feel welcome.

Which reminded Nikki why she'd come in search of Marshall in the first place. "Marshall, you know Jeremy's sister, Alison?" She glanced at her side to find her companion gone.

She'd been there just a second ago. . . .

Nikki turned to see Alison standing a couple of feet behind her, red-faced, obviously thrilled and embarrassed at the same time to even lay eyes on *the* Marshall Thunder. Nikki wondered if *speaking* to him might put Alison over the edge. Marshall had fans who became hysterical at the sight of him, mostly from the ropes at red carpet affairs. She hoped her boyfriend's sister wouldn't be one of *those* women. Nikki didn't have time to tend to fainting women; Ashton Kutcher had hollered to her across a champagne fountain that he needed her advice on a piece of property going up for sale in Malibu.

"Alison," Nikki whispered, gesturing impatiently that she should step forward. *The smile* reappeared. "This is my dear friend Marshall. I know you've heard me talk about him."

"Is there anyone who doesn't recognize Marshall Thunder?" a honey blonde with hair extensions and serious breast enhancement gushed. There was an echo of feminine giggles.

Alison took a hesitant step forward, brown-eyed gaze downcast. She was wearing a beige handkerchief dress that neither fit nor was flattering. Nikki couldn't imagine anyone who could look good in the flimsy, shapeless, colorless sheath, and felt badly that she hadn't offered to help Alison shop before the party. "This is Alison Sahira, Jeremy Fitzpatrick's sister," Nikki introduced, hoping that Jeremy's name might win Alison a place among the women, at least for a few minutes. Nikki had several people she needed to say hello to, and then there was Ashton.

Nikki flashed Marshall a look that said, *Take her. Please.*

He arched a dark eyebrow. It was a gesture *so* overused, and yet he was so good-looking, it worked for him.

"Alison has a new business. 90210 Dog Walking. I won't say who she's working for"—Nikki looked one way and then the other, as if to be certain no one was listening—"but I understand that one of her clients made quite a hit last season in a hot tub scene on *Casa Capri*," she said in a stage whisper.

Marshall's dark eyes got big and his hand shot out to catch Alison's. "Darling, let me get you some champagne." He drew her closer. "You're working for Diara Elliot?"

Obviously a friend of Marshall's was a friend of theirs and the women gathered around Alison.

Alison glanced at Nikki uneasily, then back at Marshall. Like everyone else who worked in Beverly Hills, Alison was concerned about client confidentiality, but Nikki could tell by the look on her face that she'd give up national security secrets to Marshall if he asked. "I . . . I don't think it's a secret. I walk Mr. Melton's dog, so I guess, *technically,* I work for *him.*"

"So you see them all the time." Marshall's eyes danced. "Tell the truth. Out every night partying? Crazy fights? Cops at five in the morning?"

"No, no, nothing like that." She blinked. "A-Actually, they're a pretty quiet couple. Just regular people. Mostly they stay in, that or have dinner at home with their friends."

"Borrring," Marshall groaned, making an exaggerated face. "So whom else do you work for? Tell us something juicy!"

Nikki met Marshall's gaze over Alison's shoulder. *Thank you,* she mouthed.

He grinned and returned his attention to Alison, eager for any gossip that he could pry out of her. Marshall was a gossipmonger. He loved all of the tabloid magazines, fanzines, and nightly entertainment shows on TV, even if it was about him. But he loved firsthand gossip best.

Nikki moved on. She had no doubt Marshall would entertain Alison for a while and when he was ready to pass her on to another guest, he'd do it with such aplomb that she would feel as if she were their guest of honor, instead of the hostess's daughter's boyfriend's sister.

Nikki grabbed a French canapé as a tuxedoed waiter walked by and she popped it in her mouth. It was a delicious tidbit of toasted sourdough bread, sockeye salmon, and a paper-thin slice of lemon. Scrumptious. She eyed the waiter as he made his escape and calculated when she could intercept him again. It was five-thirty in the afternoon and the only thing she'd eaten that day were a few grapes she'd stolen off a caterer's tray, midmorning.

Licking her fingertips, Nikki glanced around. She thought she'd heard someone call her name, but the pool area and grassy lawn, with its monstrous white tents, bubbling fountains, and twinkling lights, was so loud she could barely hear herself think. Everyone who was anyone in Hollywood was at Victoria Bordeaux's party this afternoon, and it sounded as if they were all talking at once. They were so loud that the big band music coming from near the west gate could barely be heard.

"Nikki!"

She spotted her dear friend, Ellen Mar, through a wave of tuxedos and grass-length gowns. Ellen was standing with a good-looking guy Nikki vaguely recognized but couldn't place.

Ellen was making quite a stir on The Food Network. As a new chef on the cooking network, she was already one of their most popular, doing a crazy show where she made one kind of food look like another, like roasted turnips that looked like miniature lemon meringue pies or cream puffs disguised as turkey sandwiches.

"Ellen." They kissed cheeks for real—no air-kissing for them.

"Nikki." Ellen was a drop-dead gorgeous biracial woman with mesmerizing blue eyes. And she was wearing a remarkable Tom Ford gown. "Do you know Ryan Melton?"

Aha, Ryan Melton. Now she recognized him. He was shorter than Nikki (six foot in her measly two-inch heels—she was a wimp when it came to heels, especially in grass) but very good-looking in a bad-boy kind of way. He reminded her of Ryan O'Neal from his *Love Story* days. He had blond hair that was a little too long; he was wearing Gucci sunglasses and a hip, two-toned black Ralph Lauren tuxedo. "It's so nice to meet you, Ryan," she said politely, offering her hand and *the smile*.

She *did* know him, but not personally, only *of* him, from the cover of *Variety* magazine. And *People* magazine. And *Men's Health* . . . and the list went on.

Nikki dug into the cobwebs of her mind and tried to pull up what real info she had on Ryan Melton. He had been a nobody who had become somebody. He was the arm candy husband of TV star Diara Elliot, who was playing a role on the wildly popular TV drama *Casa Capri*, Victoria's new TV drama. Hence his coveted invitation to her mother's party. He'd never have rated an invitation on his own. *Mother* didn't recognize his form of celebrity. Ryan had tried some modeling; he was too short. He'd tried some acting; he couldn't. He'd opened a restaurant; it had failed. Mostly, it seemed, he was good at being the trophy husband of a famous actress. But he *was* cute.

"Nice to meet you, Nikki." He held her hand a beat too long before releasing it. She could tell he was one of those guys who got along on his looks. There were plenty of them in L.A.

"Your mother has a gorgeous place," he went on. "We're over on Mulholland, but Diara and I have been talking about looking at a bigger place. I don't suppose your mother would consider selling? I'd love a Roxbury Drive address. Very classy."

"I'm afraid this house isn't for sale." She glanced up at the two-story Paul Williams Georgian. Victoria wouldn't leave here until the EMTs carried her out on a stretcher. She returned her attention to her guest. "Houses go pretty quickly on Roxbury's 1000 block, but if you want to give me a call sometime, we can have a look. I'm with Windsor Real Estate."

"I know." He gave what she suspected was his version of *the smile.* Acquired much later in life than Nikki's, she could tell.

His wife of four or five years, Diara Elliot, had become

a household name ten years ago, when she was a teenager and working for Disney Studios. Diara, Kameryn Lowe, Julian Munro, and Angel Gomez, called the Disney Fab Four, had been America's darlings in a sweet sitcom set in a private school . . . somewhere. Nikki had never seen the show, but she knew, from flipping through the channels, that it was still popular, even though the last original episode had aired five or six years ago.

Nikki knew all about syndication. It had paid for her boyfriend Jeremy Fitzpatrick's college and dental school, and would put his children through college, and his grandchildren as well. Jeremy had been a child star, then a teen idol, before leaving the footlights of L.A. for a normal college life on the East Coast. Only now he was back, his wife was dead of cancer, and she and Jeremy . . . It was complicated, but what relationship wasn't?

Nikki made herself refocus on Ryan. He'd said something to her and she'd missed it. Her right heel was killing her. She rarely bought uncomfortable shoes, but the 1960s peep toes she found in a vintage clothing shop on Santa Monica had been too amazing to turn down. And too cheap. Her frugality came from her mother. She smiled at Ryan.

Fortunately, he went right on talking. "I can introduce you, if you like," he said.

While trying to stand on her left foot and rub the right heel inconspicuously under her gown, Nikki glanced in the direction Ryan and Ellen were looking.

If there was a designated *beautiful people* area at the party, Ryan's wife and friends were standing in it. Or maybe it just followed them from place to place.

Ryan's wife was tall and blonde. Of course she was; Hollywood was blonde. And tall. And thin. The young stars, and their spouses, were all gorgeous with toned, spray-tanned bodies draped in designer gowns and tuxes.

They had their heads together in an obviously serious discussion. They were probably deciding what nightclub they'd go to tonight, after the party.

"Diara," Ryan called. "Come say hi," he said to Nikki and walked away. Leaving her no other option except to follow.

"I'll catch you later," Ellen called, going in the opposite direction.

"I want you to meet Nikki Harper." Ryan pressed his hand to the small of his wife's back. Diara was pretty; she reminded Nikki of a taller version of Scarlett Johansson.

Diara slipped something into her handbag, a cute little silver Badgley Mischka that hung from the crook of her elbow. She offered her hand. "It's so nice to meet you, Nikki. Your mother talks about you on the set all the time."

Nikki wasn't entirely sure she was being genuine. Her mother hadn't had much to say, good or bad, about Diara. The twenty-six-year-old blonde was too inconsequential a person for Victoria to have an opinion on. Everyone knew the term *new money*. In Victoria's eyes, Diara and her friends were *new talent*.

"Nice to meet you." Nikki shook Diara's hand.

Ryan introduced Nikki to the other three of the Disney Fab Four and their spouses. They all shook hands, exchanged greetings. Her first impression was that everyone in the group was pleasant and . . . very young. Two other things stood out. Julian Munro's wife, Hazel, had red hair that was almost exactly the same shade of red as Nikki's own. Victoria called it strawberry blonde. Nikki also noticed that Kameryn Lowe's husband, Gil, looked so much like star Angel Gomez that they could have been brothers.

"Oh, gosh, Nikki, your hair is gorgeous," Hazel gushed. "Who's your colorist? Please don't tell me it's Eduardo at Christophe's! I'll kill him. I just went with this shade." She stroked her shoulder-length bob. "He said it would look gorgeous on me. Don't tell me it was what he had left in the bottle after your appointment."

Nikki laughed. She liked Hazel at once; she was polished and plucked, but she stood out in the group. Maybe because she was the only woman in the Fab Four faction who *wasn't* a blonde.

"No need to harm Eduardo. This is my natural color." She ran her hand over her hair, pulled back in a simple, sleek ponytail. She'd glammed it up with a 1920s rhinestone Art Deco brooch to cover the elastic hair tie.

"Your *natural* color? You've got to be kidding me." Hazel looped her arm through Betsy's. "Can you believe that's Nikki's natural color?"

Betsy was holding on to an emerald green fox fur Sang A handbag as if she was afraid Nikki was going to grab it and run. Which was not likely. It was one of the uglier designer bags Nikki had spotted that day. And there were some *seriously* ugly, *seriously* expensive bags wandering around. The thing in Betsy's hand looked like a little green Shih Tzu hanging from a gold ring.

"Natural?" Betsy said. She kept glancing at Gil and Angel, who had their heads together again. She sounded nervous. At meeting Nikki?

That was even less likely than the possibility of Nikki stealing her $1,500 fuzzy wristlet. Nikki was so unintimidating in a town of intimidation that complete strangers were always sharing intimate information with her.

"I can't believe that's your natural color," Hazel went on, looking more closely.

Nikki smiled, feeling uncomfortable under the women's scrutiny. "I *do* highlight it once in a while," she confessed. "Myself. With one of those boxes of highlighter from the drugstore."

"You do it yourself!" Hazel gasped in awe.

"Nicolette!"

Only one person on earth called Nikki by her given name.

Nikki gave the two women a wry grin. "Will you excuse me?"

"Nicolette, darling. Do you have a moment?"

Though the words were spoken kindly, it wasn't really a question. It was a command. It meant, *come here now.*

Nikki walked toward Victoria, who was standing only a few feet away. She looked stunning, as always. She was wearing a gorgeous, beaded, long Chanel couture gown, in white of course. It wasn't a new gown; Nikki had seen it on her many times before. Victoria might spend ten thousand on a gown, but she got plenty of wear out of it. Petite and a natural blonde, Victoria, who was somewhere in her early seventies (she'd always been vague about birthdays and her birth records had been *lost* in a fire), still had that sweater-girl curvaceous figure that had shot her from a soda fountain stool to stardom more than fifty years ago. Victoria wore the Chanel the way it was meant to be, with a natural grace that everyone in Hollywood wanted, but few possessed.

"Mother." Nikki smiled, feeling a flutter of tenderness for her. She and her mother didn't always see eye-to-eye, but secretly, they adored each other. "I met Diara and her husband. She seems quite fond of you."

Victoria looked up at Nikki. Her face sparkled with perfect makeup, a perfect smile, but Nikki could tell all was not perfect in Victoria-land.

"What's wrong?" Nikki said under her breath. She nodded to Tom Hanks, who was standing a couple of feet away, talking with a group of directors. She made a mental note to be sure to find his wife, Rita Wilson, later. She adored Rita; like Victoria, she was one classy lady. She'd always admired Tom and Rita because they were a Hollywood couple who had managed to stay together. It didn't happen often in Tinseltown.

Nikki returned her attention to Victoria.

"Beatrice Andrews," Victoria said under her breath . . . through *the smile.*

"I'm sorry?" Nikki leaned closer.

Victoria waved to someone Nikki couldn't see. She froze *the smile,* talking through her teeth. "Beatrice."

"I haven't seen her."

"That's because she *isn't here,*" Victoria said pointedly. "She stood me up."

Nikki found it hard to believe anyone in this town would dare stand up Victoria Bordeaux. Although it had been ages since her last film, Victoria still had a lot of pull in Hollywood and, more importantly, everyone respected her. Just dropping her name could open doors, and everyone was looking for an open door in their business, even stars who had been around forever, like Beatrice Andrews.

But theirs was another complicated relationship. Victoria and Beatrice had a past. Nikki had never gotten the whole story. She'd gotten *none* of the story from her mother. What she knew, she'd picked up over the years. It had happened in the seventies. Victoria and Beatrice, who had been good friends, had done a movie together. Beatrice had been engaged to wealthy financier, Alexander Mason. The movie wrapped and Victoria and Alexander went to Mexico for the weekend . . . and married. Husband number four. The marriage wasn't long lived. Beatrice's hatred for Victoria, however, was.

"Maybe she had another engagement," Nikki told her mother. "Or maybe she's sick."

Victoria rolled her eyes. "I don't suppose we could hope for a case of the bubonic plague?"

Nikki laughed. "Mother, you said you didn't have a problem with Beatrice. You said you were fine working with her on this show." *Casa Capri* was set in the Napa Valley against the backdrop of the wine industry. A modern-day *Falcon Crest.* Her mother's character was the new matriarch come to town to do battle against an established matriarch, Beatrice's character. Network television was buzzing with excitement in anticipation of Victoria's permanent role.

"That was before I started working with her. She's just awful, Nicolette. Let's call a spade a spade. The woman can't act. She never could. She'll drag down the ratings and we'll be cancelled, and that will be the legacy I leave." Victoria pursed her perfectly lined and lipsticked lips. "Cancelled on a TV network."

Nikki nibbled on her lower lip. "You sorry you took the job?" Nikki had advised against taking it. Her mother was too old for the rigors of network TV. She didn't need the work, and she certainly didn't need the fame. Nikki didn't know why she'd taken the role in the first place. "It's not too late to—"

"I'm certainly not sorry!" Victoria's stunning blue eyes, the Bordeaux blues they were called, flashed with annoyance. "Did you know *that woman* is threatening to walk off the set and halt production if I'm not replaced at once? The nerve!"

"Mother, she's not going to walk off the set."

"Of course she won't." Victoria glided away, smiling. "If I kill her first, it won't be necessary for her to walk off the set, will it?"

Chapter 2

"Jeremy, I'm not saying you shouldn't let Alison stay with you." Nikki took a plate from the Louis XIV-style china cabinet and turned to the matching dining table behind her. Trapping her iPhone between her ear and her shoulder, she laid the Aynsley china plate on a stack of paper and began to carefully wrap it. "I'm just suggesting you two need to talk about her plans for the future."

"Her plans are to save enough money to put a down payment on a condo."

She could tell he was annoyed and not just with her, but with his sister, too. Maybe himself. That didn't keep her from going on. She'd wanted to have this conversation with him for weeks. Alison seemed to be making herself too comfortable in Jeremy's house and it was worrying her.

"When?" Nikki asked into the phone. "When is she going to have enough money for this down payment?"

"I don't know. Soon."

Nikki frowned as she folded one corner of the paper over the plate, then the next, making a neat bundle. "How soon?"

"I don't know."

"My point exactly." Satisfied with her wrapping job, she lowered the plate into a sturdy cardboard box on the table where it joined half a dozen identical friends. "I don't mean to be a witch about this, Jeremy, but riddle me this . . . do you want her to live permanently with you and the kids?"

"No, of course not. It's hard on them . . . and I know it's been hard on you. On us. Since she moved in, we haven't exactly had a lot of alone time."

"I could say that I enjoy sharing a glass of wine with you and Alison after the kids go to bed, but that would be a lie. You know I don't have a problem with Alison. I like Alison." She hesitated. "It's just that I'm afraid she's not going to do what she says she's going to do. She never does."

Nikki hated to sound whiny, but between her job selling real estate, his dental practice, and his three children, they had very little time alone to begin with. Since they started dating for the second time since his wife's death (a long story), Nikki had made it a habit of stopping by his Brentwood house two or three times a week, after his three children went to bed. She would help Jeremy clean up after dinner and then they'd have a glass of wine together. It had become a good way to connect regularly without involving dinner reservations and babysitters. Their relationship had been going well. Until Alison moved in.

Jeremy was quiet on the other end of the line. He knew she was right. Nikki didn't want to see Alison take advantage of him; his sister had certainly done so before. And while Alison really did seem to have her act together, Nikki just wasn't as trusting as Jeremy was.

She took another plate from the china cabinet. "I miss you."

"I miss you, too. But I need to do what I can, not just for Alison, but for Jocelyn, too. This child custody case has them both scared. Jocelyn doesn't want to live with her father any more than Alison wants her to live with him."

Alison's ex, Jocelyn's father, had taken everything in the divorce, and now hc was trying to get custody of their daughter. He was a wealthy businessman in L.A., but a shady character. Nikki suspected he didn't really want custody of their fourteen-year-old daughter; he just wanted to hurt Alison. He was the kind of man who believed his wife and child were possessions, and he didn't give up ownership easily. There had been proof of that in the divorce settlement.

"I'm not saying you should kick her out. I'm just saying—" Nikki 's hand hit the edge of the plate and the plate took a nosedive off the end of the pile of papers. "Come back here!" She caught the edge of the plate before it sailed off the table, and exhaled with relief. The plates were a hundred bucks apiece, if they were a dollar.

"What are you *doing*?" Jeremy asked.

She held the white china plate with its elaborate painted design with both hands. "My two o'clock in Holmby Hills rescheduled; his psychic told him his moon or sun or something was in the wrong place today for making large purchases. So I stopped at your house to work on the dining room. I texted Alison and she's just going to bring the boys here."

This was Nikki's contribution to the Alison cause. Alison took Nikki's Cavalier King Charles spaniels to the dog park twice a week. Which was nice, because Nikki had been so busy with work lately that Stanley and Oliver weren't getting enough exercise and it was beginning to show. Both dogs had been up a pound when they'd gone for their annual checkups with their veterinarian. Nikki had also passed out Alison's cards to clients and had acted as a reference several times. The rich and famous tended to be careful about who they allowed into their homes, which was completely understandable, considering the number of nut jobs out there. Alison was a lot of things, but she wasn't a nut job.

"I told you, you don't have to do that, Nik. I'll get someone in."

Nikki shifted the phone from one ear to the other.

It had been almost three years since his wife had died, and he was finally ready to change things in the house. He wasn't erasing Marissa's memory, just making some modifications to reflect his own taste. And maybe a part of him was doing it so that the memory of her wouldn't be so present everywhere. He'd decided to start in the dining room because he had never liked the way she had decorated it with white and gold Louis XIV furniture, a massive chandelier, and heavy gold drapes and table linens. Jeremy's tastes were simpler; he liked cleaner lines and less . . . stuff.

"I don't mind doing this, Jeremy," she answered quietly. "I know how you are about privacy . . . and keeping strangers out of the house and away from the kids. I can do this."

"Well, I don't know if I could. I want the stuff stored, but the whole idea of getting rid of things she bought . . . the things she liked . . ."

"You're not getting rid of them. You're saving them for the girls, in case they want them."

They were both quiet for a minute. She loved these moments between them. When they didn't have to speak. When they knew what the other was thinking.

"You're good to me." She knew he was smiling.

"Just remember that the next time I'm late for dinner or Mother calls you," she teased. She began to wrap the rescued plate.

He laughed. "Gotta go. I've got a patient waiting for me who needs a tooth reconstruction and he's got to be back on the set tomorrow at five a.m. I'll probably be running late tonight. Will you still be there when I get home?"

"You want me to be here?" She added the plate to the box.

"Always," he said.

Now *she* was smiling. "Go be a dental hero." She hung

up the phone and set it down so she could concentrate on her wrapping skills.

A few minutes later, the house phone rang. Nikki let it ring. Jeremy still had one of those old-fashioned answering machines in his kitchen rather than using a phone service for messages. She had a feeling Marissa had bought it. It wasn't that Jeremy was having a hard time moving on; he was just having a hard time with Marissa's *stuff*.

"Jeremy? Are you there? Jeremy?" Nikki heard come from the kitchen.

It was Alison. There was something in her tone that made Nikki leave the plate and walk toward the archway between the dining room and kitchen.

"Jeremy, pick up, please pick up if you're there." Her voice was shrill, but quiet, almost as if she were trying to keep someone from hearing her.

Nikki walked into the kitchen and picked up the phone. "Alison, it's Nikki."

"Oh, God, Nikki. Thank God. Where's Jeremy? He's not answering his cell."

"He's still at work."

"Not today." She was sounding slightly manic now. "He comes home at one on Tuesdays. He takes Jerry to karate after school."

"Not today. Karate was cancelled and Jeremy took an emergency in the office." Nikki leaned against the counter. "Alison, what's wrong?"

Alison hesitated, but only for a second. "Could you come here?"

"Where's *here*?" Nikki got a sudden, uncomfortable feeling. "Alison, are Stan and Ollie okay? Nothing—"

"They're fine. They . . . they're in kennels in my van. I . . . I need you to come here, Nik. It'll take Jeremy too long."

"I'll come," Nikki said. She made a beeline for the dining room to grab her cell and her bag.

"Now."

"I'm coming now," Nikki assured her. "Tell me where you are."

"At Diara Elliot's. On Mulholland."

"I know the house," Nikki said. "Alison, what's going on?"

"He's dead."

She picked up her Prada bag off the Louis XIV sideboard. "Who's dead?"

"Ryan . . . Ryan Melton."

"I'll be right there."

Spotting the emergency vehicles with their flashing lights a block east of the property, on Mulholland, Nikki whipped her Prius onto Sumatra Drive. She parked it illegally on the side of the road in front of a client's five-bedroom Colonial, grabbed her bag off the car seat, and hurried toward the Melton/Elliot house.

The street had been narrowed to a single lane in front of the Elliot/Melton house. A Beverly Hills police officer was directing traffic. She crossed behind an unmarked police sedan that she was pretty sure she recognized, and she walked between the line of police cars and the property's white wrought-iron fence.

Nikki hurried up the circular white driveway.

The Elliot/Melton house was a contemporary traditional worthy of the spread that had run in *Architectural Digest* the previous year. With 3,000 square feet, a limestone master bath, an incredible pool and outdoor living area, they would easily get 3.6 million for it, even in the present market.

"I'm sorry! You can't go in there," someone called behind her.

She adjusted her vintage Persol sunglasses and kept walking. *Look important, people will view you as important.*

She was halfway up the driveway, which was full of police vehicles, an ambulance, and a fire truck (a fire truck?) when she realized she was wearing sweatpants and a skintight Iams dog food T-shirt. And flip-flops. Not exactly a *someone important* ensemble. She hadn't left the house that morning looking like this. She'd been dressed in a cute short-sleeved sweater dress, equestrian blue—which complemented her own Bordeaux blue eyes—and knee-high, black, Italian leather boots. When she got to Jeremy's, she'd changed into the sweats and T-shirt because after she packed up the dishes, she planned to carry them to the attic. This was her "dish-wrapping, attic-crawling, weed the herb garden" outfit. It was not her "sneak into a murder scene outfit." Too late to change now.

She walked past Alison's white van, with a Standard Poodle and a Lhasa Apso painted on the side, along with the words *90210 Dog Walking* and Alison's cell number. The Lhasa Apso was peeking out of a Louis Vuitton dog carrier; the poodle was wearing a diamond-encrusted collar. The side door was open and she heard a familiar bark. She spotted Stanley and Oliver in individual kennels, looking like inmates behind bars.

"Oh, you're okay, guys," she crooned. "You're fine." She patted the floor of the van as she hurried by, but didn't dare stop or they'd really start to bark.

She passed two EMTs wearing latex gloves. One was talking on her cell; it didn't sound like a work-related call. Nikki caught "just brown the burger and turn on the rice," as she walked by quickly, with purpose. . . . In her Victoria's Secret sweatpant capris with the word *PINK* printed across her butt, she *knew* she shouldn't have bought these pants, even if they were five bucks, brand new with tags, at the consignment store on Sunset.

A cluster of uniformed cops stood at the double front doors, which were open. She was hoping she could just slip into the house, but there was no way around them. Nikki smiled *the smile*. "Excuse me," she said to the cop immediately in front of her.

He actually started to step aside, then checked himself. He was a big guy, mid-thirties, Hispanic. "You can't go in there, ma'am." He looked in the direction of the driveway and his first line of defense. There were at least half a dozen cops milling about; no one had stopped her.

"I got a call from my . . . friend." Boyfriend's sister sounded too convoluted. "She's here. She told me what happened. She sounded scared. I told her I would come."

"You're friends with the victim?"

"What happened?" She pushed her sunglasses up on her head. At least she was wearing makeup and her hair was brushed. "I can't believe—we just saw him Saturday night. He and Diara. At Victoria Bordeaux's." She offered her hand. "I'm Nikki Harper."

His eyes lit up with recognition. "Victoria Bordeaux's daughter." He took her hand slowly. "Right. My sister loves old films. Back when we were kids, she used to have a poster of Victoria Bordeaux over her bed. That pose from *Sister, Sister.*" He frowned. "She lost it in the fire. Our whole apartment complex went up. Somebody trying to use a kerosene heater on a chilly night. Our family got out, and the dog, but I lost my hamsters." He shook his head. "They were cute little guys. I had nightmares for weeks afterward."

Nikki ran into this all the time. Was it something about her face that made people want to tell her personal things? She wanted to hold up her hand and say, "TMI, Officer Ramos" (his name was on his uniform), but she couldn't because she needed to get into the house. She craned her neck, hoping to catch sight of Alison. She looked back at Officer Ramos. "Can I speak with Alison? She's inside."

"The house and the pool area are off limits to civilians—"

"But my friend is inside. Could you go inside and get her, then?"

"I'll take this, Officer."

Nikki looked up to see Lieutenant Detective Thomas Dombrowski, aka Detective Cutie-Pants, in the doorway.

Officer Ramos looked at Nikki, then at the detective.

"Ms. Harper and I are acquainted," Detective Dombrowski explained. He turned in the doorway and indicated with his hand that she could come in.

"What are you doing here?" she asked as she stepped into the white marble-tiled foyer. "This isn't Beverly Hills precinct jurisdiction."

"I'm sort of on loan. Going to be a high-profile case." He looked at her with Robert Redford eyes. "Of course, I'm a cop, so *I'm* supposed to be here. *You,* on the other hand, are a real-estate agent and should not be at the scene of yet another murder." He tilted his head, not even pretending not to be looking at her backside. "Nice pants."

She wanted to stick her tongue out at him. "Real-estate *broker,*" she corrected.

"What?" He blinked, as if distracted by the ad on the back of her sweatpants.

She dropped one hand to her hip, facing him again. "I'm a real-estate *broker,* not a real-estate *agent.*" She could see through the sunken living room, through glass doors, to the pool outside. Lots of guys in uniform. Someone in a medical examiner's jumpsuit. Officer Ramos had made a point of saying the pool area was off limits. Her bet was that Ryan Melton was floating in the pool. How the heck did it happen? Drug overdose? Bad dive off the board?

She looked up at Tom. They'd gotten on a first-name basis a couple of months ago when her mother's housekeeper's son, a gardener, had been accused of killing a famous producer's son. With a pair of garden shears. Good times.

"Alison Sahira called me from here. She told me Ryan was dead. She asked me to come."

"You know Alison Sahira?" he asked. He had his cop face on. Not the Sundance Kid one. "Know her well?"

"She's Jeremy Fitzpatrick's sister. Jeremy's my—"

"Your boyfriend," he finished for her. He glanced down the hall. "She's in the dining room. Waiting."

"Waiting for what? Can I talk to her?"

"You can talk to her, but just for a sec. I still have some more questions for her."

Nikki glanced down the hall, then up at him. He was tall, heavier built than Jeremy. But not heavy. Just an imposing guy. She wondered if he'd been a linebacker in a previous life. "What do you need to talk to her about? Why are you questioning her?"

"She didn't tell you?"

Nikki got a bad feeling. "Tell me what?"

"That Ryan Melton was murdered."

Chapter 3

Nikki followed the detective past a sunken living room. A guy with a long ponytail in plaid shorts sat on the end of one of the two white leather couches. He was just sitting there, staring straight ahead in sort of a daze.

"This way," Dombrowski said, leading her down a short hallway to a dining room.

"Nikki," Alison whimpered when she saw her walk in. She half-rose from her chair, as if she was too weak to make it all the way to her feet, and raised her hands for a hug.

Nikki and Alison had never been on hugging terms, but a murder scene required special allowances. Nikki walked up to her and gave her a genuine hug. Alison's shoulder blades were boney; the woman needed a few extra pounds on her thin frame.

"Are you all right?" Nikki whispered. She could feel Dombrowski behind her, hovering in the doorway.

Alison gulped and nodded.

Nikki released her and took a step back. Alison slipped into the dining room chair, again; it was a crazy ash and stainless thing. There were eleven more identical chairs around an equally modern, ugly dining table.

Nikki glanced around the room as she dropped her bag

on the dining table. Diara's taste was awful . . . and very expensive. There were original contemporary paintings on the walls, all abstract, with wild colors and designs. All originals, she suspected. All very expensive and, in her humble opinion, all looking as if they had been painted by a kindergarten class.

Nikki met Alison's gaze. "What happened?"

Alison's gaze darted over Nikki's shoulder. She had big brown eyes that seemed bigger than they were when framed by her pale face and the limp brown hair that had escaped from her ponytail.

Nikki turned around. "Detective Dombrowski, could I have a minute alone with Alison?"

"I should talk with her. The sooner we get through the interview, the sooner she can go."

"I just need a minute," Nikki said quietly.

"Sure." He sounded reluctant.

She waited until she heard his footsteps in the living room, then pulled out a chair beside Alison. There was a white furry rug under the table. It appeared to be real fur. Polar bear?

"What happened to Ryan?" Nikki asked.

Alison pressed her lips together and shook her head. Her big eyes filled with tears. "They think I did it," she whispered.

Nikki frowned. "They don't think you did it." She studied Alison's face for a moment, then lowered her voice. "They don't *really* think you did it, do they?"

Alison was the last person on earth you'd suspect of killing a man. Or a mosquito. She was a quiet woman. Timid. Always soft-spoken. She was one of those women you might say was afraid of her own shadow. She'd been that way as long as Nikki had known her—back when they were kids and Nikki and Jeremy were best friends. Alison was three years younger, so they rarely hung out, but she was never the kind of little sister you could tease or play practical jokes on. She'd always been too . . . *frag-ile* was the word that came to mind.

It wasn't that Alison was a bad person. She was just the kind who got easily washed in and out with the tide. At least she had been, in her late teens and early twenties. She'd dropped out of several colleges, had a hard time keeping a job. But after she married Farid Sahira, a businessman quite a bit older than she was, she seemed to have settled down. She'd had Jocelyn, and was a stay-at-home mom for a few years. Then she'd opened a party store and party planning business a couple of years ago—when her marriage became rocky, Nikki suspected. The business had failed and so had the marriage. The dog-walking business was less than a year old but seemed to be doing well.

"Why would the police think you killed Ryan Melton?" Nikki asked, taking care to be sure she didn't sound confrontational. She knew Alison walked Ryan Melton's Rottweiler. He was a sweet doofus of a dog that got along with Stan and Ollie; Alison took all three to the park at the same time. "Did you call 911? Were you the one who found the body?"

She shook her head.

"Okay," Nikki said slowly. "So what's going on, sweetie? Why does Detective Dombrowski think he needs to question you?"

Alison glanced toward the doorway, wringing her hands in her lap. She was wearing a pair of worn jeans, a long-sleeved T-shirt with a chocolate Lab on the front, and a pair of athletic shoes. The jeans didn't fit her well; she'd lost weight over the last few months. Something about the weight loss, about her even-more-than-usual reticent behavior hummed in the back of Nikki's mind, but she couldn't quite say why.

She took the younger woman's hands between hers. Alison was acting strange, even for Alison. "Do you need an attorney, Alison?"

She shook her head in little, jerky movements. "I can't afford another attorney. I can't afford the one I have. The child custody hearing. I had to get an attorney. A good one. It's the only way I can fight Farid."

Nikki knew she was terrified of losing full custody of her fourteen-year-old daughter, Jocelyn. And the teen didn't want to live with her father any more than Alison did. No one had said anything, but Nikki secretly suspected there had been physical abuse in the marriage. She had no evidence; it was just the way Alison behaved sometimes. The way she flinched when a man spoke too loudly or moved quickly.

Nikki leaned over, looking into Alison's face, forcing her to make eye contact. "I know you're scared, Alison, but you have to give me something here. You didn't find the body? So who did?"

"The . . . fish guy."

"The *fish guy*," Nikki repeated.

If someone said, "The fish guy found the dead body," and there was no one there to hear it . . . was it still a really odd-sounding statement?

"Mars." Alison spoke so softly that Nikki had to listen carefully to hear her above the voices of the police somewhere else in the house. One second they were talking about the deceased, the next, baseball scores. Apparently, the Angels were playing the A's this week.

"Mars?" Nikki asked.

"The fish guy. I don't know his last name." Now Alison wouldn't break eye contact. She just kept looking at Nikki with those big Jeremy-like eyes of hers. It was the only thing they had in common, physically or otherwise.

"Mars cleans the fish tanks. In the bathrooms."

"They have fish tanks in the bathrooms?" Nikki was momentarily sidetracked. "Really?"

She nodded.

Nikki refocused. "So Mars found Ryan." She didn't ask

where or in what state; she figured she'd work her way up to that. "And how did you get to be here? You came, what? While Mars was waiting for the police?"

"I brought Muffin home."

"Not knowing that Mr. Krommer was here?" came a male voice.

Nikki looked over her shoulder to see Tom Dombrowski standing in the doorway again. He had a little leather notepad, a pen poised. He glanced at Nikki. "I've really got to get her statement."

"Then she can go home?"

He nodded. Nikki nodded.

Dombrowski walked into the dining room. He was wearing a well-tailored suit and nice shoes: Italian leather loafers. Too nice for a police lieutenant's pay grade. Nikki wondered what his story was: wealthy ex-wife who gave him a nice settlement in the divorce? Born a rich kid? Or something more interesting? Married an heiress maybe? She didn't know whom she could ask. She certainly wouldn't ask him.

"Were you aware that Mr. Krommer was here at the same time that you were here?" Dombrowski asked.

Alison's face showed confusion. "Who?"

"Mr. Krommer." He flipped back a page in his notebook. "Mars Krommer."

"Oh . . . Mars. Um . . . I didn't know he was here, at first," Alison said. "I was dropping Muffin off. His Rotty. A Rottweiler," she clarified.

"You didn't see Mr. Melton when you dropped the dog off?"

Alison rubbed her hands as if washing them. "No," she whispered.

Dombrowski took a step closer. "I'm sorry, Ms. Sahira, you'll have to speak up."

"I didn't see him!" She said it loudly enough to startle both Nikki and Dombrowski. "I let Muffin in, hung the leash up by the back door and . . . went out."

"The front door?"

She nodded.

"Where Mr. Krommer stopped you?"

She nodded again. Looked down at her feet. "I was getting in my van. He came out and told me. About Ry—Mr. Melton."

"So, you would have been in the house when Mr. Krommer was making the 911 call?"

Alison didn't look at them. "I didn't—"

She was interrupted by the sound of a cell phone vibrating in Nikki's bag on the edge of the table. The ringer was off, but the sound was still loud. Really loud. Or at least it seemed so at such an inopportune moment.

Alison looked at Nikki's bag. Dombrowski looked at it.

Nikki glanced up quickly at Alison, ignoring the phone. "So you were in the house when the fish-tank guy found Ryan and called 911?"

"No. Maybe. I guess. I . . . I don't know. I'm not trying to be difficult." She took a breath and started again, her sentences short and delivered in a staccato fashion. "I never saw Mars. I didn't see Mr. Melton. I let the dog loose in the house. I hung the leash up. I went out the front door. I was getting into my van when Mars came outside. He was crying. He said Mr. Melton was dead. He said he called the police. Then I heard the sirens."

Nikki wanted to ask if Mars said where Ryan was, how he knew he was dead, the particulars, but Dombrowski didn't ask, so she didn't.

He scribbled something on his notepad, then flipped the leather cover over. "Okay."

"Okay?" Nikki asked, a little surprised his questioning had been so brief. Maybe this was a follow-up to previous questioning.

"Okay. I've got Ms. Sahira's statement. She can go."

Alison bolted out of her chair and practically ran for the door.

Nikki looked at Alison, then the detective. There was no way he couldn't have noticed Alison's odd behavior. Nikki grabbed her bag.

Alison darted past the detective and he turned to watch her go. "I've got your cell number and your address. Same address as Dr. Fitzpatrick's. In case I have more questions for you, once the security tapes are run."

Alison halted in the doorway but didn't turn around.

Again, odd. But then she always had been odd.

"Security tapes?" Alison said.

Nikki's phone started vibrating again.

Dombrowski looked pointedly at Nikki, then at Alison's back. "Sure. The house has security cameras, inside and out. Everyone in Beverly Hills has them."

"Oh." It came out as an exhalation. Nikki's phone was still vibrating. "Of course," Alison said. She still didn't turn around. "Nikki?"

"Coming."

Nikki went past Dombrowski without saying good-bye. As she walked through the house, toward the front door, she couldn't help eyeing the glass doors in the living room that led out to the pool. She glanced over her shoulder. He hadn't followed them; she heard him answer his phone. "Dombrowski."

She didn't hesitate. She took three steps into the sunken living room. Everything was white: the carpet, the walls, the leather couches, even the tables. The guy with the ponytail was still sitting on the couch, still staring into space. Mars Krommer? "Hi," she murmured.

"Hey," he answered, his voice distant. He didn't look up; obviously he was stunned by the events unfolding around him.

Nikki took another step into the living room, then another. A couple more and she was at the open doors. A cop on the pool patio talking to another moved slightly and Nikki saw what held everyone's attention.

Another dead body. Her fourth, but who was counting?

A now all-too-familiar tightness gripped her chest. She saw the back of Ryan's head over the top of a lounge chair; he had nice hair. She took another step, then another. She heard Alison go out the front door. She needed to go with Alison. She needed to be with her. But she couldn't help herself. She walked out the glass doors, right past the cops.

Ryan Melton was lying on his back in a lounge chaise, facing the pool, his back to the French doors leading into the house. He was shirtless and wearing a pair of surfer-type swim shorts. Just lying there, sunbathing. There was even an icy glass of something on the table beside him. And a laptop. A pair of Oakley sunglasses on the white stone, paved deck, near his chair. There was a second lounge chaise on the other side of the table. A white towel lay folded on top of it.

Someone had begun to put up little sign tents to mark evidence in the photographs that would be taken of the crime scene.

Nikki stared at Ryan's face. The only indication that he was dead was his unseeing blue eyes. No one had closed them yet.

"What the hell are you doing out here?"

Nikki felt Dombrowski's hand grab her wrist at the same time that she heard his voice.

"Don't you know the definition of a crime scene by now?" he asked irritably, dragging her across the deck, through the open doors into the living room.

"He didn't drown," she said, feeling a little light-headed. It was a relief to know that just because she'd already seen a murder victim up close, she wasn't immune to it. "How was he killed?" she asked softly, already going over in her mind what she had seen. The details. It was all in the details, she'd learned: the drink in the glass, still cold, the sunglasses on the deck, the laptop and scattered magazines.

"You know I can't tell you that. We haven't even finished with the crime scene yet." He halted at the front door. "Go home, Nikki."

She frowned. "I'm going."

Alison was sitting in her van, hands in her lap, staring out at nothing. Nikki snapped out of her another-dead-body fugue, confirmed that Alison was okay to drive, and promised she'd meet her at Jeremy's. Hopefully, he'd be finished with his patient soon and be able to come home. Then she took Stan and Ollie, still on their leashes, to her own car. She put them both in a single kennel in the back; neither of them was happy with her. "Just a quick stop at Jeremy's," she told them. "Then home." She gave each a scratch behind the ears, closed the kennel door and then the hatchback.

Nikki was just climbing into the driver's seat when her phone vibrated, yet again. She knew who was calling her. Only one person dialed her again and again until she answered. Then she realized the call might be important, given the circumstances here on Mulholland. She fumbled for her phone in her bag, found it, and raised it to her ear. "Mother?"

"It's about time, Nicolette. I called you twice already."

Nikki got into her Prius. "I was kind of busy. You still on the set?" It was only three-thirty in the afternoon. Even though Victoria was always on set by six a.m. the days she was shooting, she was rarely home before six p.m. She barely had time to eat and had to go to bed so she could be back up by four a.m. the next morning. Which was exactly why Nikki had been against her mother taking this part to begin with. It was too much.

"We shut down early today. Drama on the set."

Nikki gripped the steering wheel with her free hand. She had a pretty good guess what the drama was about, although that might not have been the word she would have chosen. Poor Diara. How horrible would it be to get a call on set that your husband had been murdered? "You heard?"

"Heard what? Did you hear? It's supposed to be a closed set, but you know, they never are. Everyone and their brother traipsing through wanting autographs."

Victoria couldn't possibly know about Ryan's death. Not even *she* would go on this way if she did. "Mother? Why did you call?"

"To tell you about Diara and Kameryn, of course. They practically got into a catfight."

"About what? No . . . *when?*" Nikki asked quickly.

"Just before lunch. The director sent us home. Amondo and I went to Spago." (Amondo was the patient man who had served as Victoria's assistant, secretary, bodyguard, driver, and sometimes companion for nearly two decades.) "I had a lovely celery and apple soup and the duck confit," her mother went on. "You and Jeremy should go there. For lunch. Lunch was excellent and *not as pricey as dinner.*" Victoria whispered the last words.

Nikki shook her head. She would have laughed were it not for the police and ambulance *and fire truck* on the street and Ryan's body in the lounge chair. His unseeing blue eyes. "And you never heard from anyone on the set the rest of the day? No . . . news?"

"What news? I just turned my phone on. Let me get my glasses. They're here somewhere. Ah." There was a pause. "It says I have seven missed calls. I don't know how to check those," she said dismissively. The phone beeped several times in Nikki's ear. "Come for dinner, Nicolette, and I'll tell you all about Diara and her little fit. She may find herself unemployed if she's not careful. Seven."

Ollie whined in the back of Nikki's car.

"Mother, I might have a . . . situation. I might not be—"

"Nonsense. You never come for dinner anymore. Not when there's just the two of us. Casual . . . but not *too* casual, darling. You know how I dislike denim."

Before Nikki could respond, Victoria hung up. Nikki could just picture her mother riding in the back of her white Bentley, giving Amondo instructions as to what streets to take, even though she hadn't driven a car in twenty-five years, and punching random keys on her cell phone. Victoria was smart and a quick study when she wanted to be, but for some reason she remained stubborn about cell phone use.

Nikki tossed her phone on the car seat and punched the Start button on her Prius. She'd have to go to her mother's and tell her about Ryan. But first, she'd go to Jeremy's and make sure Alison was okay.

Dombrowski had let Alison go, but she hadn't liked how he acted. What did he know that he hadn't been saying? And what had possessed Alison to run like that when he said she could go? Running should never be involved when talking to the police.

Nikki pulled away from the curb. She had a bad feeling this wasn't the last time Alison was going to hear from Detective Dombrowski.

Chapter 4

"Murdered? And they wanted to talk to you?" Jeremy kept his voice down so his three children, all in the family room doing homework or coloring, didn't hear, but he had some *tone* in his voice.

He, Alison, and Nikki were all standing in his massive kitchen in his home in Brentwood. Nikki was making pancakes on the stove while bacon spit in a tray in the oven. She didn't usually play this role in Jeremy's home, but the kids had to eat and Alison was certainly in no state to cook. Jeremy had just arrived. So Nikki had declared it breakfast night. It was one of the uncharacteristically fun things she remembered her mother doing for her as a child. Of course, on breakfast night, Victoria had never actually *cooked* the breakfast for dinner; there was a housekeeper to do that. And they had eggs Benedict. Nikki's breakfast for dinner tonight involved a box mix and the addition of eggs and water.

Jeremy looked at his sister, sitting on a stool at the granite counter. She had her head in her hands.

"Did you see Ryan Melton? Dead?" he asked.

Alison shook her head. "I didn't see anything," she whispered.

Jeremy glanced at Nikki. He was good-looking, but all-American good-looking—part of the reason he had been so popular as a teen. He had never been gorgeous in a Ryan Melton kind of way, but he was tall and had nice brown hair and dark eyes a girl could lose herself in. What was most attractive to Nikki about Jeremy—what had *always* most attracted her, even when they were kids—was that he was a super-nice guy. Jeremy was kind, loyal, smart—he was the whole package.

Nikki flipped a pancake. It was supposed to look like Mickey Mouse's head. It was for Jeremy's youngest, Katie, who would be five the following month. One of Mickey's ears tore off. Nikki neatly cut off the other with her spatula and ate the ears.

"She's upset, Jeremy. You need to stay calm."

He frowned. "I *am* calm. I'm just asking my sister why the police wanted to question her about someone's *murder*."

Nikki answered for Alison. "Because she was in the house today."

"When it happened?"

"No. No, of course not, right, Alison?" Nikki asked. Both she and Jeremy looked at his sister.

"I don't know when he was killed." Alison spoke each word slowly, as if in a daze . . . slowly, as if she needed to form the words in her head before being able to say them. "I don't know anything about what happened. I only know what I did. I took his dog to the dog park, along with Ollie and Stan. I took the dog back to the house. I let him loose in the house. I hung up the dog leash and left the house."

"See. She was there. Doing her job. That's why Tom . . . Detective Dombrowski questioned her." Nikki gestured with the spatula, then flipped another pancake.

Jeremy exhaled. He never wore his white lab coat home, but he was still in a shirt and paisley Ralph Lauren tie. "And you told the detective that? That you didn't see anything?"

"Yes," Alison said.

"And you *really* didn't?"

"Jeremy?" Nikki turned to him, surprised. "That's a terrible question to ask."

"Not as terrible as it might sound." He glanced at his sister, who had dropped her head to the counter again. "Considering previous events."

Alison didn't answer, and the look on Jeremy's face suggested this wasn't the time for Nikki to ask what he was talking about.

"Why don't you go in and see the kids?" Nikki suggested. "Alison said Jocelyn stayed after school for something, but she's getting a ride home, so no one needs to pick her up. I'll finish here. Then I have to run. Mother's for dinner. Unless you need me to stay?"

"We'll be fine. Thanks, hon." He rested his hand on Nikki's shoulder and gave her a sweet peck on the cheek before walking out of the kitchen.

Alison waited until her brother was out of the room to speak. She lifted her head to look at Nikki. She was a mess. The little bit of mascara she had been wearing had run and then smeared under her eyes. Her face was swollen and blotchy from crying. "He hates me," she said in a girlish voice.

Nikki tossed pancakes from the frying pan onto a white serving platter. Every dish in the kitchen was white or yellow. The kitchen, renovated by Jeremy's wife in the early stages of her cancer treatment, was very French Country: a brick floor, honey yellow walls, granite countertops, distressed white cabinetry, ceramic tiles, and rustic urns. Copper pots hanging from a rack over the enormous island added to the ambience.

"Jeremy doesn't hate you," Nikki said. "That's ridiculous. He loves you."

"He thinks I'm lying." There was a tremor in her voice. Again, the little voice.

"He doesn't." Nikki poured more batter into the frying pan, giving the Mickey Mouse head another try.

"Didn't you see the way he looked at me?" She sniffled. "He's never forgiven me. He doesn't believe people can change."

Nikki turned to Alison. "Forgiven you for what?"

She slipped off the stool, pushing her hair out of her eyes. "It doesn't matter," she said softly. "You'll know soon enough."

"Murdered? And you were there? Good heavens, Nicolette," Victoria said. "People are going to be afraid to associate with you."

Nikki slid back in her chair and reached for her water glass. They were eating on Victoria's stone terrace, but it was Waterford all the way. The everyday Waterford, of course. "I had nothing to do with the murder. Alison called from Ryan's house. She was dropping off his dog when the guy who cleans their fish tanks found him. She was scared, and Stan and Ollie were with her. What was I going to do? I had to go."

"You could have sent Jeremy."

Nikki sipped her water. "He was with a patient. Alison needed me."

"She's a needy one, that girl." Victoria lifted a tiny sliver of filet mignon to her mouth. "Poor Diara. Makes the fight she had with Kameryn on set today seem meaningless."

Victoria had told Nikki about the fight even before Nikki was through the front door, but there really weren't many details to give. "And you don't know what they were arguing about?" Nikki asked.

"No, the only thing I heard was Diara telling Kameryn that she better keep her mouth shut. That was when the shoving started."

"But they're friends?" Nikki asked.

"Best friends, from what I've seen on the set." Victoria was quiet for a moment. "Did anyone say how Ryan died?"

"No." The image of him sitting in the lounge chair, his blue eyes unseeing, crossed her mind and she shivered, even though it was a warm evening. "His body was on the pool deck. In a chair. I didn't see any obvious wounds."

Victoria met her gaze, Bordeaux blues to Bordeaux blues. "You saw him dead?"

"Just for a second." She looked away. She knew what Victoria was thinking now. About the first body they had seen together. Nikki had been young and foolish. Rebellious. Her mother had warned her time and time again to be careful whom she associated with. But it was Victoria who had come to her rescue that night. Victoria who had called her attorney and then the police. In that order.

Nikki's gaze drifted back to her barely touched dinner plate. "I didn't ask Detective Dombrowski."

"Alison doesn't know? The girl was there."

"She says she never saw Ryan, or the guy servicing the fish tanks. He's the one who called 911."

"But she was in the house at the same time as the fish-tank man?" Victoria patted her mouth with a pressed, white linen napkin and returned it to her lap. "And he didn't see her?" She gave a little sniff. "Someone's lying."

Nikki cut her eyes at her mother. It was twilight and the scent of roses drifted on the warm breeze. Victoria's gardener, Jorge, had a way with roses and somehow managed to keep them blooming from spring to autumn. "What makes you say that? The house is pretty big and there's a front and rear drive. Alison let the dog in through the front. The fish-tank guy was parked around back." She used her fork to poke at her wedge salad. The blue-cheese dressing Ina made was delicious, but she wasn't all that hungry.

"Maybe the fish-tank guy killed him, then laid in wait for Alison to arrive so he could point the finger at her," Victoria theorized.

"Mother, no one is pointing any fingers at Alison. What would make you say such a thing? She was questioned. Routine stuff." Nikki didn't know why she was defending Alison so hardily. Jeremy had been acting so strangely. What did she *not* know about Alison?

Victoria sat back in her chair, pushing her plate away. She was wearing her typical comfy evening attire: a white jogging suit and pearl earrings. It was a very casual evening; she wasn't wearing one of her strings of pearls. A pair of dollar-store reading glasses hung on a very expensive white gold chain from her neck.

"Do you think the girl had anything to do with Ryan Melton's murder?" Victoria asked pointedly.

"Of course not. And she's not a girl. She's a grown woman. She's only a few years younger than I am."

Victoria gave Nikki a look Nikki knew all too well. Victoria would never accuse anyone of being stupid; it wasn't in her nature, but she was more than willing to tell you when you were behaving or speaking foolishly. "Nicolette, some women are always girls." She looked out over the rippling pool. Stan and Ollie were both sitting on the edge, watching something. Maybe a stray leaf the pool boy had left behind. "Not everyone is as fortunate as you and I." She looked at Nikki with those breathtaking blue eyes of hers. "To be born women. You were never a girl." She looked away, her mind seeming far off for a moment. "Nor was I."

Nikki gazed out over the gorgeous manicured lawn and gardens. The white tents, fountains, and twinkling lights were gone. There wasn't a single cigarette butt or a fluttering paper napkin to be seen. There wasn't a speck of evidence left of the party Saturday night or the celebrities who had attended. "I don't think Alison had anything to do with Ryan's death," she said quietly. Honestly. "I think she was in the wrong place at the wrong time."

Victoria waved dismissively. "But you're going to leave that all up to Detective Dombrowski. Aren't you, Nicolette? You've learned your lesson after your last *two* encounters with dangerous murderers?"

"Aren't all murderers dangerous?"

Victoria smiled sadly at her daughter. "Not all, darling."

Friday morning, Nikki was punching buttons on the copy machine in the copy room in the Windsor Real Estate office, cursing under her breath at it. "There's no paper jam," she declared to the machine. She lifted the top of the scanner and closed it none too gently. She pulled out the paper tray and shoved it back in. Then she pushed the Copy button again. The display screen flashed "paper jam." Again.

Nikki growled out loud.

"Need some help there?"

Nikki turned around to see Detective Cutie-Pants standing in the doorway. He was wearing another expensive suit and holding two paper cups of gourmet coffee from a shop down the street.

"Hey. What are you doing here?" she asked suspiciously. She had a bad feeling he hadn't *just been in the neighborhood.*

"Bringing you coffee." He offered one cup. "Vanilla latte. I took a guess."

She accepted the cup. It was a good guess. She loved vanilla lattes.

"And fixing that paper jam, if you like." He motioned to the copy machine with his cup of coffee.

She groaned impatiently. "It doesn't have a paper jam." She sipped from the cup. It was perfect.

"Suit yourself." He raised his cup as if in toast and took a sip.

She had that bad feeling again. "You didn't come to bring me coffee, did you?" she asked.

"Not exactly."

She walked past him, through the doorway. "Come on." Whatever he had to say, she suspected she didn't want her colleagues to hear it.

He followed her down the hall to the tiny office she had once shared with her good friend Jessica. He closed the door behind him.

She took her chair behind her desk. He didn't sit. She looked up. "It's about Alison."

He nodded. "I wanted to give you a heads-up. This is totally off the record."

The bad feeling just kept getting worse.

"We've got a warrant for her arrest."

For a moment Nikki got that light-headed feeling you got when receiving bad news. It was an all-too-familiar feeling. It was as if all the oxygen had been sucked out of the room. Nikki remembered feeling this very same way the morning her mother came to tell her that her father had been murdered in New York City. Victoria and John Harper had been divorced for years, but Nikki had seen the tears in her mother's eyes. Victoria had still loved John Harper. She guessed she always would.

"I don't understand," Nikki said when she was able to breathe again. "The fish-tank guy found the body. He called it in. What about him? Maybe he killed Ryan."

"Did Alison tell you how Ryan was killed?"

Nikki made herself look up at the detective. She didn't answer.

"He was strangled. With a dog leash."

Chapter 5

"A dog leash?" Nikki murmured.

"We'll have to wait for the autopsy and lab reports, but we're pretty sure—*I'm* pretty sure—that's what was used. The assailant approached from behind the lounge chair where Mr. Melton was sitting, dropped the leash over his head, and tightened." Dombrowski crossed his fist over his coffee cup and pulled back, making a motion as if to strangle someone with a rope. Or a dog leash.

Nikki's bad feeling turned to slight nausea. She closed her fingers around the paper coffee cup. Felt its warmth. "That doesn't mean the dog walker did it."

"Her fingerprints on the leash came up as a match."

"Wait," she said, confused. "You fingerprinted Alison?"

"Didn't have to. She was already in the system. Priors."

Nikki was quiet for a second. She didn't know what *priors* Alison could have had. Was this what Jeremy was referring to the other day when he suggested Alison might not be telling the truth? "Okay, that does sound incriminating."

"Thus the warrant."

"But she's the *dog walker*. Her prints are on Stan's and Ollie's leashes, too."

He drew his eyebrows together. "Laurel and Hardy had leashes?"

She almost smiled. She was surprised by how many people *didn't* make the connection. "My dogs, Stanley and Oliver. Alison walks them, too. They were with her the day Ryan died. She took them and his dog to the dog park."

"The dogs tell you that?" He didn't wait for her to answer. "Her story's shaky at best, Nikki." He actually seemed to feel bad about it.

"You sure you have the right leash?" She took a sip of the coffee. "Maybe you've got the wrong leash. I have half a dozen, at least."

"We confiscated five from the Melton/Elliot house. We'll check them all, but I'm fairly certain we have the right leash. It matched the ligature marks on his neck."

Ligature marks. Nikki hadn't noticed marks on Ryan's neck. She had been too busy looking at his gorgeous, dead face. At the objects around his chair, assuming they might hold significance: the drink glass, the laptop, his sunglasses. "Do you know when he was killed? The beverage in the glass was still cold."

Dombrowski arched one eyebrow.

"I noticed that the glass was still sweating a little when I walked out onto the pool deck."

She got a half smile. "Good pickup. I saw that, too. There was actually still a sliver of ice in the glass when I arrived. The ME will give us an approximate time of death, once he does the autopsy, but I think Mr. Melton was killed less than an hour before the 911 call was placed by the guy servicing the fish tank."

"If the fish-tank guy and the dog walker had access, who knows who else could have walked in the back or the front doors?" She looked at him, thinking out loud. "What kind of security is on the gates, front and rear? The front gate was wide open when I got there, but that might have been because of all the emergency vehicles."

He looked at her for a long moment, then lifted the coffee cup, holding it short of touching his lips. "I came here to let you know what was going on, not to pick your brain on the evidence. Obviously, this is a police matter." He took a sip.

"Obviously."

"Which means I don't want real-estate agents—"

"Broker," she interrupted.

"*Brokers* interfering with my investigation."

"The way brokers have *interfered* in investigations before?" she said, referring to the murder of her mother's next-door neighbor the previous fall. Nikki was the one who had figured out who actually killed him, and even called Dombrowski to hand the murderer to him on a silver platter.

"Stay out of this, Nikki. Please," he beseeched with one hand. "I'm saying please."

She scrutinized him. "So *why* did you come here to tell me about Alison's arrest?"

He shrugged. "I don't know. Because I thought you'd want to know. Your boyfriend will want—with Ms. Sahira having a teenage daughter and all. Someone might want to pick her up from school before it hits the news. Or maybe I came because it was an excuse to see you."

Nikki shot out of her chair, his last comment barely sinking in. "I have to go." She pulled open the bottom drawer of her desk and grabbed her ancient, beloved Prada shoulder bag. It was supple tan leather, shaped more like a feed sack than a handbag, with a long strap and only a few pen marks and water stains. "I don't want Jeremy to hear from someone else that his sister's been arrested." She came around her desk. "Has she already been picked up?"

He checked his watch. "Should have been. I told them to wait until the daughter had left for school, but get there before Ms. Sahira left Dr. Fitzpatrick's house for the morning."

Nikki crossed her office.

Dombrowski opened the door for her.

She halted in the doorway and looked up at him. "Thanks, Tom. I appreciate this."

He nodded and she was out the door.

Jeremy had a high-end office in a high-end building not far from Windsor Real Estate, on Wilshire in Beverly Hills. He practiced general dentistry, but his *star* past made him popular with celebrities. They appreciated the confidentiality he and his staff offered and the spa-like atmosphere of the office itself. That had been his wife Marissa's idea.

Nikki entered his waiting room. It was plush and decadent, decorated in gold and red as if Jeremy's patients were royalty. Which in a way, many were. She walked past Brad Pitt and one of his kids. At the front desk, Jolene, a cute blonde, smiled. She was wearing khaki pants and a tight, low-cut, green T-shirt. The two additional receptionists behind the counter were wearing identical T-shirts. Monday, they would be wearing the same T-shirts in teal. But Fridays, Fridays were green tee day. Jeremy liked order. He didn't mind that his staff wore different colors on different days, as long as they wore the same color, the same day every week.

"Ms. Harper, nice to see you."

"You, too, Jolene," Nikki said, subdued. "Is Dr. Fitzpatrick busy? I mean, I know he's *busy,* but I need to speak with him."

"He's just finishing up with a patient."

"I'll wait in his office. Can you tell him I'm there?"

"Sure thing," Jolene sang.

Nikki went through a closed door, into the back, and walked into Jeremy's office. It was expensively furnished, but in good taste: oxblood leather and cherry wood with one wall covered in paneled, cherry wainscoting. She dropped into one of the two leather armchairs in front of his massive desk. His desk was clean, of course. Neat. A computer monitor and keyboard. His cell phone. Framed, candid photos of the kids and a leather cup of pens. She noticed that the picture of Marissa on his desk was gone. He must have removed it recently because the last time Nikki was here, maybe a month ago, the framed photo had been there, behind the children's. Another sign Jeremy was moving on, recovering from his wife's death from cancer. As much as anyone could recover from such a thing.

Nikki didn't dare contemplate what that would mean for her and Jeremy. They'd been in sort of a holding pattern for a while. He had definitely moved to boyfriend status, but they'd never talked about what that meant. What it *could* mean in the future. Which was just as well, because Nikki didn't know what she wanted or how she felt about Jeremy. She knew she loved him, but they had been through so much, together and apart, that she didn't know where their relationship could lead. Her mother's seven marriages had turned her off to the whole institution, but she'd learned a long time ago to never say never. Something else her mother had taught her.

"Hey, everything okay?" Jeremy walked into his office, looking very handsome and very professional in his shirt and tie and white lab coat. He took one look at her face and closed the door. "Everything's not okay."

She shook her head. "Jeremy—"

"Alison did it, didn't she?"

"No, no, of course not." She was momentarily taken aback, not only by his accusation, but by the way he made it. As if he'd thought all along that his sister had killed someone. She rose from the chair. "But she's been arrested."

There was a glisten in his eyes and he looked away. His hands hung at his sides. "I'll have to get money together to post her bail."

She rested her hand on his chest. This was the Jeremy

she knew, not the accusing one. He was the kind of man who would bail his sister out because it was the right thing to do, not because he thought she was innocent. "Tell me what I can do."

"I'll have to call my attorney. He can find out what her bail will be set at." He was talking to himself, not really her. "Move money around." He swore under his breath, something he rarely did.

"Jeremy, this is a mistake. She didn't do this."

He turned his gaze on her, his facial expression hard, something she wasn't used to seeing. Jeremy was usually so easygoing, so slow to pass judgment. "No? How do you know?"

"Because this is Alison. Your little sister. She wouldn't hurt anyone."

"No? Ask her to tell you about the armed robbery she was involved in."

Nikki's mouth dropped open. For a second, she thought she might have to close it manually. "Armed robbery?" she whispered. "When? Not recently?"

He wiped his mouth with the back of his hand, as if speaking of it literally tasted bad. "No, it was before she met Farid."

"Alison was involved in an armed robbery?" Nikki repeated. "You mean she was *accused* of being involved."

"She *was* involved. A man was seriously wounded. Alison didn't pull the trigger, but she knew it might get pulled."

Nikki was flabbergasted. "But . . . but she never went to jail."

"Not for more than a couple of nights, because I bailed her out. She lied to me. Promised me she had nothing to do with robbing this convenience store in East L.A."

"But . . . but if she was guilty, she would have served time in prison."

"Doesn't always happen that way, Nik. There was an error on how the evidence was filed or something. She got away with it. They all did. She and her friends."

Nikki didn't know what to say.

She didn't think Jeremy did either. He walked around his desk and sat in his high-backed, leather-upholstered chair. "I need to make some phone calls."

"For a murder charge, a judge will have to set bail," Nikki said quietly. "That could take a few days."

He nodded. "Right. I still want to call my attorney now. And catch one of my stockbrokers before he heads off for a long weekend in Catalina. Could you tell Jolene to reschedule the rest of my day?"

"Sure, of course." She picked up her bag, hovering.

He lifted the telephone from its cradle and looked at her across the desk. "Jocelyn," he groaned. "I need to get to Beverly Hills High School and get her out of there before someone starts tweeting that her mother's been arrested for Ryan Melton's death."

"That's what Detective Dombrowski thought. He's the one who told me that Alison was being arrested. I can't sign Jocelyn out, though. I don't have her mother's prior permission."

"I can." He lifted the phone to his ear. "I'll take care of it. Can you be at the house when the kids get home from school?"

"Sure, of course." Nikki was relieved to have something to do. "I'll see you later," she said as she went out the door.

He didn't answer.

At four-thirty in the afternoon, Nikki was in the kitchen making Jeremy's youngest a snack when Alison rushed into the kitchen.

"Is she here? Is Jocelyn home?"

Nikki was surprised, bordering on shocked, to see Alison. She couldn't imagine how she could have posted bail so quickly. Jeremy must have pulled some strings somehow. She glanced down at little Katie. "Would you like to take your snack in the living room and bug your big sister?"

Katie bobbed her head and grinned.

Nikki gave her a plastic Hello Kitty plate with cut-up carrots, apple slices, and peanut butter on it. "Go for it."

Katie galloped out of the kitchen.

Nikki turned to Alison. "Jocelyn's not with you?"

"With me?" Alison's usually pale face was even paler. She had no makeup on and looked as if she'd had a rough day. Maybe been arrested and spent time in a holding cell. She wrung her hands. "Nikki, I was arrested this morning for Ryan Melton's murder. How could Jocelyn be with me?" She was beginning to sound panicky. "She was in school. Did she not go to school?"

"I'm sure she's fine." Nikki wiped her hands on a dish towel and approached Alison. "She went to school as far as I know. Jeremy was going to pick her up early . . . in case someone heard about your arrest before we . . . before Jeremy had a chance to tell her himself. But weren't you with Jeremy? Didn't he bail you out?"

"He was going to post my bail?" Tears filled her eyes and she looked at the floor. "I can't believe he'd do it again. After . . . the last time. After what I did."

Nikki exhaled. She didn't know when the right time to talk about that with Alison was, but she was sure it wasn't right now. "I'm confused. How did you get here? Did Jeremy post your bail and then not pick you up?" That didn't sound like him, but she was beginning to realize that Jeremy wasn't the same person with his sister as he was with everyone else on the planet.

"Jeremy didn't post my bail," she said in a small voice.

Nikki waited for an explanation. When Alison didn't go on, Nikki pressed, "Okay, so who did? Your ex-husband?"

Alison laughed, but there was no humor in her voice. "Farid? Are you kidding? He'd let me die of thirst before he offered me water from the hose in the backyard."

Again, Nikki waited. Again, Alison wasn't forthcoming with information. "Then who posted your bail?" Nikki asked pointedly. To Nikki's knowledge, Alison had no friends; it was the way Farid had liked it.

Just then the door to the garage opened into the kitchen. Jocelyn walked in, backpack flung over her shoulder. When she saw her mom, she ran to hug her. "I thought you were in jail," the teen cried, her arms tight around Alison. "I'm so glad you're not in jail."

Jocelyn was gorgeous in all the ways her mother wasn't. Even at fourteen, it was obvious she was going to be a beauty. She had her father's dark complexion and dark eyes, and an athletic build. She carried a certain air of confidence you didn't usually see in teenagers, which amazed Nikki, considering the fact that Alison was the polar opposite in that area.

Jeremy walked in behind his niece and frowned when he saw his sister. "I went to post your bail and they said you'd already been released. Who the hell posted your bail, A?"

Alison still had her arms around her daughter. She looked over Jocelyn's shoulder sheepishly. "I can't tell you."

Chapter 6

"What do you mean you can't tell me?" Jeremy bellowed.

Nikki turned to look at him, wondering who the heck this guy in Jeremy's kitchen was. It certainly wasn't Jeremy. Had aliens taken over his body?

Aliens? Where did that come from? She'd been reading too many Dean Koontz novels.

"Jeremy," Nikki said calmly. She took a step toward him and placed both hands on his chest. "Let her catch her breath. Let Jocelyn get something to eat and then maybe you and Alison can—"

Jeremy brushed by her, jerking at his Gucci watercolor tie. "I'm going to change." He walked past his sister without saying a word to her. "Is Maria here?"

"She's putting laundry away." Nikki waited until she heard his footsteps in the hall before turning to Alison. "You need to tell him what's going on."

Jocelyn had let go of her mother's shoulders but was still holding her hand. "You need to tell *me* what's going on, Mom," the teen said. "Uncle Jeremy wouldn't tell me anything in the car. He had me called to the office in the middle of a biology quiz and said he was signing me out for the day. Then we went to his lawyer's office, but he made me sit in the lobby. Like, for hours. Mom, were you really arrested?"

Alison just stood there in the middle of the kitchen, looking scared and lost.

"Mom," Jocelyn urged, "you should sit down. You look like you're going to pass out."

Nikki followed the teen's lead and took Alison's other arm. They led her toward one of the kitchen stools.

Jocelyn was not only beautiful, but she was wise beyond her years. Nikki had a feeling she'd seen more of real life than most Beverly Hills kids had.

"Sit," Nikki instructed. "I'll get you a glass of water."

Jocelyn backed her mother up to the stool. "What were you arrested for? Please tell me you haven't been calling Dad and hanging up again."

Alison just shook her head.

Nikki came back around the island, carrying the glass of water. "Jocelyn's going to find out, Alison," she said as gently as she could. "It's going to be all over the news. It's probably already been tweeted across the country."

"It's not true, Jocelyn," Alison whimpered, tearing up. "What they're saying. I didn't do it."

"Now you're scaring me, Mom." Jocelyn sat on a stool next to Alison's and rubbed her mother's arm. She was wearing jeans and a cute, flowered, fuchsia T-shirt. "What do the police think you did?"

Alison sat on her stool, frozen.

"Drink," Nikki insisted, pushing the glass into her hand.

Alison drank as Nikki and Jocelyn watched. "They . . . they think I . . . I . . . I can't even say it." She looked up at Nikki. "I'm going to lose custody. I'm going to lose my baby." She set the glass on the counter, spilling some of the water with her wobbly hand. She lowered her head to her arms on the granite countertop.

"What's she talking about?" Jocelyn pleaded. "Tell me

the truth, Nikki. She never wants to tell me the truth. She thinks I'm still five years old."

Nikki glanced at Alison, who still rested her head on the counter. She didn't like the idea of getting in the middle of a mother/daughter thing, but how could they not tell Jocelyn? Ryan's murder had made the headlines of every newspaper and had been the opening piece on all the news magazine shows on TV. An arrest would land the case on the front pages again. The kids in school would be talking about it. They'd all be talking about Jocelyn.

Nikki took a deep breath. "She was arrested for Ryan Melton's murder."

"Ryan Melton!" Jocelyn stared at Nikki. Blinked. "The star?"

"Actually, *he's* not a star," Nikki clarified. "His wife is Diara Elliot. *She's* the star."

"But Mom doesn't even *know* Ryan Melton." She looked at her mother. "Mom, you don't know Ryan Melton, do you?"

"He was a client," Nikki explained when Alison didn't say anything.

"My mom knew *Ryan Melton*? She walked his dog? For real and true?" It was the first time Jocelyn sounded like a teenager since she'd come in the door. She looked at her mother. "Why didn't you tell me, Mom?" When Alison just sniffled, Jocelyn looked to Nikki.

"Client confidentiality," Nikki explained.

"For a *dog*?"

Nikki shrugged. "People are funny in Hollywood."

"Right," Jocelyn exhaled. She glanced at her mother, then back at Nikki. "Why do they think she did it? My mom would never hurt anyone. When my goldfish died, she couldn't flush it. I had to do it. And I was, like, six."

"I don't know the details," Nikki said. Which was true. Mostly. "But I'm going to find out." That, at least, wasn't a lie.

Nikki heard Jeremy's footfalls on the stairs. She reached out and gave Jocelyn a half hug. They had never been on hugging terms either, but it seemed like the right thing to do.

Jocelyn didn't pull away.

"It's going to be okay," Nikki assured the girl.

Jocelyn nodded bravely.

Nikki gave the teen some space. "Why don't you go see what the girls are doing? Maybe start homework? Give your mom and Uncle Jeremy a few minutes to talk?"

"He's really mad," Jocelyn murmured. "I've never seen Uncle Jeremy mad like this. He's always so nice." She walked over to her mother and laid her hand on her shoulder. "You going to be okay if I go hang out with the kids for a while? I've got a big geometry test on Monday to study for."

"I'll be okay." Alison's voice was muffled by her arms.

Jocelyn looked at Nikki as if to say, *Will you take care of her?* Nikki nodded.

Jocelyn was walking out of the kitchen with her backpack on her shoulder at the same time that Jeremy was walking in. He closed the pocket doors behind him.

"All right, Alison. Tell me what the hell is going on."

At the sound of his abrupt tone, Alison lifted her head from the counter and turned on the stool. "I . . . I don't know."

He took another step toward her. "You *don't know?* You spent the day in jail and you *don't know* what's going on?"

Alison trembled at the sound of his voice.

"Jeremy." Nikki brushed his arm with her hand.

He took a deep breath. Exhaled.

Alison sat there on the stool, hanging her head, staring at the Italian tiled floor.

"Why were you arrested, Alison?" Nikki asked. "What

evidence was strong enough for them to actually arrest you? Was it just because your fingerprints were on the dog leash?"

"What dog leash?" Jeremy looked at his sister's teary face. "Ryan Melton was killed with a dog leash?"

"With Alison's fingerprints on it," Nikki admitted. "But that's not enough evidence to convict someone," she went on quickly. "I'm surprised Dombrowski would issue a warrant on that lame evidence." She looked at Alison. "Is that all they have on you? Just the dog leash?"

Alison's lower lip quivered.

"Jeez," Jeremy muttered, shaking his head. "What'd you do, Alison? Huh? What'd you do?"

"I didn't kill him. You have to believe me." She burst into tears. "I . . . I didn't . . . k kill him, but . . . but . . ."

Nikki let go of Jeremy's arm and stood in front of Alison. Now she was getting annoyed. "You didn't kill him, but you *what*?"

"I . . . I . . . I . . . lied . . . to . . . to the . . . p-police. I . . . I think they . . . they know. The . . . the security tapes."

"You lied to the police? Not again. Really, Alison? What, you didn't learn your lesson the first time?"

"I was scared!" Alison shouted, surprising not only Jeremy and Nikki, but, apparently, herself.

Nikki threw both her hands up as if refereeing a boxing match. Jeremy turned away and strode to the other side of the kitchen.

"You lied about what, Alison? What did you tell the police that wasn't true?"

Jeremy was now pacing.

"Oh, this is bad," Alison moaned. "This is so bad. Farid's going to take Jocelyn." She began to rock back and forth. "He's going to take Jocelyn, and then he's going to move back to Saudi Arabia and I'm never going to see her again."

Nikki grabbed both of Alison's hands in hers. "You're not going to lose custody. Now look at me. Look at me and listen."

Alison slowly raised her gaze. Tears ran down her sallow cheeks.

"Tell me what you lied about."

Again, Alison's lower lip trembled. "I . . . I said I was in the house because I was bringing Muffin back. But . . . but that . . . it wasn't exactly true."

"You *weren't* returning the dog?"

"No. I mean, yes, I did take Muffin home. But . . . then I went back again. That's when the fish guy told me he was dead."

"Why did you go back after you dropped off the dog?"

"I can't tell you," Alison blubbered.

Nikki exhaled. Alison continued to sob. Jeremy continued to pace.

"Okay, okay," Nikki said after a moment. She patted Alison on the back. "It's all right. But you can't lie to the police. Do you understand me? You can't lie to Detective Dombrowski. He's a good guy. He's a fair guy, but he's smart. He'll catch you in a lie." She had a whole mouthful of questions, but she knew she wouldn't get any answers as long as Alison was hysterical. "Just tell me you understand."

She nodded, taking a shuddering breath. "I understand."

"And you can't lie to me either," Jeremy said.

Nikki looked over her shoulder at him, then back at Alison. "Who bailed you out?" she asked quietly. Calmly.

"I . . . I don't know. I . . . I'm not supposed to say anything to anyone."

"Who told you that?"

Alison tried to hang her head, but Nikki tugged at her hands.

"Who?" Nikki repeated.

"My attorney."

"What attorney? You hired a defense attorney already?"

Alison shook her head. "I don't have money for an attorney. I don't know who hired her. The attorney . . . she said it was a . . . a concerned citizen."

"A *concerned citizen*?" Jeremy asked. "What's that supposed to mean?"

Alison shrugged, fighting another wave of tears. "I don't know, Jeremy. I swear, I don't. She . . . she took care of my bail; then she picked me up at the holding facility and she dropped me off here."

"*She* who?" Nikki asked.

Alison fumbled in her pants pocket and pulled out a business card. "Lillie Lambert."

"Lillie Lambert?" Nikki took the card and stared at it. Lillie Lambert was one of the most well-known, highest-paid hotshot lawyers in Hollywood. Word was, Lillie Lambert was the woman to hire . . . if you or a member of your family were guilty. Just the previous year, she'd gotten a producer's son off on vehicular homicide. It had been a crazy case, worthy of plenty of Nancy Grace airtime. In the end, Lillie Lambert's client had gotten off scot-free, and another producer was forced to live with the death of his son and the knowledge that the young man responsible would never actually be held responsible.

Nikki turned to look at Jeremy. He must have been thinking the same thing, because now he was pale, too.

"I have to go to the powder room," Alison said. She got up from the bar stool, tucked a straggly piece of hair behind her ear, and walked out of the kitchen.

Nikki walked up to Jeremy. "She didn't do this," she said.

He wouldn't look at Nikki. "You don't know that."

"I do," she whispered. She looked up at him and slowly he shifted his gaze until it met hers.

"What if she did, Nik? I can't have her in my house . . . *with my kids.*"

"Why would she kill Ryan Melton? She doesn't know him. She *walks his dog.*"

"She lied to the police," he said. "She admitted it."

"I lied to the police once. I told them he forced me into that car."

"That's different. You were a kid."

"I *wasn't* a kid. I was nineteen and I knew exactly what I was doing when I got into that car."

He put his arms around her shoulders. "Nikki," he breathed.

"She didn't do it," she repeated, slipping her arms around his waist. She rested her cheek on his chest for a minute. He smelled good. Jeremy always smelled good.

They just stood there that way for a minute; then he let go of her. "That time when she was arrested. For the robbery. She told me she wasn't with them in the car when they shot a man while robbing his store. She said it was a girl named Alice. There was no Alice."

"Jeremy, how long ago was that?"

"I don't know. Fifteen, sixteen years ago. Right before she met Farid."

"Has she done anything since then to suggest to you that she would do something like that now?"

He closed his eyes and rubbed one temple. "I just don't know that I can trust her. That I should. I mean . . . she's been arrested. The police don't arrest you without serious cause." He opened his eyes and looked at her. "Why are you so quick to come to her defense? You've never been a big Alison fan."

"Because she didn't do it."

"You don't know that," he said.

I know it, she thought to herself. *And I bet I can prove it.*

*   *   *

"So why *did* you come to her defense?" Marshall asked.

Nikki looked up from the fanzine she was flipping through while lying on her stomach across Marshall's enormous bed. She'd taken the magazine off a pile on the nightstand. She was scanning an article on the Ryan Melton murder.

Marshall was going through his closet, choosing clothing he no longer wanted that he could donate to a charity auction. His partner, Rob, an undercover cop, was working the nightshift. Usually, when Rob was working nights, Marshall stayed at his official residence on Beverly Drive in Beverly Hills. He was big box office and he had a public image to keep up. Nikki didn't necessarily agree with his decision to remain in the closet. She didn't know that it was healthy, after all these years. But it wasn't her call.

Tonight, against his manager's advice, he'd decided to stay at Rob's—which happened to be next door to Nikki's—which was how they met in the first place. He said he didn't feel at home in his enormous, opulent mansion in Beverly Hills. Here, he said, he felt safe. Here, he could sleep, even without Rob.

Marshall came out of the walk-in closet in a lavender sweater and white linen pants. He strutted, then posed as if modeling for a *GQ* magazine cover. "Stay or go?"

She looked up from a splashy page of Ryan and Diara's wedding photos. "I thought you were going for the rugged look these days." She made a face. "Go."

"But I *love* this sweater," he protested.

"The pants are wrinkly."

"Egads, Nicolette," he said, his imitation of Victoria awfully damned good. "They're linen!" He leaned over the bed. "Oh my God! Isn't she gorgeous? I've never seen that photo before." He pointed to a photo of Diara in her wedding gown, standing in an array of white rose petals.

"There're two pages." She turned the page. "They married four years ago. You must have seen them on the first go-round. I remember they were splashed all over the magazines."

He sat down on the edge of the bed, taking the magazine out of her hands. "My God, my God. No, I never saw these." He flipped the page, then flipped it back again. "These are new releases. Look at that cake. Isn't it gorgeous?"

Nikki looked at Marshall. "Diara would have never released wedding pictures to the press the same week her husband was murdered. Would she?"

"Maybe." He closed the magazine and held it up. "This kind of publicity is expensive: a glossy front cover with a two-mil circulation? With exposure like this, she'll be in meetings next week renegotiating her *Casa Capri* contract."

Nikki stared at the front cover, a photograph of Ryan and Diara walking hand in hand down a red carpet. Two beautiful people. One now dead.

She thought about poor Alison, lying in her bed at Jeremy's . . . scared she's going to lose her daughter. She thought about Diara. Diara and Ryan had appeared to be the happy couple at the party last Saturday night, but were they?

Was the evidence at the crime scene so obvious as to be *too* obvious? Had someone set Alison up?

Who could have afforded to pay Alison's bail so quickly? Diara certainly could have. But if she had something to do with the murder, why would she bail Alison out? Nikki felt like she had more questions now than answers.

Chapter 7

"I'm sorry," the young man on the other end of the phone line said. "Ms. Lambert is in court today."

Nikki gazed up at the yellow light in front of her, judged her speed and distance, and then reluctantly hit the brakes. Traffic was heavy on Beverly Boulevard. But then it was always heavy midday. "Would it be possible for me to make an appointment?"

"Regarding?"

Nikki couldn't say she wanted to talk to her about Alison and the Melton case. There was no way she'd agree to that. No attorney would. "It's . . . confidential," she said.

"Of course." He then named an astronomical fee for a fifteen-minute appointment and offered a day and time.

"That's three weeks from now," Nikki protested. And there was no way she was paying that kind of money for fifteen minutes with Lillie Lambert. Nikki wasn't as frugal as Victoria, but she was still her mother's child.

"Yes," the receptionist said, not even bothering to apologize.

"Well, that just won't be acceptable," she said, quoting Victoria.

"Have a good day," the young man responded.

"You too." Nikki hung up using the button on her steering wheel. The traffic light had just turned green when her phone rang again. The screen on the dash identified the caller as Victoria. "Hello."

"Are you coming, Nicolette?"

"I'll be there in five minutes." Someone honked his horn behind her as she slipped around a panel truck. "Traffic."

"I only have an hour."

Nikki glanced at the dashboard. "You said one o'clock. It's twelve forty-five. I'll still be early." She signaled and changed lanes. It wasn't cutting someone off if you signaled first, was it? "You sure you don't want me to stop for takeout somewhere?"

"Goodness, no. I told you. The amount of food they throw away here, it's a sin. I've left your name at the gate. Hurry, Nicolette, I'm starving."

Ten minutes later, Nikki walked into the studio where *Casa Capri* filmed their indoor scenes. The director had declared a closed set after Ryan's death, to protect Diara, no doubt, but no one beyond the studio front gate stopped her. After only one wrong turn down a dark hallway, Nikki found the set where they were filming that day: the office of the family vineyard where Victoria's character and her sons and daughter schemed and double-crossed. She heard Victoria before she spotted her.

"Well, that looks like an eggroll to me. Can you explain the difference?"

Nikki ducked to avoid being hit by a microphone on the end of a pole being carried by a young man talking on a headset who didn't look old enough to be on a TV set without his mother. She sidestepped around a corner and saw Victoria, dressed in character in a pink Jackie O suit and kitten heels, standing in front of a food service table. The long table, covered with a white linen tablecloth, was laden with lunchmeats, salads, fruits, vegetables, and sweets.

A cute redhead in her late twenties, wearing a headset

over pigtails, was talking with Victoria. "Good question. I don't know . . . except that spring rolls are smaller."

Spotting Nikki, Victoria waved her over. "Try one of these little eggrolls, Nicolette. Megan says they're spring rolls. They're divine."

The young woman smiled shyly at Nikki.

"Nikki Harper." She offered her hand.

"Megan Larson." She tucked a clipboard thick with paperwork under her arm and shook Nikki's hand. "Nice to meet you."

"Megan is the assistant director's assistant, but everyone knows she's in charge here," Victoria explained. "Megan knows everyone, knows everything, and, most importantly, knows where to get a cup of decaffeinated Earl Grey tea." She motioned to Nikki. "What are you waiting for? Take a plate, dear. And try one of these spring rolls. They're vegetarian." She handed Megan plasticware wrapped in a napkin. "Could you hold this?"

Megan met Nikki's gaze as she accepted the cutlery. "You better get a plate."

Nikki liked her sassy tone. "Mother's mentioned you." She picked up a plastic plate. "I appreciate the way you look after her."

"Oh, Ms. Bordeaux doesn't need anyone to look after her. She does fine all on her own."

Nikki put some Asian coleslaw on her plate and glanced around the enormous room with the office set, directly in front of them. Men and women moved around, adjusting cameras while munching on sandwich wraps and, apparently, spring rolls. "So, production is running on time, despite Ms. Elliot's loss?" she said, trying to put it as delicately as she could. It was Monday: Ryan hadn't been dead a week yet.

"What can I say? She's dedicated to her craft." Megan gave a shrug. "Maybe it's easier to be here, working, rather than wandering around that big house of hers. All alone. Knowing he died there." She shuddered. "I can't imagine."

Nikki doubted Diara had even been allowed to enter her house yet. It was probably still taped off as a crime scene. She was most likely staying with friends, or maybe at the Beverly Wilshire Hotel. It was where everybody who was anybody stayed.

"Have you heard when the funeral will be?" Nikki asked.

"He's being cremated." Megan nodded to another young woman with a clipboard and headset walking by. "One of the stylists told me. Then a private memorial service, but no one knows when. I guess that's how you keep it private. Have you been by their house on Mulholland? People are leaving flowers and notes and teddy bears and stuff in front of their gate. I heard there were even people there with candles Saturday night, some kind of vigil."

"The girl will be lucky if she can ever go home," Victoria injected. "Is that turkey or chicken? I hope it's turkey."

"Is Diara around?" Nikki glanced behind her. The studio was full of people coming and going: actors and actresses, the film, sound, and lights guys and gals. "I'd like to express my condolences."

"Probably in her trailer." Megan stood patiently at Victoria's side. "She's been totally professional, but she's not socializing with us much. Kameryn, Julian, and Angel were here all day Friday and again today. Mostly in Diara's trailer. You know, supporting her. Being there for her. They've been friends a long time. My little sister was into their show. She cut pictures from fan magazines and plastered them all over our bedroom wall. She was crazy-excited when she heard I got this job. She's in college now, but I bet she'd love autographs from the Disney Fab Four. I just haven't had the nerve to ask. It wouldn't really be appropriate right now, anyway. You know?"

Nikki's gaze settled on Kameryn Lowe, standing in the middle of the office set; she had joined the cast recently. She wasn't dressed for filming, though. She was wearing sweatpants, a T-shirt, and glasses. She faced Nikki, and was talking to her husband, Gil, whose back was to Nikki.

Nikki eyed Kameryn and Gil as she moved from dish to dish on the table, trying to only take a little of anything that looked too good to pass up. She couldn't hear what Kameryn and her husband were saying, but it seemed to be an intense conversation. Kameryn appeared upset; Gil was trying to calm her down. He reached out to put an arm around her shoulder, but she pulled away.

Victoria had mentioned that Diara had been instrumental in getting Kameryn the part of the lead male character's girlfriend. It really was about who you knew in Hollywood. It only made sense that Diara would have put in a good word for Kameryn. They'd been friends since middle-school age when they'd been cast on Disney's *School Dayz*, and had remained friends into adulthood.

"This okay, Ms. Bordeaux?" Seeing that Victoria had nearly finished making her selections, Megan had carried her cutlery and a bottle of water to a table with chairs set up in the food service area.

"Perfect," Victoria called, now checking out the petite desserts.

Nikki skipped the desserts and walked to the table. "Mother said this was supposed to be a closed set since Ryan's death, but it doesn't look all that closed. Daughters, husbands . . ." She glanced at Kameryn and Gil.

Megan looked in the same direction and rolled her eyes. "Things would move faster around here if it was a closed set *all the time*. No offense meant," she added quickly.

Nikki smiled, taking a seat. "None taken."

"Kameryn's always got guests." Megan returned her attention to Nikki. "And that's not even her husband."

"It isn't?" Nikki did a double take. The two were still engaged in their intense conversation.

"Nope." Megan leaned closer so no one walking past them would hear. "It's easy to mistake one for the other, but that's not Gil, that's Angel. Angel is a little taller," she explained. "I think she and Angel dated at some point, but his wife is Betsy. She's super nice."

"She is. I met her at Mother's." Nikki stabbed a miniature-sized meatball with her plastic fork.

"See, Angel was in *School Dayz* with Diara, Kameryn, and Julian," she said in a conspiratorial tone. "They're like this." She wrapped her middle finger around her index finger. "They're here all the time."

"They are?" Nikki popped the mini meatball into her mouth.

Nikki was still looking at Kameryn and Angel when Kameryn looked right at them. Nikki dropped her gaze to her plate.

"Megan?" Kameryn waved her over. "Could you do me a favor?"

"Gotta run. Nice to meet you." Megan gave Nikki a quick smile as she headed over. "Duty calls," she tossed over her shoulder.

Nikki watched as Megan joined Kameryn and Angel. She couldn't really hear what Kameryn was saying, but it was something about the shooting schedule the following day. The three walked away.

"Nice girl," Nikki observed as her mother joined her.

Victoria sat in a chair across the table from Nikki and spread her paper napkin across her lap. "Too nice sometimes. Did you try this?" She tapped something on her plate that looked like a miniature tamale. "Maybe I should take some home to Ina in a napkin. I imagine she could make them."

"You said Megan is *too* nice." Nikki nibbled on one of the spring rolls. Her mother was right; it was divine. "How so?"

"Kameryn and Diara." Victoria pointed her plastic fork in the direction Kameryn, Angel, and Megan had gone. "She runs and fetches for them constantly." Two men walked up to the food service table and Victoria lowered her voice. "These young women, they have Queen of the Nile Syndrome."

"Queen of the Nile Syndrome?"

"They think they're deities. They're entirely too impressed with themselves and their fame. They have fancy trailers. They want a masseur and to have sushi delivered when there's perfectly good food here—" Victoria indicated her plate and then took another bite.

"Mother, you asked Megan to hold your plastic fork and knife for you. That's not acting like a star?"

Victoria looked at Nikki as if she had said something ridiculous. "I *am* a star," she whispered.

Nikki couldn't resist a grin as she sampled a bit of smoked salmon.

"So, what have you found out?"

Nikki looked up at her mother. "About . . ."

"You know what about." She glanced around as she patted her pink lips. They seemed to be able to retain lipstick even when she ate. "About Jeremy's sister. Did she do it?"

"Of course she didn't do it."

Victoria did this thing with her mouth that always annoyed Nikki. It was her skeptical look.

"She *didn't* do it," Nikki repeated.

"Maria told Ina that Jeremy's considering kicking his sister out of the house and getting custody of the child himself."

Nikki exhaled in exasperation and leaned closer to her mother. The two men had filled their plates and taken seats at the other end of the table. "Jeremy is *not* kicking Alison out of his house, and he is *not* filing for custody of Jocelyn.

Jeremy's housekeeper shouldn't be saying such things and yours shouldn't be repeating them."

"So Jeremy doesn't think his sister had something to do with that young man's murder? Ina says Maria says there's a lot of tension in the house. That Jeremy and his sister went all weekend without saying a word to each other."

Nikki pushed her plate aside. "Alison . . ." She groaned, debating how much to say. "Oh, it's going to come out in the papers anyway." She looked up at her mother. "Alison had a run-in with the law. Years ago. Before she married and had Jocelyn." She hesitated. "She may have participated in an armed robbery where a man was shot."

Victoria pursed her lips. "May have?"

"She did," Nikki conceded. "She was in the car, but, anyway, she got off on a technicality. But Jeremy was the one who bailed her out and then paid her legal fees. And she lied to him about the whole thing."

"And now he doesn't trust her."

Nikki nodded.

Victoria was quiet for a minute. "Why do the police think she did it?"

"Alison was there when a guy servicing the fish tank at Ryan and Diara's house found him dead. Alison had taken his dog to the park. With Stan and Ollie. Ryan Melton was killed with a dog leash. Strangled. Alison's fingerprints were on the leash."

Victoria scowled. "Well, I would certainly hope so."

"You would hope what?"

"That her fingerprints were on the leash. She wasn't doing her job if they weren't. Walking the dog." She spread pâté on a cracker. "That's nonsense. What other evidence do they have?"

"I don't know. I'm not sure they have any. If they had a stronger case, would they have let her out on bail?"

"Marshall said Lillie Lambert is her lawyer. That woman could get Jack the Ripper out on bail."

"You've been talking to Marshall?" Nikki couldn't help but feel perturbed. "Since when do you two chat?"

She lifted a delicate shoulder. "We've become friends, Marshall and I. We talk all the time."

"About me?"

"Of course." Victoria took a bite of the cracker. "But about other things, too. Anyway, he also said that your friend, that nice-looking police detective, is in charge of the case. Can't you just ask him what evidence the police have against the sister?"

"Detective Dombrowski is not going to tell me what evidence they have in a murder case."

Victoria arched one perfect brow. "Well, how do you know that, if you don't ask, Nicolette?"

"What makes you think I even want to ask?"

Victoria continued to nibble on the cracker. "Because I know you and I know you won't just let it go. Ina says that Maria said you and Jeremy had words about the sister."

"Alison."

She patted her mouth with her napkin again. "Ina says that Maria says that you're convinced the sister didn't do it."

Nikki could feel the lines on her forehead. "Does Ina say that Maria said anything else?"

"The daughter leaves wet towels on the bathroom floor."

Nikki couldn't tell if her mother was trying to be funny or not.

Victoria met Nikki's gaze. "You're not going to let this go, are you?"

"I'm curious, that's all. Alison just isn't the type to do something like this. She's not even the type that a man like Ryan Melton would ever notice, let alone *speak* to. Something just doesn't add up."

"So find out what that is, Nicolette."

Nikki half-smiled. Her mother never ceased to amaze her. "Are you saying you think I should look into this?"

Victoria unscrewed the cap on her water bottle. "Are you seeking my approval?"

Nikki's gaze shifted to the sounds of laughter as Kameryn, Diara, and Angel appeared on the opposite side of the studio. Their laughter didn't seem quite like grief counseling to her.

Victoria glanced over her shoulder, then back at Nikki. She took a sip of water. "I'd check with the nice-looking detective."

Chapter 8

The next morning, Nikki walked into Jeremy's kitchen. Alison sat at the kitchen counter. She was still in her pajamas. Her hair was a mess and she hadn't put her contacts in. Her wire-frame glasses sat too far out on the end of her nose.

She looked up, startled when she saw Nikki. She pushed up her glasses. "Jeremy's gone . . . to work."

"I know." Nikki dropped her Prada on the counter and nodded to Maria, the housekeeper, who did far more than just keep the house. She washed clothes, ran errands, and supervised the children. She'd been with Jeremy and his family since Katie was born, and had been a godsend when Marissa was dying. "Good morning, Maria."

"Good morning, Miss Nikki." Maria was a slender woman in her early fifties who had been born in Mexico but claimed Mayan descent. There was something about the way she carried herself that made Nikki see her as an exotic Mayan queen or princess. Even in khakis and a polo. She and Victoria's housekeeper, Ina, were neighbors and good friends. Which explained how Ina knew what had transpired at Jeremy's house over the weekend.

Maria dried her hands off with a kitchen towel, threw a disapproving look in Alison's direction, and walked out of the kitchen.

Nikki opened a cupboard and pulled out a coffee mug. She was on her way to work; fortunately, she kept her own hours at Windsor Real Estate. She poured herself a cup before turning to Alison. "Okay, so what do they have on you?"

"What?"

"What do the police have on you?" Nikki asked. She opened a drawer, grabbed a spoon, and dug a spoonful of sugar out of the bowl on the counter. Jeremy didn't have sugar substitute in his house. He didn't believe in it. He jogged to keep his waistline trim.

Alison stared into her cup as if coffee grinds would rise up and give her the answer.

Nikki reached into the refrigerator behind her and retrieved a carton of milk. "I can't help you convince Jeremy that you didn't do this if you don't talk to me."

Alison slowly lifted her gaze, tears in her eyes. "Why would you do that?" she whispered. "Why do you care if he believes me or not?"

Nikki poured milk into her coffee. It was a good question. One she'd been asking herself since she defended Alison to Jeremy days ago. "Because I don't think you did it," she said simply.

Alison pressed her lips together. "I have a lawyer. She says I won't go to jail."

"Considering your track record and Lillie Lambert's, that doesn't mean you're innocent. At least it won't to Jeremy." Nikki returned the milk to the refrigerator and took a sip of her coffee before she spoke again. "I'm not saying that to be mean, I just—"

"I know. Because of what I did before." Alison hung her head. "But that was a long time ago. I'm not the same person I was. You have to believe me." She looked up. "*Someone* has to believe me," she added in a little voice.

Nikki nodded and sipped her coffee. That was it. That was why she was here. That was why she would do whatever needed to be done, to prove to Jeremy that people could change. That Alison wasn't the same girl who had been in that car the night of that robbery and that she didn't kill Ryan Melton.

Alison looked up at Nikki. "Do you think he'll ask me to leave? Jeremy? If he asks me to leave here, I . . . I don't know where we'll go. I can't go," she said, her voice quavering. "If I leave here, this *stable environment,* the judge will give Farid custody and I"—she looked up at Nikki—"I can't live without my daughter."

"She's the one you need to think about, Miss Alison."

Nikki looked up to see Maria coming back into the kitchen, a laundry basket in her hands. The woman washed a lot of laundry.

"I'm trying, Maria," Alison bleated.

Nikki walked around the corner of the island to give Maria room to put away the dish towels from her basket. "So try hard to think what evidence the police could have against you. They have to have something other than the dog leash. Did they find something on the security tapes?"

"No." She shook her head. "No way."

"Then why did Detective Dombrowski issue a warrant for your arrest?"

Alison grabbed both sides of her head. "My lawyer said I can't talk about the case."

Nikki groaned and took another sip of coffee. Maybe it didn't matter. Maybe Alison really didn't know what the cops had on her. When she was arrested, she would have been told what she was charged with, but the police wouldn't necessarily have told her what evidence they had against her. According to the episodes of *Law & Order* that Nikki watched, that information might not be divulged until the discovery phase of the case in pre-trial.

"Okay," Nikki said, refocusing. "Can you tell me who cleaned Ryan's fish tank? What was the guy's name?"

Alison looked up, her eyes big.

"Alison, Detective Dombrowski mentioned his name in front of me. I saw the guy in the living room at the Melton house. I spoke to him. It's not a State secret."

"People who won't help themselves," Maria muttered. She slid a drawer shut maybe a little harder than she needed to and carried her basket out of the kitchen.

"Maria hates me," Alison whimpered. "Everyone hates me. Everyone thinks I did this terrible thing and I didn't."

"Everyone doesn't hate you. But everyone is getting a little impatient with you. What was his name, Alison?" Nikki thought for a minute. "It was something bizarre, wasn't it? A planet?" She wracked her brain. *Pluto? No, that's a cartoon dog.*

"Mars," Alison whispered. "Age of Aquarius Aquariums in Venice. He's got a store there."

"Okay." Nikki blinked. Crazy name. But it worked with *Mars*. Sort of. "Okay, that's a good start. I'll talk to Mars. See what he knows."

"You will?" Alison stared at Nikki. "Are . . . are you allowed to do that?"

"What? Talk to a guy about a fish tank?" Nikki grabbed her bag. She had a house to show on Mulholland Drive. Then she'd head to Venice and try to catch Mars at his store. "Sure. Why not? I've been thinking about getting a fish tank."

"Really?" Alison asked.

Nikki scowled. "Of course not. But he doesn't have to know that."

The house Nikki went to see was just east of Sumatra Drive on Mulholland. A private driveway led to an amazing Mediterranean villa with soaring cathedral ceilings, custom plaster treatments, and hand-carved moldings. It was 8,000 square feet with five bedrooms, seven baths, and had a hand-leaded glass double door that opened into the front entryway. What was most incredible about the house were the paintings by a renowned Italian artist who had supposedly made his name restoring paintings in the Vatican. Nikki would have to do some research into the artist, but she was pretty certain she could find a buyer at the ten million–dollar price the owners were looking for.

Leaving the gated property, Nikki turned west to head toward Venice. She only passed two houses before she came to the Melton/Elliot house where she'd been the week before. As Victoria had told her, by word of mouth from the housekeepers, people had, indeed, set up a shrine outside the gate. Nikki slowed down, unable to keep from staring. Interestingly enough, there were people at the gate, too. Fans, she guessed.

Nikki didn't know why, but she pulled over, parking behind a yellow VW Bug. She got out and walked back toward the closed gate of the Melton/Elliot house. Fans, mourners, whatever you wanted to call them, had heaped flowers on the driveway in front of the gate. There were photographs of Ryan Melton, some torn out of magazines, two in photo frames. There were candles and stuffed animals; a large white teddy bear stared back at Nikki from the wrought-iron gate.

Nikki couldn't decide if the tribute to Ryan Melton was touching or creepy.

There were two young women on the edge of the driveway. One was crying. The other stood like a mourner, her head down, her hands clasped.

Nikki made eye contact with the crier. She was in her early twenties, dark hair, wearing a Carney's employee T-shirt under her jacket. Nikki nodded.

The girl nodded in return, then offered a half smile. "It's hard to believe, isn't it?" the girl said.

Nikki looked at her.

"That someone could kill an amazing man like Ryan Melton." She looked at Nikki, her pale blue eyes entirely serious. "Who would do such a thing? Who would rob the world of such beauty?"

"He was perfect for Diara," the mourner, a blonde, put in. "They were the perfect couple. So beautiful together."

Nikki noticed that she, too, was wearing a Carney's T-shirt. Both must have worked at the iconic restaurant/diner world famous for its hot dogs.

"I mean . . . what kind of world are we living in?" the crier continued. "That we can't appreciate such beauty. That we have to destroy it."

Nikki didn't know what to say. Fortunately, it didn't seem to matter.

"I mean . . . all human life is precious, obviously." The crier wiped at her wet face. "But . . . Ryan . . . he was . . . special. A gift from God. Wasn't he?" She looked at Nikki with her big, teary eyes.

"He . . . he was," Nikki agreed, feeling completely awkward. What was she doing here? She had a fish specialist to call on in Venice and she had a pile of paperwork sitting on her desk. "Special." And, she recalled, she'd promised her mother she'd pick up a birthday gift for her half brother.

"Have . . . have you heard any news?" the mourner asked Nikki. Her hair was pinched off in little dreadlocks that were actually kind of cute. "I . . . I saw that they arrested someone—the dog walker—but that doesn't make any sense. If she did it, they wouldn't have let her out on bail, would they?" She leaned down to adjust an eight-by-ten glossy photo of Ryan at her feet.

"I . . . I haven't heard anything."

The blonde looked up at Nikki, then got that look on her face that Nikki knew all too well. "I know you," she said slowly. She pointed. "You . . . you're that famous old actress's daughter. I just saw you on TV on E! with your mom. You were at some fundraiser for the Christopher Reeve Foundation."

Nikki smiled. "Nikki Harper."

"Just shoot me! It is you! And your mom is Victoria Bordeaux. I'm Jessie Bondecker. It's really nice to meet you." She grabbed her friend's arm. "Monica, this is Nikki Harper." She pressed her hands to her cheeks, which were growing red. "I can't believe that you're here. But, of course, I bet you were friends." She got a tragic look on her face. "I'm so sorry for your loss."

Nikki wondered how she could make a graceful exit.

"It's really nice to meet you," the brunette said. "I heard that last night Heidi Klum was here. Did you hear that?"

Nikki gave a quick smile. "I . . . I wouldn't know."

"Jessie and I once waited all night outside Greystone Manor, you know, the fancy nightclub, because we heard Rihanna was going to be there," the brunette explained. "But we never saw her. Oh," she added quickly. "But we think we spotted J. Lo."

"Nikki was a friend of Ryan's," Jessie explained to her friend Monica.

Nikki would have protested that they weren't really *friends*, that she'd just met him once, but she doubted it would make a difference.

"You know," Jessie said, "Monica and I were talking, and I think the police just arrested that poor dog walker woman to throw the real killer off." She adjusted her frameless glasses. "Do you know if he had any international ties? We wondered if he was involved with some Saudi prince or something. Or . . . or maybe he was working with the CIA. They took his computer, you know—"

Nikki's ears perked up. "His computer?"

"Uh-huh. There had to be something on it, right? Otherwise, they wouldn't have taken it."

"How . . . how do you know the police confiscated Ryan Melton's computer?" Nikki asked.

"My brother told me," Jessie said enthusiastically. "His roommate works for a computer company or something.

They have a contract with the Beverly Hills police and he heard that one of their IT guys was called in to look at Ryan's computer."

"His computer?" Nikki said. "You're sure?"

A car went by behind them and someone beeped. Nikki took a step closer to the gate, trying not to step on a bundle of daisies.

"I'm sure," the girl said earnestly.

"When was this? Do you know?"

"Right after it happened. Can you imagine, getting to touch Ryan Melton's computer? Your fingers touching the same keyboard he touched?"

Nikki knew that people didn't always tell the truth, but this was too weird not to be true. "I . . . I should go," she said. "It was really nice to meet you. Both of you."

"You too." Jessie whipped a pen out of her handbag. "Would . . . would you mind giving me your autograph?"

"Um . . . sure. I . . . I guess." Nikki gave a little uncomfortable laugh. This never got any easier. "I'm not really famous or anything."

"You are to me." She thrust out the pen.

Nikki took it. "What would you like me to sign?"

"My bag." She held out the cheap canvas rucksack, the strap still over her shoulder.

The surface wasn't the easiest to write on, but Nikki signed her name anyway. She couldn't think of any way to get out of it.

"Just shoot me," Jessie breathed. "Thank you so much. If . . . if you ever want to stop by Carney's and say hi, we're there all the time, me and Monica. We can give away free fries without getting into trouble."

"Thanks." Nikki walked away with a wave and strode toward her car.

Ryan's computer. What on earth could there be on the computer, and what did it have to do, if anything, with Alison?

Chapter 9

With the help of her fancy new iPhone (she'd always been a BlackBerry girl), Nikki found the address of the Age of Aquarius Aquariums on Nielson Way in Venice. The GPS in her car took her right to it. It was only a few blocks off the beach, a cute shop with underwater scenes painted on the glass windows. A bell rang overhead as she entered.

There were rows of fish tanks filled with bright fish that immediately entranced Nikki. She lightly ran her finger along the glass of the nearest tank, watching an electric-blue school of tiny fish swim by.

"Hi, I'm Moon. Can I help you?"

Moon? Nikki looked up, thinking she probably had the right place. "Hi . . ."

The girl was tall and slender with long, blond hair tied back with a hot pink bandanna. She was wearing board shorts and a surfing tee, and was barefoot.

Nikki smiled. "Is . . . Mars in?"

"Sure, hang on. Daddy!" the young woman hollered over her shoulder.

Nikki guessed the girl was in her early to mid-twenties. She had a hot bod, super-healthy look with a gorgeous sun-glowed face. She didn't wear a bit of makeup. Nikki wistfully imagined the girl's life in Venice, California: working in a fish store, hanging out at the beach, rollerblading the famous boardwalk.

Nikki and Moon waited for Mars; they got no response but the bubble of fish tanks.

Moon rolled her eyes. "Dad!" she hollered again; then she looked at Nikki. "Sorry. He's a day trader when he's not being fishy. He had some kind of alarms going off in the back. I guess one of his stocks is tanking—no pun intended. He's got six or seven computer monitors." She grabbed a little net and scooped something out of the tank with the little blue fish.

It wasn't until the girl dumped the object into a trash can on the floor that Nikki realized it was a dead fish.

"Be free," Moon said.

Nikki must have had a look on her face that begged explanation.

"When I was little," Moon said, "and I played here, I thought I had to have a funeral for every fish that died. A box, a hole in the backyard. The whole thing." She wrinkled her delicately freckled nose. "It got old. Now I just wish their little souls good luck." She peered into the next tank. "You think fish have souls?"

"I . . ." Nikki hesitated. "I don't know."

The man Nikki had seen in Ryan Melton's living room walked into the room from the back. He was dressed similarly to his daughter. He was wearing a Grateful Dead T-shirt that looked to be from the seventies. He was also sans shoes. "Hi, can I help you?"

When he looked at Nikki she could tell he was trying to place her.

"Nikki Harper." She offered her hand.

He shook it hesitantly.

"We met," she said. "Actually, we didn't *meet*. I'm a friend of Alison Sahira's. I was at Ryan Melton's house last week right after the murder. I saw you in the living room."

"Right," he said slowly. Then he shook his head. He

was one of those people who took his time before he
spoke. "Crazy, awful day."

There was an awkward silence. Now that she was here,
Nikki wasn't sure how to proceed. "What kind is that?"
she asked, pointing to a black and white fish that looked
more like a piece of ribbon.

"Pennant Butterfly. She's gorgeous, isn't she?"

She could tell by the change in his expression that he
felt passionate about his fish. "And this is a saltwater
tank, right?" Nikki asked. "That's why the fish are so
beautiful."

Mars tugged on his ponytail. He was a nice-looking guy
in a California beach hippie kind of way. Nikki guessed he
was about her age.

"Only way to go," he said. "You have a tank?"

"No, I'm not sure I'd be good at taking care of it."

"That's where we come in," he explained with a lazy ca-
dence. He seemed like a man who had all the time in the
world. It was actually kind of refreshing.

"We set up the tank," he said. "Add the fish. Fifteen-
day guarantee on all the fish."

"He says that"—Moon walked by them with her little
fish net—"but he's a pushover. Some lady in Beverly Hills
called him the other day complaining someone was floating belly up in the tank in her husband's office. A doctor's
office. They've had the tank at least three months. Dad
drove a new Nemo all the way over to Beverly Hills."

"Nemo?" Nikki watched a miniature skate-looking fish
glide along the bottom of a tank.

"You know, a clown fish. *Finding Nemo*. Pixar flick."
Mars rested his hand on the tank Nikki was peering into.
"We're having a special on these hundred and fifty gallon
tanks." He named a price. "I can have you rolling in a
couple of days."

Nikki tore her gaze from a school of thumb-sized orange fish. "I didn't come to buy a fish tank."

"I didn't think you did." He had a nice smile beneath his blond mustache. "But they brighten up any house." He glanced at her, taking in her business attire. "Or office."

A phone rang and Moon trotted to the back of the small store.

They both watched her go, suntanned bare feet soundless on the tile floor. "Nice girl," Nikki said. "It must be great having her here to help you with the shop."

"It's the only way I ever get to see her." He was still watching his daughter, his eyes looking misty. "When she plays hooky and comes home to hang out with me."

"Hooky?" Nikki wondered if she'd misjudged the girl's age. Was she still in high school? She couldn't be.

"Getting her PhD in marine science at UCLA."

Nikki cut her eyes at the young girl leaning on the counter, talking on a cell phone.

"Following after her pop, I guess."

"Wow." Nikki looked at him. "Congratulations." *So much for stereotypes,* she thought as she adjusted her Prada on her shoulder. "Mars, I came to ask you about Ryan Melton. About that day."

"You a cop?" His gaze narrowed, causing tiny lines to form at the corners of his dark brown eyes.

"No, a real-estate broker in Beverly Hills. I knew Ryan." Barely a fib.

He hesitated. "Not much to tell you. I gave Detective Dombrowski my statement. He seemed cool with it." He shrugged. "At least I think he was. He didn't arrest me."

"But he did arrest my friend Alison Sahira," she said quietly. "And she didn't do it either."

He nodded. "I saw that in the *L.A. Times* and was kind of surprised."

Nikki found it hard not to jump in. She was so used to the lightning speed life of Beverly Hills. Everyone talked fast there. Interrupted each other. Venice and Mars seemed a million miles from there. She waited patiently for him to go on.

"No way she did it."

Nikki met his gaze, surprised he would offer that information so easily. "What makes you think she didn't kill Ryan?"

"Her aura was all wrong for a cold-blooded killer." He pointed to a tank with hot pink fish in it. "What do you think of these? They're cardinal fish. They'd look great in your tank."

Moon was now walking around the store, her cell phone to her ear. She was laughing, obviously talking to a friend.

"Um . . . they're beautiful." Nikki wasn't sure how to respond to the aura remark. It was great that Mars didn't think Alison did it, but she was relatively certain that a *wrong aura* defense wouldn't hold up in court. "Did you tell Detective Dombrowski that you don't think Alison did it? I mean, she just happened to be at the house, right? Like you."

"He wasn't asking for my opinion. Just the facts, so I gave him just the facts. I was pretty freaked out. I never saw a dead man before. Just in a funeral parlor. My grandfather. I had nightmares for months after, and he died last year." He pointed to the tank that had caught Nikki's eye when she'd first come in. "Electric Blue Cichlids. I could see you being happy with these, too."

"So . . . what *did* happen when you arrived at the Melton house that day? Alison's so upset. She's not really sure what happened, and now that she's been arrested, her lawyer doesn't want her talking to anyone. Not even to friends."

"Just trying to make sure she doesn't get run out on a rail, huh?"

Nikki wasn't quite sure what he meant, so she smiled *the smile.*

"That's good. She's lucky to have a good friend like you."

Moon, who was one aisle over, lowered the cell phone. "Dad, Tulip says the Dalai Lama tickets at USC are all sold out. Think there's any way you can get them for us? We were going to go for her birthday."

Mars grimaced and dropped a pinch of food into a tank. "Doubtful." He glanced at Nikki. "I'm just an adjunct professor."

"You're a professor at USC and you service fish tanks?"

Moon walked away. "He doesn't think he can get the tickets."

"On sabbatical," Mars told Nikki. "Writing a textbook for the marine biology department."

He didn't look like a college professor. Nikki wasn't entirely sure she believed him. Did college professors service fish tanks in Beverly Hills bathrooms? "That day," she said, going back to their previous conversation. "You arrived and . . ."

"Well, I went in the back gate like I always do. I've got the security code. Ryan was a hell of a nice guy. Used to bring me a beer while I worked. Anyway, I went in the back door as usual. I checked the tank in the master bath first. There was a pH issue."

"Did you speak to Ryan before you checked the tank?"

"Nope, a lot of houses, I just go in, do what needs to be done, and go out. They're on a monthly billing plan. Goes right to a credit card."

"Was Alison there when you arrived?"

"Not in the house. I'd been there about fifteen minutes when I heard the dog bark. I was finishing up the powder room. Not long after that I heard the front door open—"

"Wait a minute," Nikki interrupted. "You heard the Rottweiler bark? That doesn't make sense. Alison was bringing the dog back from the dog park."

He shrugged. "I'm just telling you what happened, Nikki. It's what you want to know, right?"

He looked at her with such sincerity that she glanced at the clean tile floor. She followed his lead and paused to think before speaking again. "If the dog was already in the house, do you know why Alison came back?"

He shook his head. "Didn't really think about it. There are service people coming and going all the time in houses in Beverly Hills. I didn't know it was her until I saw her in the hall. She was headed down the hall one way, I was headed the other."

"You saw her?" *Alison had said she never saw Mars until he came out to tell her Ryan was dead. Had she forgotten? Or lied?*

He nodded.

"Was she going toward the front of the house?"

"For the front door, I assumed."

"Did she say anything?"

He thought for a second. "Nope. I said, 'Hi.' She just sort of nodded. She was in a hurry."

Nikki closed her eyes for a second. She didn't know what to say. Clearly Alison had lied . . . to her and to the police. She opened her eyes. "How did you find Ryan? I mean . . . how did you come upon him if he was out on the pool deck?"

"I just wanted to let him know that I was on the pH problem. He'd left me a voicemail the evening before. Usually, if he's home, he's out on the pool deck. So I went out to the pool."

"And that's when you found him dead?"

Mars pressed his lips together. He looked like he might cry. "He was lying there on the lounge chair, his eyes open. But I knew his soul was gone. His eyes were empty. You know?"

"So you called the police?"

He nodded. "That's when I saw Alison again. Through the window. When I went back into the house to make the call. I couldn't stay with him. I just couldn't do it. So I went out the front door."

"Alison was in her van?"

He nodded. "She was on her cell. I made the 911 call. Then I went out the front door and told her about Ryan. I thought she might want to come in and put the dog up. Muffin would probably get scared, all the police and everyone there."

"Did Alison seem upset?"

"Of course she was upset. Who wouldn't be?"

"Did she act . . . strange in any way?"

"Strange how?" he asked.

"I don't know . . . guilty?" she dared.

He blinked. "No, she acted upset. She started crying when I told her." He stared at the pink fish. "So what do you say? Can I interest you in a hundred and fifty gallon fish tank?"

A few minutes later, Nikki sat in the front seat of her car, staring at the receipt in her hand for a fish tank. She couldn't believe she'd bought a fish tank. What the heck was she going to do with a 150-gallon fish tank?

She had no idea why she'd done it. It was just that Mars was so nice, and he seemed to really think she would enjoy the tank.

Nikki tossed the receipt on the passenger's seat and started her car. She was just pulling onto the street when her cell phone rang. An unfamiliar number flashed on the screen in the center of the dashboard. She'd splurged and traded in her old black Prius for a new one, just so she could have the integrated phone and navigation system.

She pressed a button on the steering wheel. "Hello?"

"Hey, Nikki, it's Moon."

Nikki slowly eased into traffic. "Hey." She hesitated. "How'd you get my number?"

"On the receipt for the tank. It was nice of you to buy it. Dad's tickled. He thinks you need some relaxation in your life. You being famous and all."

Nikki thought it interesting that Mars had made no indication he knew who she was. Was he so accustomed to working for *celebrities* that it didn't faze him? Or was he one of those rare individuals who just didn't care if she appeared on E! occasionally or that her mother was a movie star? *The* Victoria Bordeaux?

"How can I help you, Moon?" Nikki asked.

"I heard what my dad said about your friend. About her aura. Dad's a little wacky about that sort of thing. He always wants to assume the best about people."

Nikki slowed for a yellow traffic light. "Okay . . ."

"He said he didn't think the dog walker killed that guy, but I'm not so sure. You seemed nice. I'd hate to see you get wrapped up in the whole thing. You know, if she did do it."

"What makes you think she might have done it?" Nikki asked, thinking this was a really odd phone call. Could she trust Moon? But what reason would the young woman have to lie to her? Moon was the one who had initiated the call.

"I don't know if I should be telling you this. No, I'm sure I shouldn't be, but I just had this feeling I needed to call you. Daddy doesn't know I'm calling."

Nikki waited.

"I have a friend who works for a security company. That's who I was talking to when you were in the store. Can't be coincidence, right? Anyway, her name's Tulip. Yesterday, she mentioned that the police had come to the security company where she works the day after the murder. They had a warrant to get a digital copy of the security footage for the Melton house."

"So . . . there were no physical tapes?" Nikki knew that some people still used VHS tapes to record security footage, but more and more houses were utilizing digital feeds that could be recorded and/or sent to monitors in the house, but also to an outside site.

"I don't know the particulars. Tulip didn't really say. We were actually talking about warrants, not about the murder."

"Where does she work?" Nikki eased through an intersection and signaled to turn.

Moon was quiet on the other end of the line for a second. "Adam Ace Security in Beverly Hills. I'd appreciate it if you'd keep this on the down-low. I'm sure Tulip's boss would be pissed if she knew she was gossiping about what went on in her office."

"Sure. I really appreciate you calling me, Moon."

"Yeah, well, my horoscope this morning said I would provide vital information to a stranger, so I felt like I needed to call you."

That tidbit caught Nikki off guard and it took her a beat to respond. The girl was in her mid-twenties, getting a PhD, and read her horoscope every day? "Thanks, Moon. I mean it."

"You enjoy that fish tank," she said.

Nikki disconnected.

So had Alison been arrested because she lied about the dog . . . possibly about what she had been doing in the Melton/Elliot house? Or had there been something incriminating on the surveillance footage the police confiscated?

Nikki needed to talk to Tulip. But first . . .

"Victoria, mobile," she said.

"Calling Victoria, mobile," a voice replied.

Chapter 10

Nikki left a message for her mother, then pulled over to get an address for Adam Ace Security and punched it into her GPS. She was almost back to Beverly Hills when Victoria returned her call.

"Crazy question," Nikki said, changing lanes on Santa Monica Boulevard.

"I'll attempt not to provide a crazy answer," Victoria returned dryly.

Nikki assumed this would be a waste of time, but in the past, her mother had been able to provide her with items she could use to barter for information. Or at least give in thanks for cooperation. Victoria had an armoire full of gifts and gift certificates she'd received in green rooms before a television or red carpet appearance. She also had access to concert, performance, and sporting event tickets long after they had been sold out. It was all about who you knew in L.A., and Victoria knew everyone.

"You don't know the Dalai Lama, do you?" Nikki asked.

"What a ridiculous question."

Nikki laughed. Traffic was moderate to heavy. She stayed in the center lane and did her best not to get plowed over by the trucks and enormous SUVs. "I just wanted to check."

"Could you hold a moment, dear? That nice Megan is here scratching at my door. I'm in my trailer powdering my nose."

Nikki wasn't sure why her mother couldn't just say she needed to use the restroom. After all, she was human like everyone else, but that wasn't a word in Victoria's vocabulary.

She heard her mother's muffled voice, then a higher-pitched voice. A moment later, her mother was back on the phone. "Apparently we're reshooting a scene." Victoria sighed with obvious annoyance. "One of the *gentlemen* doesn't like how his hair looked in the last take."

Nikki smiled to herself. Victoria could be difficult at times, mostly with Nikki, but she was never, *ever* a diva on set. She learned her lines, showed up on time, and was always professional. She had little patience for those who did not behave in what she perceived as a professional manner.

"So, the Dalai Lama," Victoria said. "Have you decided to become a Buddhist, Nicolette?" She pronounced it "Bud-ist."

"Not this week. I was just wondering if you knew him because apparently he's coming to California. He's speaking at the University of Southern California and . . . there are these two girls I was hoping to get tickets for."

"Well, of course I can't call His Holiness directly," Victoria said. "I don't even know that there *are* phones in Buddhist temples." Again, *Bud-ist.*

"Mother, I don't think he actually lives in a temple."

"Let me make a few calls after we shoot this silly scene again. I'll call you later? This cell phone is very handy. I can call you. I can call Amondo to bring the car around. I suppose I could call and make an appointment to get my hair done, if I wanted."

"Which is why I've been telling you for years that you'd like having a cell phone, if you could just start keeping

track of it." Nikki was about to launch into another dia-
tribe about the conveniences of modern telephone technol-
ogy. Then she realized what her mother had just said. She
was getting as bad as Victoria with her digressions. "Wait
a minute." She gripped the steering wheel. "You *do* know
the Dalai Lama?"

"Well, it's not as if we're bosom buddies. His Holiness is
busy . . . doing whatever it is that a Lama does. You know,
people believe he's the reincarnation of the most learned
Lama. He's reached enlightenment. He can't be reincar-
nated as a fly or a beetle."

Nikki couldn't resist a chuckle. "Mother, how do you
know about Buddhist lamas?"

"Well, Richard, of course."

"Richard?"

"Heavens, I don't remember his name. He was in that
sweet film where Julia Roberts played the prostitute."

"Richard *Gere*?"

"That's him. I only have a minute, dear, so will you let
me finish?" Victoria paused and then went on. "I'm not
friends with the Dalai Lama, but I've met him. When I was
in India, years ago. He was very kind. He had a pleasant
smile. And he knew who I was . . . though I can't imagine
he would have seen any of my films," she mused.

"And you really think you could get me tickets?"

"I don't see why not. I know someone who makes the
arrangements when His Holiness is in the U.S. Two, for
USC. Anything else, Nicolette? I have to run."

It was on the tip of Nikki's tongue to say, "Just that I
love you," but she didn't. Couldn't. It wasn't something
they said to each other. "Thank you."

"You're welcome, Nicolette. Have a grand day. I'll call
you when we wrap for the day."

Nikki found Adam Ace Security on Brighton, off Rodeo
Drive. It was in a four story modern glass office building.

She parked in the garage below and took the elevator to the third floor.

Nikki introduced herself as a real-estate broker at the reception desk and asked to speak with Tulip. It turned out she was a technician; she was out on a service call, but the pleasant older woman behind the desk said she was expected anytime.

Nikki had spent less than ten minutes answering e-mails on her iPhone when a young woman with inky black hair and multiple piercings and tattoos walked in carrying a laptop bag.

Nikki stood. "Tulip?"

"Yeah?"

"I'm Nikki Harper. I . . . Moon gave me your name." She eyed the receptionist. If Tulip was going to be willing to give her any information, she was certain it wouldn't be in front of another employee. She took a chance. "She said you were looking at a property I'm listing?"

Tulip glanced at the receptionist, then back at Nikki. "Nikki. Right, right. Come on back." As she led Nikki through a swinging half door, she said to the receptionist, "North Canon is up and running again. Kids had a loose guinea pig and it chewed a wire."

"I'll let the clients know."

Tulip led Nikki down a hall, past several offices with glass doors. As Nikki followed her, she took in the baggy knee-length shorts, short-sleeved T-shirt over a long-sleeved T-shirt, and canvas sneakers . . . all black. Tulip was also wearing black knit gloves, the kind without fingertips. Like Moon, she was probably in her mid-twenties.

"We can talk in here." Tulip led Nikki into a conference room and closed the door.

Nikki wondered if Moon called and warned Tulip that Nikki might try to contact her. Had she been expecting Nikki? Was that why she was going along so easily?

"Thanks for seeing me," Nikki said quietly.

"Look, let's cut to the chase. I don't know anything about his association with any drug cartel. I haven't even seen him in at least a year." Tulip dropped her laptop bag on an oval glass table. It was a nice conference room, done in light-colored wood and clean lines; very Ikea. "I told that to the last Fed who came here."

"Fed?" *This girl had had contact with Feds?* "No. No, I'm not with the FBI," Nikki assured her. "I'm a real-estate broker."

Tulip studied her suspiciously. She was a pretty girl, despite the heavy black eyeliner that encircled her bright green eyes . . . and the tattoo of a snake with a long, forked tongue on her neck.

"You're not with the FBI? Because if you are," she said defensively, "I think you have to tell me."

"I'm Nikki Harper, with Windsor Real Estate. You can call my office and check, if you like." She reached into her bag and pulled a business card from the inside pocket. She offered it.

Tulip scrutinized the card, then Nikki. "Wait a minute. I know you. Aren't you—" She snapped her fingers. "I know you! Your mom is Victoria Bordeaux. You have her eyes. The Bordeaux blues." She tucked the card into her back pocket and clasped her gloved hands. "Oh my gosh. I can't believe it! I *love* her movies. My grandma and I watch them all the time. *The Widow's Daughter* has to be my favorite. I've seen it a hundred times."

Nikki smiled. She was always amazed by the different kinds of people she met who said they loved Victoria's films: cops, sanitation workers, grandmothers . . . and Goth techies.

"I apologize for coming to your work, but this is kind of important. Moon didn't call and tell you I might be coming?"

"Actually, I think she left me a message half an hour ago, but I didn't get a chance to call her back. Can I get you a Coke or something? Oh, gosh. I'm nervous. Sit down." She indicated a chair and waited for Nikki to sit before she took a seat across from her. "I can't believe Moon sent you here. She's the best. I didn't know she knew how much I liked Victoria Bordeaux."

"Actually, I didn't tell Moon I was coming. I . . . I wasn't sure you would talk to me if I called ahead of time."

"Wouldn't talk to you? Are you kidding? What do you want to know? Brad and Angelina's code to their front gate? State secrets? I don't know any, but I'd tell you if I did."

Nikki laughed and waved her hand. "Nothing like that, but . . . what I need to ask you is a little delicate." Nikki quickly related her relationship to Alison.

Tulip knew all the details of the murder. She said it had been the hot topic of conversation, in the break room, all week.

"So, she's in jail?" Tulip asked, wide-eyed.

Nikki had thought Tulip was an odd name, especially for a girl in black eyeliner and tats, but she seemed more and more like a tulip with every minute that passed. There was something sweet about her. Innocent.

"No," Nikki said. "She's out on bail."

"And *why* are you investigating the case?" Tulip asked. "You're not like some kind of double agent, are you? Real-estate agent by day, cop by night?"

"I'm not a cop." Nikki exhaled. "I'm here because . . . because I feel like it's important that her brother—"

She pointed. "Your boyfriend."

"My boyfriend, believe his sister." She waved her hand. "It's more complicated than that. I'm sure my psychiatrist would have a field day with this, if I had one. Anyway, it's important to me not only that Alison not have to stand trial, but that she be proved innocent, in Jeremy's eyes. So, what I want to ask is if you know what the police found on the video surveillance of the Melton/Elliot house that day."

"Actually, I probably couldn't tell you that. It's against company policy, and I like my job too much to break the rule of client confidentiality. But it doesn't matter because they didn't see anything."

"They didn't see anything?" Nikki asked.

Tulip shook her head. "Nope, everything had been erased."

"*Erased?*" Nikki repeated.

"Yup, from the home. I didn't install that system, but they probably have a laptop or a notepad that records the digital images and feeds them to us. But once they erase their images, ours are erased."

Nikki shook her head trying to understand what Tulip was saying. "Someone in the house erased footage?"

"Sure did." She leaned closer. She narrowed her green eyes. "Want to know my theory?"

"I do." Nikki held up her finger. "But first, let me make sure I've got this. Ryan's murder was not recorded?"

"Nope, the computer was clean until just before the police arrive . . . and find Ryan Melton dead. Whoever did it knew what he or she was doing."

Nikki sat back in her chair, thinking. "Can you tell when the cameras were shut off?"

"No, but whoever erased it went back to five a.m."

Which was about the time Diara would have left for the set. Victoria left at five. Nikki returned her attention to Tulip. "So what's *your* theory?"

"That Ryan erased them because there was something recorded that day that he didn't want his wife to see. Like maybe he was cheating on her. A hot-looking guy like him? You know girls had to be throwing themselves at him. I know I would be."

Nikki gave her a quick smile. "So . . . I'm still not entirely clear on the whole erasing thing. If he erased the evidence of whatever he had been doing in the house, wouldn't that have made his wife suspicious?"

Tulip shrugged. "I don't know. Someone erases stuff in that house all the time. But a lot of clients do it."

Nikki sat back in her chair. "It doesn't make sense," she said as much to herself as to Tulip.

"Maybe the killer did it."

Nikki looked up, smiled, then nodded. "I think maybe you're right."

"You bought a what?" Jeremy asked. He was cranky. He'd invited her for dinner and now was acting as if he didn't want her there. Dinner had been awkward. Jocelyn had been at play practice. Alison hadn't said a word through the entire meal. Nikki spent the meal chatting with Jeremy's kids. She now knew that Lani was on a horse kick and was reading *National Velvet*, Jerry was excited about some new comic book series release, and Katie had fish sticks at school for lunch.

Jeremy had been almost as quiet as Alison. Now, at least, he was speaking to Nikki.

She slid a dirty plate into the dishwasher. "A saltwater aquarium."

"What are you going to do with a saltwater aquarium?" He sounded judgmental.

"I don't know." She sounded defensive. She shrugged and reached for another dirty plate in the sink. "I thought maybe your kids would like it. We could have it set up in the living room. We can have it serviced so you don't have to do a thing."

"Nik, we've got two turtles and a lizard the kids don't take care of. We don't need fish."

She loaded another plate in the dishwasher. "I found out something interesting today."

Jeremy was putting leftovers in plastic containers. "Okay."

"Someone erased the security tapes at the Melton household the day Ryan was killed. And shut off the security cameras so there's no record of who came and went that day."

"Someone?" he asked. He sounded less than enthusiastic. He'd already made it clear that he thought she should stay out of the investigation into Ryan's death.

"I think it was Ryan," she said, pointing a dirty fork at him.

"Why would he do that?"

She shrugged. "I don't know." She thought out loud. "But, you know, it's interesting that he was so famous. I mean . . . he didn't *do* anything other than marry Diara."

Jeremy didn't say anything, but at least he seemed to be listening to her.

"He was in the news all the time: pictures of him playing golf, working out at the gym, just walking down the street. Articles about what charity event he was appearing at, or what award ceremony he had escorted his wife to." She turned to face him, leaning against the counter. "Do you ever remember hearing anything connecting him with another woman, other than his wife?"

Jeremy frowned and slid two sealed containers into the refrigerator. "Me? You know I don't read that kind of stuff. I certainly don't have time to watch any TV that isn't a family movie."

"Yeah, I don't really follow the news either," she mused. "But I know who does."

Chapter 11

"I really appreciate you getting this appointment for me, Marshall," Nikki said into her phone the next day. "Especially on such short notice." She'd just had her hair washed in the posh Byron & Tracey salon in Beverly Hills. She was waiting for her stylist, who was finishing up with another client.

"Not a problem, sweetie. Byron and I are buds. I hope you like McCale. He's super sweet. I think you should go for the bangs."

"No bangs. I'm just getting a trim." Nikki liked her natural red hair (Victoria called it strawberry blonde), but she wasn't very adventurous when it came to styling. She wore it parted on the left side, and it hung below her shoulders. Often it ended up in a ponytail.

"Be bold. Be brave. Go for the bangs," Marshall teased. "They're very in right now."

"No bangs," she repeated, glancing up to see Kate Bosworth, in dark sunglasses, slipping out the door. She lowered her voice. "So you're sure there hasn't been any gossip about Ryan and other women?"

"Positive. Never, ever," Marshall said. "In fact, there was a spread in some magazine last year. I can't remember which. It was about faithful husbands and wives in

Hollywood. Let me tell you, the list was short, but he was on it."

"But that's so un-Hollywood," she said, thinking out loud.

"Right. Monogamy, it's just not done. Ashton and Demi. It broke my heart when they split up."

"You think Ryan was smart enough to keep his extracurricular activity a secret?"

"I don't know," Marshall hemmed. "You met him. Nice guy. Gorgeous, for sure, but *not* the sharpest arrow in the quiver."

Nikki groaned and fussed with the collar of the white terry robe she'd been given to wear. She'd left her blouse in a locker, but unlike some of the women she saw walking by, she kept the rest of her clothing on. She wasn't here for a spa day. She was here on reconnaissance . . . and to get her split ends trimmed. "We'll see what McCale has to say," she told Marshall. "Then I'm going to run over to the gym where Ryan had a membership and see if I can bump into his trainer."

"Well, if he *was* cheating, those are the people who'll know. Hairdressers hold all the secrets in Hollywood. There's something about that chair. I know I can barely keep my mouth shut when I'm sitting in one. Hairstylists are worse than bartenders with good Scotch."

Nikki heard voices in the background.

"Gotta run," Marshall said. "Photo shoot for *GQ*."

Nikki groaned. "Please, your celebrity status is killing me. Weren't you just in *GQ*?"

"Cover, this time," he sang. "Somehow my manager talked them into running it the same month my next movie comes out. I'm coming, sweetheart," he said to someone.

"You coming to Movie Night tomorrow night at Mother's?" Victoria's Movie Nights were famous in Beverly Hills. Once a week, she had dinner for a dozen or so people and then showed a classic movie in the media room that she'd built before the days of media rooms. An invitation to a Victoria Bordeaux Movie Night was as coveted as an invitation to a family dinner at the Spielbergs'.

"*Lawrence of Arabia*?" Marshall said. "Wouldn't miss it for the world. Behave yourself . . . and be careful," he added.

"Be careful?" she asked. "I'm getting a haircut."

"And putting your nose into police business again. I'm just saying. Be careful. I don't want you ending up on the wrong end of a semiautomatic."

"I'm rolling my eyes," she told Marshall. "Can you see me rolling my eyes?"

A man in his late twenties walked into the shampoo area. He was tall and slender, and was dressed head to toe in black. "Nikki?"

"Talk to you later, Marshall," she said into the phone. She hung up and got to her feet, accepting the young man's hand. "McCale. Nice to meet you."

"And you," he bubbled. His bleached blond hair was chin length and appeared to have been chewed off with . . . a chain saw, maybe? And he had seriously dark roots. Were they intentional? She couldn't tell. Nikki was beginning to wonder if she ought to reconsider having McCale cut her hair.

"Right this way to my station," he went on. "I couldn't believe it when Byron said that Marshall Thunder had called asking for an appointment with me for you. God, he's a hunk and a half. I wouldn't be surprised if they didn't make him the next James Bond."

Nikki smiled at the thought. "British Native American?" she asked. "*That* would be interesting."

"Wouldn't it, though?" He led her behind a long row of styling chairs; every single one was occupied. Everything in the salon was white: the chairs, the tile, the carpet. White scared Nikki; she couldn't wear a pair of white pants or a white blouse without getting salad dressing or diet soda on it. "I can take your bag and hang it right here. Have a seat." He motioned to a chair three quarters of the way down the row.

Nikki handed him her bag.

"Vintage Prada," he murmured. "Very classy."

She sat down. The woman to her left getting blond hair extensions was talking on her cell, a mini mop dog on her lap.

"I'm going to throw a cape on you, if you don't mind. Just to be extra cautious. A beverage?" McCale snapped the black cape, as if he were a bullfighter, and draped it over her, securing it at the nape of her neck. "Coffee, tea, mineral water? A nice pinot grigio?"

She held up her hand. "No, thanks. Just the trim."

"Beautiful hair. Gorgeous, natural color. God, I love a natural ginger," McCale fussed, holding up a strand of her hair and letting it fall. "Now, I understand you want bangs. I think they'll frame your face magnificently."

Nikki looked in the mirror in front of her to see McCale leaning over her shoulder. He lifted a thick lock of hair and held it over her forehead, demonstrating a thick fringe of bangs.

"I don't think I'm ready for any changes," she told him. "Just the trim today."

"Whatever you say, sweetheart." He walked around her and went to his station on the wall. "So, how long have you known Marshall?"

"Years. My mother introduced us."

"Victoria Bordeaux," he sighed, fiddling with one pair of scissors, then another. "I *adore* that woman. I once held a door open for her at a restaurant. She was very pleasant. Very genuine."

Nikki smiled. "She is that."

McCale returned to his place behind the chair and Nikki watched as he combed out her wet hair.

"But you must be used to celebrities," she said, hoping her segue was smoother than it sounded. "I know you have a long list of star clients. Marshall said you were Ryan Melton's stylist. Shocking, wasn't it? His murder."

McCale clutched his comb to his chest. "I was a mess! I had to call out sick the next day. I took a Xanax and went back to bed. *Devastated,*" he declared, shaking his shaggy head. "You can't imagine."

"Awful," she agreed. "I'd just talked to him a few nights before it happened. At my mother's garden party. He seemed like a nice guy."

"Nice, nice isn't the half of it!" McCale gushed. He began to snip at her hair.

"I met Diara, too."

"Did you?" *Snip. Snip.* "Please tell me she's as gorgeous in person as she is on the screen."

"Gorgeous." She flicked a piece of hair off her arm. "They'd been married a few years. What, five? Six?"

"Going on five, I think."

"And you know," she said, "I never heard a single rumor about him. You know, with other women."

"He was totally devoted to Diara. Of course, *Diara . . .*" His tone changed.

Nikki met his gaze in the mirror in front of her.

"Yes?" she said quietly.

"I'm not sure the fidelity was reciprocated," he whispered.

"No," she breathed. She didn't know why that surprised her. How chauvinistic of her to assume *he* was the cheater. "*She* was cheating on *him*?"

"So I heard." He snipped as he talked. "But it was all very hush-hush. You know, to protect her squeaky-clean image. It wouldn't have done her well to have her name plastered all over the tabloids, not with her being a Disney deb and all."

"Do you know with whom?"

"Well, you know, I always wondered about her relationship with Angel Gomez and Julian Munro."

Nikki frowned as she remembered seeing Julian that day on-set. Her thoughts flew. Megan had said he was there all the time. Were Diara and Julian having an affair? Or Diara and Angel? Had Diara been the one who erased the security footage? Had Diara and Julian, or Diara and Angel, killed her husband so they could be together? It seemed far-fetched, but cops always looked at the wife first, didn't they? At least in the movies.

"So, what do you think?" McCale asked, holding her hair over her forehead. "Just a few wisps to try it out?"

"You're not coming?" Nikki said quietly into the phone. She'd spent the morning at work on the phone, then gone for the haircut, then met clients for a walk-through before settlement in Bel Air. She'd ended up running late and had to throw her vintage blue lace Valentino cocktail dress on in the bedroom Victoria still kept for her. Short of hospitalization, one was *not* late to Movie Night.

Nikki stepped into a pair of taupe Christian Louboutin heels. "And you're just cancelling now, Jeremy?" She tried not to sound too witchy.

"I'm sorry," he said, "but I'm just not up to it. I had a lousy day at work. The kids are arguing. It's Maria's day off, so the house is a mess, and my sister can barely drag herself out of bed to see to her own child."

Nikki could hear Victoria greeting guests downstairs at the front door. She needed to get down there and help her mother host. "It's just that I was looking forward to seeing you," Nikki said. What she really wanted to do was talk to him about everything she'd learned in the last couple of days. It was all just a jumble in her head. She couldn't figure out which details were important and which weren't. She was thinking that maybe if Jeremy could get Alison to confide in him... but by the tone of his voice, she doubted that would be happening anytime soon. She sighed. "It's fine. I understand."

He was quiet on the other end of the line and she felt the emotional distance between them widening. She wondered if she was making a mistake siding with Alison in this mess. Was she risking her relationship with Jeremy to come to his sister's defense? Was this really any of her business?

But someone had to believe in Alison, didn't they? If Victoria hadn't stood by Nikki that night at that marina, hadn't believed her when others hadn't, she might not be who she was today. Where she was.

"I have to run, Jeremy," Nikki said. "The guests are arriving." She paused, wanting to tell him not to worry, that everything would be okay. But what if it wasn't? "Talk to you tomorrow?"

"Sure."

Nikki ended the call and tossed her phone on the pile of discarded clothes on the bed. With a swipe of lipstick and a touch of Versace perfume, she went down the curved staircase to the elegant black and white tiled front hall.

"At last, Nicolette." Victoria turned to her distinguished guest. "You know Jerry," she introduced. "Governor, my daughter, Nicolette Harper."

"Nice to meet you, Governor." Nikki gave him *the smile* as she shook his hand.

"Could you show Jerry out to the terrace, where we're serving cocktails, dear?"

"This way." Nikki and the governor of California made small talk as they walked through the house and out onto the candlelit terrace. There, he excused himself to speak with a Silicon Valley start-up CEO.

Nikki made her way to the bar and ordered a club soda. She was just accepting the glass when a man behind her spoke to her.

"And there you are again, Ms. Harper."

She turned to see Detective Cutie-Pants: nice suit again, club soda in a glass in *his* hand.

"Okay, I really *am* surprised to see you *here*," she said. "What are you doing here?"

"I was invited." He raised his glass to her. "I like your hair. Something different. The bangs."

"Wisps," she corrected, sweeping the fringe of red hair off her forehead. She wasn't going to tell him about the haircut or the fish tank. She took a step toward him. "My mother really invited you?" She kept her voice low.

He tipped his head down and moved so that they stood beside each other. "I know . . . a cop. We don't exactly travel in the same circles, you and I, but then, in a way, we do."

She nodded and sipped her drink, gazing out at the other guests milling around on the stone terrace. "Dead people. Right. Sure."

He smiled. He was good-looking, and for the first time since she met him she had a feeling maybe he knew it. Maybe he used it to his advantage. If she didn't know better, she'd think he was flirting with her.

"Flying solo tonight? No Dr. Fitzpatrick?" he asked.

"He couldn't make it. He's home taking care of his sister. Someone had her arrested."

"Touché."

She turned to him, suddenly serious. "Tom, you don't really think Alison did it, do you?" She studied his face, trying to read him.

"We had enough evidence for an arrest."

"That's not an answer, Detective."

He glanced at her. "How do you keep getting involved in cases like this?"

She shrugged. "I don't know. They sort of find me."

He narrowed his eyes, holding her gaze for a moment. "You really *don't* think Alison Sahira killed Ryan Melton."

"Do you care what I think?"

"I shouldn't, but I have to admit, you've apparently got a knack for this."

"Alison didn't kill him, Tom. I'm telling you, I know her and she doesn't have it in her. And with a dog leash? Come on. Use your Spidey sense." She frowned. "Someone obviously set her up. Maybe your arrest was premature. Now, you don't have the evidence on the security footage that you thought you had."

His mouth tightened, but he didn't lose his cool demeanor. "How did you find that out?"

"I'm not going to tell you."

He held her gaze for a second. "Nikki, I know I said this before, but you really *do* have to stay out of this. You have to let us perform our investigation."

"You've made an arrest. How much more investigation will there be?"

He was quiet for a minute. Maybe because he knew she was right, or at least a little right. "How'd you find out about the security cameras?" he asked.

"Can't reveal my sources." She waited a beat. "What was on the laptop?"

This time he chuckled. "You want a job? I think we've got a detective position opening up."

"Got a job." She smiled and nodded to two of her mother's guests, a Spanish film director and his wife. "What's on the laptop?" When he didn't answer, she asked, "Does Alison know what's on it?"

"I don't know." He sipped his drink, looking over the rim of the glass at her. "Does she?"

"She's not talking."

"She say who hired Lyin' Lillie?"

Nikki did the eyebrow thing. "Lyin' Lillie?"

"Lillie Lambert."

"Yeah, I know who you mean. I just thought that only cops on TV talked that way."

"Nah." He grinned. "I'm sorry to say, we really do talk that way."

She studied him for a minute, taking in the expensive haircut, the designer suit. "What's your story, Tom? Because you don't add up."

"I don't add up?" He gave her a Sundance Kid half smile. He was *definitely* flirting with her.

"You don't seem like a cop. You seem more like . . . someone who's used to cocktails on the one thousand block of Roxbury Drive."

"Buy me a drink sometime. You tell me your story and I'll tell you mine." He glanced away, then back at her. "Excuse me. I need to say hi to the governor."

Nikki watched the detective walk away. She was still standing by the bar when Marshall made his entrance onto the terrace, a skinny blond model she recognized from the cover of *Cosmo* on his arm. The Amazonian waif was Swedish and barely twenty-one. He left her with a glass of champagne by a potted palm and came over to stand beside Nikki.

"New girlfriend?"

He groaned. "My publicist arranged the date. You know how paranoid he is, especially with the new film being released. We have to keep up my heterosexual reputation, you know." He ordered a Scotch, neat, at the bar and then stood beside her and swirled the amber liquid around in the Baccarat crystal glass the bartender handed him. "But you might actually enjoy talking to her."

She studied the young woman for a moment. She looked good on the *Cosmo* cover, but in person, she was emaciated. "You think we have a lot in common, she and I?"

He smiled, nodded, and took a sip of Scotch. "More than you'd guess." He leaned and whispered in her ear.

Nikki looked at him, her eyes going wide; then she grabbed his arm, pulling him toward his date. "Introduce me."

Chapter 12

"Nice to meet you, Oda." Nikki offered her hand. The model was at least six foot tall. Maybe six-one.

Oda had a surprisingly firm handshake.

"If you'll excuse me, I'll leave you ladies to chat." Marshall put one arm around Nikki's waist and the other around his date's. He kissed Oda's cheek, then Nikki's, and walked away.

Oda's gaze followed him and Nikki felt a little sorry for her. Did the poor thing really think she had a chance with Mr. Sexiest Man Alive?

"Such a gentleman." Oda spoke with only a slight Swedish accent. "It's a shame I prefer the ladies."

Nikki met the model's gaze and found herself smiling. "Blind date?" she asked.

"My publicist set it up." She pouted her gorgeous, full lips. "I hope Marshall won't be too disappointed."

Nikki's smile turned to a grin. "He'll get over it."

"So . . . Ryan Melton," Oda said, sipping from her fluted champagne glass. "Marshall told me about your friend who was arrested for his murder." A waiter, in a classic black tux, walked toward them, carrying a tray of hors d'oeuvres. "Ooh, food!" she said. "I'm starved." She accepted a white napkin from the waiter and chose not two, but three canapés. "These look amazing," she exclaimed.

"Ma'am?" The waiter held out the silver tray.

Nikki wondered when she'd gone from being "miss" to a "ma'am." Was there something magical that happened once you were over forty? Even if you were barely over the line? "Sure, why not?"

"Try one of the little crackers with the caviar," Oda bubbled. "Excellent."

Nikki took one of the beluga caviar hors d'oeuvres and a tiny crepe filled with avocado and goat cheese.

Oda grabbed another caviar cracker as the waiter walked away.

Nikki looked at Oda's stick-thin figure. "Don't tell me you actually eat?"

"And I don't purge." She giggled. "I guess I just have a crazy metabolism. My mother is the same way."

Nikki was trying to juggle her appetizers and her glass, and not doing a good job of it. "Shall we go over here?" she asked. She led Oda to a tall, small, round cocktail table, covered with a white linen tablecloth. Victoria had bought a half dozen of the tables years ago and constantly had Amondo dragging them out of the basement. They were perfect for standing at; this one, in particular, was perfect because it was a little out of the way of the other guests.

"So you and Ryan . . . were friends?" Nikki asked.

"Acquaintances. Not even. A friend's brother, Marcos, owns a club on Sunset Strip, Allegro. I ran into Ryan Melton there a couple of times."

Nikki nibbled on the avocado goodie. "Pretty exclusive club." It was one of those places where there were velvet ropes on the sidewalk and people waited in the hopes of being admitted. They rarely were.

"If you'd ever like to get in, let me know. I can leave your name at the door."

"My boyfriend and I aren't really into clubbing, but thanks." Nikki refocused. "Was Ryan with his wife?"

"No, I never met her." She licked her fingertips like a woman who knew how to enjoy a good canapé. "It seemed like his being there was more business-related than social. He was, what's the American word? *Schmoozing.*"

"Business schmoozing?" Nikki knew from the Internet research she'd done on Ryan a couple of nights ago that he was presently unemployed. Neither modeling nor acting had worked out for him. "What kind of business?"

"He wanted to open a nightclub. A nice one. He was looking for investors willing to drop a million each. He was pressing Marcos pretty hard. Mr. Melton had already made a financial commitment. He was desperate, I think. He was trying to act casual about it, but he had a look in his eyes. It was a little sad."

"You wouldn't think he'd need investors," Nikki thought out loud. "Diara's got to be worth . . ." One of Victoria's rules to live by was never to discuss one's income or net worth. "A lot," she finished lamely.

Oda leaned over the table, lowering her voice. "I got the feeling his wife wasn't backing him. That was the problem. Marcos said that Mr. Melton lost a large sum of his wife's money last year in a real-estate venture that failed. He said she cut him off. All he was getting was an allowance."

Nikki was liking Oda more by the second. "Interesting."

"I don't know much more than that, but if you'd like to come by the club, I could meet you and introduce you to Marcos. Maybe he could tell you more than I can." Her smile was genuine. "We could have a drink." She glanced up. "Who knows, you and your boyfriend"—she nodded over Nikki's shoulder—"might enjoy yourselves."

Nikki turned, spotted Detective Dombrowski looking

right at her, and turned back to Oda. "That's not my boyfriend."

"No?" Oda smiled her gorgeous smile. "The way he's looking at you, maybe he should be."

Friday afternoon, Nikki took off at three after making a sale on a Nantucket-style Cape Cod on the beach in Malibu. It was a gorgeous house, just renovated, with two ocean-side decks and an interior garden, stone countertops, and walnut floors. She figured a $9.5 million sale gave her the right to take off early on a Friday. But then she felt guilty and decided to hit the gym on the way home. Penance.

She was on her second mile on the treadmill when her phone rang. She glanced around; the gym was fairly empty this time of day. She hated it when people talked on exercise machines beside her, but after a mile, she was willing to use any excuse to slow to a walk. She dialed back the speed of the treadmill, surprised to see Adam Ace Security come up on the screen.

"Nikki Harper."

"Miss Harper, hi, it's Tulip. I hope it's okay . . . Moon gave me your number."

Nikki hit the STOP button on the treadmill and grabbed her towel. "Not a problem. Please, call me Nikki."

"I just wanted to thank you . . . Nikki. The tickets arrived by courier." She was obviously excited. "To see the Dalai Lama. You didn't have to do that."

"I hope you and Moon will enjoy the talk."

"I know we will. It was really nice of you."

Nikki stepped off the treadmill. "I don't suppose you'd like a fish tank?"

"You serious?"

"Completely," Nikki said.

Tulip laughed. "Nah, too much work. But thanks."

"No, thank you. You've been a big help."

"Just glad I could. You know, it's nice to help someone. Well, you have a good weekend."

"You too."

As Nikki walked to the locker room, she thought about what Tulip had said . . . about being happy to help. On a whim, she used directory assistance and made plans for dinner. After a shower, she was just finishing dressing when her phone rang: Victoria.

"Mother." Nikki tucked her iPhone between her chin and her shoulder, and stepped into her seventies Hermes black skirt with equestrian detailing. "How was your day?"

"Short. I had to shoot only one scene. I'm going shopping. Come with me. I need a new pair of flats. The darned heel popped off one of my Ferragamos again. I'll have to send Amondo to have it repaired, but I can't wait on them." She sighed. "Seems a waste, because then I'll have *two* pairs of good black flats."

Nikki stepped into her black boot, chuckling to herself. She was pretty certain her mother was the only woman in America in her tax bracket having shoes repaired. "Sorry, I . . . I have plans. For an early dinner."

"You and Jeremy patch things up?"

"Not really." Nikki pulled the zipper on her boot.

"I'm sorry." Victoria paused. "Well, heaven knows I can't give you advice in love. How many marriages did I have?"

Nikki grabbed her other boot. "Nine, if you count the second time you married Syd and Daddy."

"That was a rhetorical question, Nicolette. I know that still makes you angry that I married your father twice."

"The fact that you *divorced* him *twice* is what makes me angry, Mother. You were soul mates."

"And now he's dead. And since you felt you needed to bring that up, I think you need to go shopping with me and make it up to me. Then I'll go to dinner with you."

"I . . . I'm not sure where I'm going is your style, Mother."

"Oh, heavens, it's just dinner. I can eat wherever. I'll meet you on Rodeo. Amondo can drop me off. I'll even ride in the toy car of yours. See you at five in front of Chanel, darling."

Click.

Victoria didn't say good-bye. She never did.

Victoria bought black flats at Gucci, they window-shopped at Harry Winston's, and Nikki picked up some *delicates* (as Victoria liked to call them) in La Perla. Nikki loved shopping at secondhand stores for her clothes. She loved a bargain, but she always splurged on undergarments.

At six, they were in Nikki's Prius, headed down through West Hollywood on Sunset.

"So what's the big mystery? Where are we going for dinner? Not that Cuban place again, I hope. It was ridiculously expensive."

"Cuban place?" Nikki frowned.

"Where you and Jeremy took me for my last birthday. It was near here."

Nikki laughed and changed lanes. "Asia de Cuba? Mother, it wasn't a *Cuban* restaurant, it was Asian fusion. You were the one who said you wanted to try something different."

Victoria sat in the passenger's seat, her hands wrapped firmly around her black and brown circa 1970 Fendi bag. "I just hope we won't be late getting home."

"You're not shooting tomorrow." Nikki glanced at her. "You don't have to be up early."

"*It Happened One Night* is on TV tonight at nine. Clark at his best. Everyone made a fuss when he didn't win the Oscar *for Gone With the Wind,* but Bobby Donat deserved it."

Nikki eased the brake down as she stopped at the corner of King's Road and Sunset. She didn't bother to remind her mother she could record the movie and watch it anytime she wanted . . . sans commercials. Victoria was perfectly capable of using the DVR on her TV, but for whatever reason preferred not to.

"I promise you'll be home in plenty of time to see Clark."

Minutes later, Nikki pulled into a parking lot.

Victoria craned her neck. "A diner in a caboose? How quaint."

"It's Carney's, Mother." She pulled into a parking spot.

"Well, I can read that on the sign." She looked at Nikki. "And who did you say we were meeting?"

"We're not *meeting* anyone." Nikki got out of the car and waited for her mother. "There's someone I'm hoping I can speak with. She's supposed to be working tonight," she explained as she and Victoria walked across the parking lot.

"A Santa Fe caboose. On Sunset Boulevard," Victoria remarked as she climbed the stairs in front of Nikki, still clutching her Fendi. "Now I've seen everything."

"I can't believe you never noticed it before—it's a yellow caboose. There's another on Ventura."

"It's not as if I spend a great deal of time on the Sunset Strip, Nicolette."

Inside, a single row of tables and chairs ran along the left wall. Ahead, the counter was on the right. "Would you like to sit and I can order you something?" Nikki said.

Victoria looked around. "Won't the waitress take my order?"

"No waitresses, Mother. You order at the counter."

"Well, then I'll order at the counter."

Nikki couldn't help smiling as Oscar-nominated Victoria Bordeaux hustled herself to the diner counter, her

Fendi hanging off her arm. She looked as out of place as a pair of Jimmy Choos on a teamster.

Victoria leaned on the counter where a guy in a Carney's T-shirt and blue apron was lining up boxes of French fries and hot dogs. "Is there a menu?"

Nikki took her mother's arm and backed her up a step, pointing to the menu on the wall.

"Oh, my. There's so much to choose from," Victoria exclaimed, obviously enjoying the adventure. "What do you think? A burger or a frankfurter? Amondo will be disappointed he missed out."

"I . . . I don't know." Nikki scanned the employees behind the counter.

"Chicken parmesan," Victoria read out loud. "That doesn't sound like any fun. Who eats chicken parmesan in a railcar caboose on the Sunset Strip? What in heaven's name is a burger dog?"

"It's, um . . . a hamburger with a hot dog on top," Nikki answered, spotting blond dreadlocks under a red ball cap at the grill.

"Fascinating! I don't know how I'm going to decide," Victoria went on. "A Polish sausage with sauerkraut and mustard. Sounds divine."

A young Hispanic man leaned over the counter. "Can I help you?"

"Um . . . still deciding," Nikki said. "Is . . . Jessie available?"

"Jessie!" the young man hollered.

The young woman turned from the grill, spatula in hand. "How can I—" She froze. "Just shoot me. Just shoot me." She ran to the counter. "Miss Harper. I know I invited you, but I didn't think you'd really come."

"Hey, Jessie. How are you? I brought my mom for dinner. I was wondering . . . if you had time to talk to me for a minute?"

Jessie leaned over the counter and stared at Victoria,

who was still trying to make up her mind what she wanted to order. "Just shoot me," Jessie breathed. "Monica is going to be so upset that she called in sick." She looked back at Nikki. "I . . . let me see if I can take my break." She stepped away from the counter, then back. "Did Jose get your order? Let me buy your dinner. I get a discount."

"That won't be necessary," Nikki assured her.

"Jessie! Those your burgers smokin'?" someone hollered.

"I'll be right out." Jessie tapped the counter with her spatula. "I swear."

Five minutes later, Nikki and Victoria sat at a table, waiting for Nikki's name to be called. "So who are we here to talk to?" Victoria asked, lowering her voice. "I assume this has to do with Jeremy's sister. Is this one of her hangouts or something?"

Nikki glanced out the window, watching the traffic on Sunset. "You make me laugh, Mother."

"Well, I'm glad I'm good for something." She propped her designer handbag on the table against the window. "I don't know why you didn't let me buy you dinner."

"Because I invited you," Nikki answered firmly.

"Nikki!" the Hispanic man called from behind the counter.

"I'll get it! I'll get it!" a woman called. Jessie.

Nikki looked at her mother across the table. "I'm hoping this girl can help me find out what incriminating evidence the police found on Ryan Melton's laptop. Her brother's roommate works for the computer firm the police subcontracted to have a look at it."

"Oh, goody." Victoria swiped on pale peach lipstick. "A caboose with frankfurters and spies."

Chapter 13

"I... I guess I could ask. You know, kind of sneaky like." Jessie clutched her soda cup. Her short fingernails were painted fuchsia and blue, alternating nail to nail.

"Heavens, this is the best frankfurter I've ever had." Victoria chewed delicately and dabbed at her mouth with a brown paper napkin. "You know, Jessica dear, it's not as if anyone will be hurt by this brother of yours telling us what's on that laptop. It will all come out in court."

"Brother's roommate," Nikki corrected.

Jessie stared wide-eyed at Victoria sitting across from her at the diner table, munching a hot dog with sauerkraut and mustard. "Just shoot me. I still can't believe you're here," she breathed. "No one's going to believe me."

"Leave your address with Nicolette. I'll send you a personally autographed photo. Nicolette, are you going to eat all your fries? I don't dare order more. I won't fit into my costumes Monday, but these fries are extraordinary. Just the right amount of salt."

"We have to change the oil all the time. That's what makes them so good," Jessie offered.

Nikki pushed the flimsy, brown cardboard box of fries across the table. "I'm done. Have them." She looked at Jessie sitting beside her. "You and Monica were talking about standing outside a nightclub. What would you say if I could get you *inside* one of those exclusive nightclubs? Allegro."

"*Allegro?*" Jessie breathed. "Just shoot me. Do I have to get him to steal the computer?"

"No, of course not." Nikki touched Jessie's arm. She would have laughed, but the girl was entirely serious. "I just want to know what your brother's friend found on the computer. I don't even need the details."

"That's it? And you'll get me and Monica into Allegro?"

Nikki raised and dropped her shoulder. "I'll see what I can do, either way. I feel a little bad, stalking you like this."

"Oh, no, Miss Harper." Jessie sipped on her straw. "Stalk me anytime."

"Could you pass the ketchup, Nicolette? It's nice of you to do this, dear," Victoria said to Jessie. "This young woman who's been accused of killing the Melton boy, she's already got the cards stacked against her. I'd hate to see her go to jail for life if she didn't do it."

"And leave the killer still on the loose," Jessie breathed. "What about the police? No, wait, they're on the take, right?"

Nikki took a drink of her diet cola. "I'm just doing this for my friend."

"Jess!" a man hollered from the counter. "You plan on working any more tonight?"

"Shoot me now, I've got to get back to work." Jessie came out of her chair. "We're only supposed to take fifteen-minute potty breaks."

Nikki fished a business card out of her bag hanging on the back of her chair. "Call me if you find anything out."

"Definitely. I'm seeing my brother tonight. Party at his neighbor's." She pushed in her chair.

"Jess!"

"I'm coming!" she shouted over her shoulder. Then looked back at Nikki and Victoria. "Thanks so much for stopping by." She clutched her drink cup to her chest. "I can't tell you how much this means to me, you trying to find Ryan's killer." Her eyes started to tear up.

Victoria occupied herself squirting ketchup beside the last of the fries, from a plastic ketchup bottle.

"Um . . . you're welcome." Nikki got up. "Is there some way I can contact you? I'll have to talk to my friend about getting you into Allegro."

"Oh, yeah. Definitely." She pulled a pen from her pants pocket, leaned over the table, and scrawled a number on a napkin. Then she wrote her name, putting a heart over the *I*. "Thanks again." She backed away from them. "Ms. Bordeaux." She nodded.

"Nice to meet you, dear." Victoria smiled kindly and popped a French fry into her mouth. "Nice girl," she told Nikki when Jessie walked away. She leaned on the table, licking her fingertips delicately. "Now tell me what Marshall's leggy date had to say about Ryan Melton. She have any dirt on him and Alison?"

"No. What gives you that idea?"

Done with her meal, Victoria wiped her mouth with a clean napkin and then dug into her bag for her lipstick. "I think she did it, and I think you're going to ruin your relationship with Jeremy over it."

"Alison didn't kill Ryan Melton," Nikki insisted, speaking under her breath.

Victoria applied her lipstick. "I think she did, so let's see if we can get this investigation going and you can prove it."

Nikki dropped her mother off in plenty of time for her hookup with Clark Gable, then on impulse, headed back toward West Hollywood. Half an hour later, she was ringing the doorbell of a cute, two-story, yellow Cape Cod on a residential street. A young Asian girl with orange hair answered the door.

"Hey-ya." She wore cutoff jean shorts and a yellow Cheerios graphic T-shirt. Sounds of automatic weapon fire blasted from behind her. TV, Nikki hoped.

"Hi." Nikki absentmindedly jingled her keys in her hand. She'd left her bag in her car. She looked down at her feet, then back at the young woman. "Elvis in?"

"Elvis! Someone at the door for you!" She looked back at Nikki. "You wanna come in? Quentin Tarantino night on TBS."

Nikki smiled. "No, thanks. I'll just wait here."

Nikki had just settled on the wooden bench swing and given herself a push when Elvis walked out onto the porch and closed the door behind him.

"Hey there, little lady," he crooned with the lopsided grin that she always found eerily spot-on. He sauntered toward her.

Her half brother was dressed casually this evening, rather than in a replica of one of Elvis Presley's famous costumes. He wore black pants, a white shirt, and a blue tie that hung loose below his unbuttoned collar. The men's leather ankle boots were a nice touch.

"That the same shirt you wore for your mug shot in Colorado in 1970?" she asked, even though her little brother Jimmy wasn't alive in 1970.

He grinned, winked, and gave her the old "pistol fire" acknowledgment. "You know, it wasn't really a mug shot. I was awarded an honorary police badge."

She stopped the porch swing and he sat down and gave it a push.

"Nice place, E." She'd never been here before, but he'd texted her the address when he moved here a few months ago. It was a residential treatment facility for folks with mental disorders.

E, like his deceased father, was schizophrenic. When he

was on his meds, as he appeared to be now, he could seem totally sane . . . if you could look past the blue/black pompadour and upturned lip. He made his living, as it was, doing Elvis impersonations, often on street corners. He did private parties and karaoke bars when he was lucky. He was on a good run right now and had been working at a used car dealership on Sunset for the last six months or so.

"People are a little nutsy here, but it beats the alley off Hollywood and Vine," he quipped.

"So, how've you been doing?" she asked, patting his knee. "Really. Because you look good."

"She send you?" He sounded hopeful.

He always referred to their mother as *she*. He'd had a falling out with Victoria ten years earlier and they didn't speak. *She* maintained it was because her son refused to seek help for his mental illness, help she was willing to pay for. Jimmy insisted it was because she was jealous of his talent. Nikki tried to remain neutral; it was hard for her to see him ill. After his years of drug abuse and arrests, after years of trying to help him, she'd realized she couldn't help him if he wouldn't help himself. She hoped he was doing as well as he appeared to be.

"She wanted me to get you a birthday present," she said. "I thought I'd stop by the car lot one day. Maybe we could have lunch."

He looked away. It was dark now and the only light on the porch was the glow that came through the curtains on the windows of the house. Agitated voices came from the TV inside. The light in the windows flashed, as the images on the TV screen probably changed. The air was cool and smelled faintly of freshly mowed lawn and hydrangeas.

Jimmy looked at her. "So, what's up, big sister? Who's dead now?"

She cut her eyes at him.

"Come on, little lady. The last two times we saw each

other, you were knee-deep minding business that wasn't yours to mind. In fact, if I seem to recollect correctly, you were in a spot of trouble and *The King* had to come rescue you."

All true, or mostly so. She was glad his memory was clear; it wasn't always. "I'm not in any trouble. I just . . ." She exhaled, dropping her keys in her lap. "Actually, I have no idea why I'm here."

"So you're not championing another innocent soul headed for the *Jailhouse Rock?*"

She turned to him. "You haven't seen the papers?"

"Bad for my recovery." He smiled and this time it was Jimmy's smile, not Elvis Presley's. "Real world already overwhelms me."

She smiled back. "It's Jeremy's sister, Alison. She's been accused of killing Ryan Melton."

He shook his head. "Bad news for her. Who's Ryan Melson?"

"*Melton.* You really don't read the papers, do you?"

He pushed back the lush, dark hair that was his own and not a wig. He certainly looked like Elvis, the Elvis before the pills and overindulgence in peanut butter and smashed banana sandwiches.

"Ryan Melton was married to Diara Elliot."

Jimmy raised his black eyebrows.

"One of the Disney Fab Four? Then played Ellie on *Smart Avenue* for two years," she said, naming an Emmy-nominated TV drama.

He shook his head.

"Has her own perfume? She's got a billboard on Santa Monica? Gorgeous blonde with big brown eyes?"

"I don't get out on the freeway much in my caddie."

"Guess you don't watch much TV either?"

He shook his head.

"Okay, well, she's a big star and he was a big star because he was amazingly handsome. Sexy—"

"And now he's dead. And the police think Alison did it?"

She gave the swing another push and told him about meeting Ryan and Diara at Victoria's party. About the phone call from Alison. About her dog-walking business. About meeting Alison at the Melton/Elliot house and her arrest. Even about Detective Dombrowski and Jeremy. Jimmy sat and listened. He had always been a good listener, even at his craziest. And when she was done, they just sat together, swinging in silence for a couple of minutes.

"Okay," he finally said. "So, tell me again how all this is your problem? I mean . . . it sounds like Jeremy is pretty pissed at you for getting involved anyway."

She nodded. "He's that, all right."

Jimmy waited.

"I . . . I guess I just don't want Jeremy to believe Alison did this. She needs someone to believe her. She needs someone to prove to Jeremy that she didn't kill Ryan, and it doesn't seem like she's willing to fight for herself right now."

"And you don't think this detective will get to the truth?"

"I don't know." She thought for a moment. "Tom's a good guy, but he's got his arrest. Obviously he's got evidence against Alison, all of which I don't know yet. What if she gets to court and the evidence says she did it, even though she didn't? Even if she gets off with her fancy lawyer, what if Jeremy believes for the rest of his life that his sister murdered someone?"

"So . . . just so I understand why you're putting yourself at risk for her—"

"I'm not putting myself at risk." She opened her arms. "I'm just asking some questions."

"Like the last time? And the time before that?"

"There's no danger, E."

"Unless you get too close to the person who really did it . . . again."

She was quiet.

"So is this about you, or about Alison?"

She scowled. It had been a mistake to come here. What was she thinking? She needed to get home and take Stan and Ollie for a walk. She needed some sleep. "How would this be about me, E?"

"I don't know. You tell me."

She looked at him through the darkness. It was weird, looking at Elvis Presley . . . but talking to her brother. "I think it's important that someone believe in Alison. Believe that the person she was isn't the person she is now. She could lose her daughter over this mess. It can't go to trial." She pressed her lips together. "And Jeremy can't go through life believing his sister murdered someone."

"Fair enough."

She glanced at him. "You get it? Why I need to do this?"

"No, I think you're crazier than I am, little lady." He gave her the Elvis smile, upper lip curled perfectly.

Nikki got up. "Thanks, E."

He followed her to the step. "Thanks for coming by. Good to see you."

"You too. Glad you're doing well." She turned away and was halfway down the dark walk when Jimmy called out to her.

"For what it's worth?"

She turned. He looked young and handsome and . . . healthy in the dim light.

"From what you told me, I'd check out the little woman. The gorgeous one on the billboard."

"Diara? You think?"

"Trust me. Cases like this"—he winked—"it's *always* the little woman."

Nikki's phone rang at seven the next morning. The number that showed on the screen was unfamiliar, but that wasn't all that unusual in her line of business. One of the downsides of her job—everyone had her phone number. "Nikki Harper," she said, throwing her legs over the side of her bed.

"Porn."

"I'm sorry?" Her dogs began to bark and dance at her feet. "Who is this?"

"Just shoot me. I'm sorry, Miss Harper. Nikki. It's Jessie, Jessie Bondecker. Sorry to call you so early, but I talked to my brother's roommate last night."

Nikki could barely hear Jessie for all the barking. She pushed her hair out of her eyes and padded barefoot out of her bedroom. The dogs followed. "Hush, guys."

"I'm sorry?" Jessie said.

"Not you, Jessie. My dogs." Nikki snapped her fingers and led them down the hall toward the stairs. She lived in an amazing little Craftsman bungalow on Wetherly Drive in West Hollywood, a bungalow with a backyard. "Sorry. Can you start again?"

"I woke you up. I am *so* sorry."

"It's okay. Really. Just hang on one sec." Once downstairs, she walked through the living room, into the kitchen, and opened the back door. The dogs sailed out, cute ears flopping. "Can you start again, Jessie?"

"I talked to my brother's roommate last night at the party. The one who works for that computer place. He was *so* wasted. I beat him playing beer pong like four times. He's kind of cute, but I don't think he knows I'm alive. You know what I mean? I mean, he *knows* I'm alive. He played beer pong with me, right? But you know, like he's not interested in me."

Nikki made her way to the kitchen counter and added water to her electric kettle. Coffee was definitely in order this morning. "Jessie, when you first called, did you say something about *porn*?"

"Yeah, that's why I called. Like I said, I'd never take advantage of having your phone number and call all the time or anything."

Nikki leaned against the counter. The refinished maple flooring under her bare feet was cool. She was just wearing boxer shorts and a ratty T-shirt. She wished she'd grabbed a sweater on her way down. "What were you talking about when you said 'porn,' Jessie?"

"That's what was on the computer."

Nikki switched her cell from one ear to the other. "Ryan Melton's laptop had porn on it?"

"Yup," the girl said triumphantly.

Nikki grabbed a mug from the cupboard. "So? What's that got to do with Alison?"

"It was her."

The teakettle whistled. Nikki was still fuzzy from sleep. Or maybe Jessie was just hard to follow. "Who was her?" She rubbed her forehead. "What are we talking about, Jessie?"

"That's what I'm trying to tell you. The skin flick on Ryan's laptop. Your friend who was arrested. She was in it."

Chapter 14

Nikki was upstairs getting dressed when she heard someone knock at her door. Her back door. She pulled on a pair of jeans. Her backyard was enclosed by a nine-foot privacy fence to keep the boys safe.

Nikki hurried downstairs. "Coming!" she hollered. Sometimes Stan or Ollie, or both, squeezed under the fence and ran into Rob and Marshall's backyard. They didn't mind if the dogs dropped in once in a while, but they did mind the gifts the dogs left behind, usually on their pool patio. "Sorry. I was upstairs getting dressed," she said as she opened the door.

It was Marshall, dressed in expensive Italian athletic pants, a tight black Under Armour T-shirt, and running shoes. He didn't dare run in their neighborhood, for fear of being spotted by fans or paparazzi, but he liked to hit the treadmill first thing in the morning.

The dogs shot through the door ahead of him and disappeared into the front of the house. Probably because they knew they were in trouble.

"You're not going to believe what I just read on this crazy blog I follow." He came into the kitchen. "I'm pretty sure the blogger is somehow connected to the Beverly Hills police force, because she knows *way* too much to just be a casual observer. Maybe a wife or a girlfriend of a cop who talks too much?"

"Coffee?" she offered. "I'm on my way out the door. I'm kind of in a hurry."

"Where you headed so early?"

Nikki pulled another cup from the cupboard and reached for her French press on the gray soapstone counter. "I've got to talk to Alison."

"I'd say. You're not going to believe what I just read."

She poured the coffee. The smartest thing was to go to Alison and just ask her outright what Jessie could possibly have been talking about. Pornography? No way. Obviously there was a mistake. Maybe miscommunication or exaggeration? Maybe Alison posed for some semi-nudie pictures or something once upon a time? Maybe that was what Jessie's drunk beer-ponger was talking about. A topless photo of Alison when she was nineteen. Not good news for her child-custody case, but that certainly didn't make her a murderess.

She added cream and artificial sweeter to both cups. "What'd you read, sweetie? I really have just a minute."

"It can't be true! It's too shocking, in every sense of the word."

Nikki took a sip of her much-needed liquid caffeine and pushed the other cup into Marshall's hand. "What now?"

When Marshall ran out of gossip rags to read, he surfed the Net for Hollywood gossip blogs. He was featured in them all the time. Nothing delighted him more than to hear what beautiful female costar he was now dating.

"Don't tell me," she said. "Another Victoria's Secret angel is having your baby?"

"No one's having my baby. Rob and I aren't ready." He held the hand-thrown pottery mug between his big hands. "It's Alison, honey." He grimaced. "You may have been a little premature in jumping to her defense."

Nikki looked up at him over the rim of her coffee cup. "Let me guess. Nudie photos."

He frowned, an exaggeratedly sad look on his face. "Victoria wasn't even sure I should tell you. She—"

"My mother knows?" She laughed, amused more than annoyed. "You already talked to my *mother*?" She grabbed a banana off the counter, but seeing it had a big brown spot, dropped it. "Don't you have your own mother?"

"You don't get up until seven on Saturdays and my mother has water aerobics. I can always count on Victoria being up when I'm on the treadmill."

She took another swallow of coffee. "I *really* have to go. Can you tell me on the fly? I need shoes." She walked out of the kitchen, past a handmade mirror she'd bought in an antique shop in Mendocino. She glanced at her reflection and tugged on her saggy ponytail. "And maybe a comb."

"And lipstick. If you're headed to Jeremy's, there may be paparazzi." He followed her through the living room. "Go with a nice peach. And some mascara."

At the bottom of the stairs, Nikki turned on her heels, coffee mug still in her hand. "Paparazzi? Why would there be paparazzi at Jeremy's?" She got a sinking feeling in the bottom of her empty stomach. "Marshall, I'm not following you."

"It's bad, Nik," he said gently.

She waited, nibbling on her lower lip. "Okay."

"Porn."

It was the same word Jessie had used. "You . . . you mean like photos, right?" She stubbornly clung to her assumption. Her prayer. "Topless on the beach. She was in France that summer—"

"I'm afraid it wasn't photos they were talking about."

Nikki held her coffee cup against her chest as if she could protect herself. "You're kidding me. You've *got* to be kidding me."

"Porn as in pornographic movie. Miss Tinseltown Tattletale says authorities believe Alison murdered Ryan Melton after he tried to blackmail her with the thought-to-be-long-lost footage."

Nikki groaned. "Really, Marshall? Alison? Making pornography?" She turned and headed up the steps. It couldn't be true. It was more nonsense, like the alien spacecraft and Emma Stone's secret triplets he'd read about the previous week. "Sweet, innocent, *boring* Alison?"

Marshall remained at the bottom of the staircase and called up to her. "It's always the boring ones who surprise you!"

Nikki used the code to open the security gate to Jeremy's house in Brentwood and made sure it closed behind her before she proceeded up the driveway to his two-story Colonial.

She called him from her car. "Just coming up the driveway," she said when he picked up. "What'cha doing?"

"Eating cereal. Reading the paper." He sounded as if he was in a good mood for the first time in a week.

Nikki suspected she was about to ruin his good mood. Bringing up the word *porn* in association with a guy's sister was never fun. Maybe she wouldn't have to talk to Jeremy about it. Maybe she could get Alison alone and clear it all up.

"Did I know you were coming?" Jeremy asked. "Yesterday I forgot Katie's pediatrician appointment. This whole thing with Alison, it's got me rattled, I guess."

"I . . . I was just stopping by before I go to Mother's, to . . . help her with some stuff in the attic." Not exactly a lie; Nikki had been promising Victoria that she'd help her go through some boxes. Victoria had it in her head that she didn't want people pulling through her possessions after she was gone. Nikki had been arguing that while she agreed the chore should be done, she didn't suspect her mother was going anywhere soon. Maybe today really would be the day to start the project. "I thought I'd say hi. Fortify myself with some of that fresh ground Colombian of yours."

"Ah, I won't ask about the attic," Jeremy said. "Front door's open."

Once inside, Nikki stopped in the living room to say hi to Jeremy's girls, who were watching cartoons while big sister Lani tried to show little sister Katie how to play Candyland. Lani informed Nikki that their thirteen-year-old brother had gone camping with his Boy Scouts troop and that she hoped rattlesnakes got him. Apparently, he'd taken her pillow instead of his own.

"Morning," Nikki said when she walked into the kitchen. "You sure you don't want a fish tank? I think the girls would love it."

Jeremy sat at the granite counter with the *L.A. Times* open, an empty cereal bowl pushed to the side. "Morning. No fish tank. And you might not want to kiss me," he said as she leaned over for said kiss. "I ran, but I didn't shower yet."

"I don't care." She kissed him soundly, happy to see him acting like himself again.

He smiled. "Coffee's made. Want me to get you a cup?"

"Nah, I'll get it myself." She stalled, taking her time making it, wiping up spilled milk on the counter, hoping Alison would appear.

"Alison here?" she asked finally, trying to sound casual. She sipped her coffee.

He cut his eyes at her. "As far as I know. I assume still in bed. Jocelyn had a sleepover and then some kind of science bowl practice today. My sister doesn't get out of bed unless she has to."

Nikki sipped her coffee. "She's not working?"

"I don't know what she's doing." He began to fold up his paper, sounding tense again. "I know she's still working for some clients, but it seems like she spends most of her day moping around here."

"Do you blame her?" Nikki asked as gently as she could. "I mean . . . this is pretty awful. Being accused of killing someone."

He didn't say anything. He got up and rinsed out his cereal bowl. "I don't want to fight about my sister," he said as he shut off the water and wiped his hands on a towel.

"Me neither." She met his gaze and they stood there for a second just looking at each other, neither sure where to go from there.

"You staying a few minutes?" he said finally. "I'm going to run up and grab a shower."

"Sure, I'll be right here."

Nikki had read the front page and skipped to the world news when she looked up, surprised to see Alison walk into the kitchen. It wasn't nine yet. She was dressed. Hair combed. She was wearing one of her 90210 dog-walking polo shirts. "Alison? Going to work?"

"I promised a client I'd be there. I have to make my car payment, I guess."

Nikki glanced in the direction of the living room; she could hear the girls laughing. Jeremy was still upstairs. "I need to talk to you."

"*Please,* let's not start again. I don't know who hired Lillie Lambert." Alison moaned. "And I'm not really in a position to care too much."

"What if the real killer hired her?" Nikki asked. The thought hadn't occurred to her until the words came out of her mouth.

Alison scowled. "That doesn't make any sense."

"None of it makes any sense." Nikki got up from the stool and walked around the counter, trapping Alison between her and the coffeepot. "Ryan Melton's computer was taken at the scene of the murder."

"Was it? I guess that's pretty routine, isn't it?" Alison's voice sounded airy. She poured herself a cup of coffee.

"They're saying there's something on that computer . . .

something that Ryan could have been . . . trying to hold against you."

Alison began to add sugar to her cup. One teaspoon. "Hold against me?" Another.

"Blackmail you."

Alison added a third spoon of sugar. "Who's *they*?"

She tried to catch a glimpse of Alison's face to get a better read on her, but she was facing the sink, her body turned slightly away from Nikki. "Could the police have found something on that computer that they could think is evidence against you?" When Alison didn't answer, Nikki went on. "Because, what they're saying. It's crazy. There's no way it's true. So if you just tell me, honestly, what's on that computer, I—"

Alison turned to look at her, her face stricken.

Nikki halted midsentence. "Oh, no, Alison. You're not serious."

"It was a bad time in my life." She started to blubber. "It was just the one. My boyfriend at the time, he said it would make us rich. He said . . ." She took a gasping breath. "I never thought I'd get married, have a daughter . . ."

"What is it? Not just pictures?"

Alison shook her head.

So Tinseltown Tattletale knew what she was talking about. Nikki felt like an idiot. No, just naïve.

"How . . . how did you know that's what was on his computer?"

"He told me," Alison whispered.

"*When?*"

"I'm sorry," Alison sobbed, covering her face with her hands. "I'm so sorry. I've disappointed you. I've embarrassed Jeremy and Jocelyn. I'm so sorry!"

"It's okay." Nikki put her arms around Alison, who was shaking all over. "It's okay. We'll figure this out."

"I don't want to go to jail. I don't want Jeremy to think I belong there!"

"Shh," Nikki soothed, patting her back.

"I can't believe I've made such a mess of my life!" Alison was crying so loudly that neither of them heard Jeremy come into the kitchen.

When he saw the two of them hugging, he cursed under his breath and closed the door between the kitchen and the living room. "What's going on?"

"I didn't want to tell him," Alison whimpered. "I'm not supposed to tell anyone anything. Lillie was very specific. She said they wouldn't pay my bill if I ran my mouth."

Nikki smoothed Alison's hair. "It's going to be all right."

"It's not," Alison whispered.

"Tell me what?" Jeremy had changed into jeans, a green polo, and boat shoes. His wet hair was combed and he was wearing the Chopard watch Nikki had given him for Christmas.

"The police have some incriminating evidence on Ryan Melton's laptop," Nikki said slowly.

Alison sniffed and stood up, letting go of Nikki. She'd left a wet spot on the shoulder of Nikki's T-shirt. "It's not what it sounds like. I mean, *it is*. That is me." Alison's voice quavered. "But he wasn't trying to blackmail me."

Nikki grabbed a paper towel off a spool on the counter and handed it to Alison.

"Is someone going to tell me what's going on here?"

He was back. Angry Jeremy. Nikki didn't know him.

"You tell him," Alison said softly. "I can't do it."

Nikki exhaled and turned to Jeremy. "Sit down."

"I don't want to sit down."

"Jeremy—" Nikki started.

"I made a mistake, okay?" Alison surprised them both with the strength of her voice. "I did a lot of stupid things in my early twenties. You already knew that."

"What did you do?"

Nikki felt so bad. For both of them.

"What'd you do, Alison? And I want the truth."

She looked down at the floor. "I made an X-rated film."

"You what?"

"Jeremy, please." Nikki reached for his arm. They were all standing in the relatively small space between the kitchen counter and the island. "Let's sit down and talk about this."

"You made pornography?" Jeremy asked his sister.

She pressed her lips together, tears running down her cheeks. But she didn't fall apart.

Good for you, Nikki thought. *Hang in there, sweetie.*

"When? This year?" Jeremy demanded. He wasn't shouting, but there was no doubt about his anger.

"No, of course not. A long time ago. Before I met Farid. It was a small production company. We made it out in the desert. They only printed a few copies. It was a bad film. Even for porn. I never thought anyone would ever see it, or make the connection between me and . . . and that girl in the film," Alison said, speaking quickly but clearly.

Jeremy just stood next to them. Silent. Angry. Staring at his sister.

"I'll move out," Alison said.

Nikki didn't know what to say, to either of them. She understood why Jeremy was upset, obviously, even if this had nothing to do with Ryan Melton. But she also knew that Jeremy was already aware that Alison had done some foolish things when she was younger. That didn't really change who she was now, did it?

"Jeremy," Nikki said. "I think you need to be calm and think about this. It happened a long time ago."

"Pornography?" he said to Nikki. "She made pornography? Why are you defending her?"

"You know why." Nikki heard her voice crack. "Because someone needs to. Because someone stuck by me when I needed her most. Because Alison is not who she was and someone needs to defend her. It ought to be you. You're her brother, Jeremy."

"I need a minute." He held up his hand. Took a breath. "Excuse me."

Nikki watched him walk out the back door. She didn't know where he was going. Just to cool off, she hoped. He was always so sensible. He'd come to his senses. Wouldn't he?

"I think I . . . we *should* go," Alison said. "Jocelyn and I. And stay somewhere else. Get our own place." She reached for her coffee cup. Her hand was shaking. "It would be best. If this gets out . . . it could hurt Jeremy. His business. His kids."

"He didn't say you had to leave."

Alison met her gaze. "He didn't tell me to stay, did he?"

"I don't think you're in a position to buy a place right now, are you?" Nikki asked. As far as she knew, Alison hadn't even been looking at properties before Ryan was murdered.

She shrugged. She wasn't drinking her coffee, just holding it. "I guess I could rent. I hate to use my house savings right now, but—"

"You could come to my house," Nikki blurted. "I have two spare bedrooms. One's full of junk, but we can clean it up."

"Are you serious?"

"Completely. Maybe it *would* be better," Nikki said. "To separate the two of you. Give you both a little space."

"I don't know what to say." Alison set her cup down. "I don't get it. You and I . . . we were never friends. I . . . I didn't even think you liked me."

"Well, it's not true. You're a good mother, Alison. You're a good person. I can see that. I know you didn't do this. Kill Ryan Melton, I mean."

Alison stared at her with those big, brown, teary eyes.

"I want to help you," Nikki said.

"Lillie says—"

"How do you know you can trust Lillie? How do you

know you can trust whoever is paying for your defense? I'm serious, Alison. What if the killer is footing your bill and it turns out not to be an altruistic act? What if the person paying your bill is who really killed Ryan?"

Alison was silent.

Nikki could see that she was teetering on the edge of tears again. "I'm going to prove to Jeremy that you didn't do this, Alison. But you have to start talking to me. And you can't just keep saying that Lillie Lambert told you to be quiet." She hesitated. "I won't tell anyone what you tell me. Not even Jeremy. Okay?"

Alison stood in front of Nikki, her arms wrapped around herself.

"So come sit down and talk to me." Nikki took her hand and led her to the kitchen table. She pushed aside a pink bowl with mushy, unidentifiable cereal in the bottom. "Sit down." She pushed Alison into the chair Jeremy usually sat in. She went back for their cups of coffee, removed Katie's booster seat, and sat down. She slid Alison's cup across the table to her. "Now tell me why Ryan Melton had your porn movie on his laptop."

Chapter 15

"I don't know how he found the skin flick," Alison said in a soft voice. "He had a lot of free time, I guess." She chewed on her thumbnail. "What with Diara's career taking off the way it has. She was shooting *Casa Capri*, modeling. He didn't have a job. He had no place to be but with her, and she didn't like having him on the set. I guess he sat at home and watched a lot of porn." She met Nikki's gaze across the table. "I was a bleached blonde then. I don't know how he recognized me. I didn't even use my real name." She laughed without humor. "Jez Jewel. You know, like Jezebel." She hesitated. "There's no excuse for what I did. I thought I loved the guy I was with at the time. I was going to make us rich."

Nikki offered a grim smile. She wouldn't pass judgment. She'd made many a bad decision in her lifetime. "So how did you know Ryan had seen the film?"

"He told me a couple of weeks ago." She looked away, her eyes tearing up. "Not because he was going to black-mail me or anything. Because he wanted to know if I . . . you know, wanted to have sex with him. He said he liked what he saw in the movie. He didn't care that I'm older now." It was obvious it was hard for her to talk about it, but she went on. "He said he knew I could be discreet. That it could just be our little secret. He said he was tired of being the good guy when Diara could do whatever she wanted with whomever she wanted."

This was the second time it was suggested that Diara might have been cheating on Ryan, and from an entirely different source. Maybe there was some truth to it.

"He was angry about money," Alison continued. "Diara made a lot, but I guess she controlled it all. He said something about her throwing him a few pennies to keep him quiet. To get him to protect her image. They're all about their images, you know. The Fab Four."

Nikki was trying to absorb everything Alison was saying. "Did you have sex with him?"

She made a face of disgust. "No, of course not."

"I can understand how that could happen," Nikki said as diplomatically as possible. "He was really good-looking. And famous . . ."

"I don't sleep around," Alison answered firmly. "And certainly not with my clients. Besides, he's married."

"Okay . . . so that day." Nikki tried to think about what information she'd already gathered. The trick was trying to figure out who was lying and who wasn't. Sadly, her experience had been that there was always someone lying. Sometimes, someone you didn't expect. "You told me you never saw Mars in the house. That you didn't see him until he came outside, after dialing 911. *After* he found Ryan's body by the pool. But that's not true, is it?"

A tear slipped down Alison's cheek. She wiped it off her cheek. "I'm not supposed to tell you anything. Lillie said it could ruin surprises she has for the prosecution."

"What surprises?" Nikki pressed. She didn't trust Lillie Lambert as far as she could run downhill in the woman's hot pink Jimmy Choo stilettos. She knew that Lillie's job was to get Alison off, but what if she went for a plea bargain instead? The attorney had made her name defending guilty parties. For all Nikki knew, Lillie believed Alison was guilty. So in the end, she didn't really have Alison's best interest at heart.

"I don't know what she wants to keep from the prosecution. We haven't talked that much."

"So tell me what happened that day. Start from the beginning." Nikki reached across the table and squeezed Alison's hand. "Tell me the truth. Please."

Alison took a deep, shuddering breath. "I . . . I arrived at his house about ten-thirty in the morning. I had already picked Stanley and Oliver up at your house." She gazed off, unseeing. "I left your guys in my van and went into the house to get Muffin."

"Was Ryan there?"

"He was waiting for me," she murmured. "He'd just showered. He . . . he was wearing only a towel."

"Okay." Nikki drew out the word.

"He . . . he said he'd been watching my movie and that he . . . really wanted to have sex with a porn star." She shook her head. "I wasn't a star. I wasn't even the lead."

"What did you tell him?"

"No, of course."

"Where were you?" Nikki asked. "In his house. Out on the pool deck?"

"No, in the living room. He was sitting on one of the couches when I came in the front door."

Nikki thought about the layout of the house. There were two steps down into the living room. "You went into his living room?"

"First, I got Muffin's leash from the utility room in the back of the house. Muffin was with Ryan. In the living room. The dog wouldn't come when I called him, so I went into the living room to get him." She began to chew on her thumbnail again. She didn't look at Nikki. "Ryan, he . . . touched me." She pressed her hand to her chest. "I shoved him. Hard."

"Good for you."

"I wasn't going to let another man do that." She lifted her lashes. Now she was looking Nikki right in the eye. "Before, I let men manipulate me. I let them hurt me. I can't do that anymore. I can't let Jocelyn think that's okay. No matter how rich they are, like Farid, or how famous."

"So you pushed Ryan?"

She nodded. "And then I snapped Muffin's leash on his collar and I walked out the door."

"Where did you go?"

"Runyon Canyon Park. They like it there, Stan and Ollie. And Muffin was learning to get along with the other dogs. That's a good time of day. Not too many people there. Rotties can be really nice dogs. He's just a big clumsy oaf."

"Okay. Then what?"

"I let the dogs run for a while, and then I took Muffin back to Ryan's house."

"What time?"

She exhaled. "One, maybe? I had an appointment at three, so I was going to take Stan and Ollie home and be in Bel Air by three. I remember thinking I had enough time, if I didn't hit traffic on the freeway."

Nikki looked at Alison across the table. "What happened when you got to the Melton/Elliot house?"

"Nothing. I let myself in like I'm supposed to. A lot of my clients don't make me knock. Most of the time, no one's home."

"Was the door locked?"

Alison shook her head. "The gates have codes, front and back. If the gate's closed, the house is unlocked."

"But Ryan *was* home."

"Yeah." She went on, "I let Muffin loose and I hung the leash on the hook in the utility room."

"Does he have more than one leash?"

She made a face as if it was a ridiculous question. "Like,

ten. Some are designer leashes. He wears a Louis Vuitton collar."

"You know which one you used that day?"

"Maybe. But I just grab one, any one. I walk him four days a week."

"So your fingerprints could have been on the leash that killed Ryan?"

"Sure. Ryan's would have been on them, too. He walked Muffin sometimes, too."

But Ryan didn't strangle himself, Nikki thought. "Okay. Go on. Did you see Ryan when you dropped Muffin off?"

"Yeah, I was dreading going back in. I even thought about keeping Muffin until Diara got home."

Nikki noted that Alison was calling Ryan and Diara by their first names. She tried to recall if Alison called all of her star clients by their first names.

"But then, I decided that if I wanted to keep the job, I couldn't be afraid to go into the house. And I needed the job. And I . . . I didn't do anything wrong."

"Where was Ryan when you dropped Muffin off?"

Alison had pushed her coffee cup aside and now rested her hands on the placemat on the table. "Out by the pool. The French doors were open between the living room and the pool deck."

The same doors Nikki had walked through that day when she saw Ryan's body. "Did he speak to you?"

She shook her head. "He just waved as I was on my way out."

"He was in the pool?"

"No, his lounge chair." She took a shuddering breath. "Where they found him dead later. When I went through the house, he was sitting in the chair with his back to the house. He didn't even turn around; he just waved. I guess he was just embarrassed by the way he'd behaved."

"But you definitely saw him when you returned the dog?"

"Definitely." Alison exhaled. "I can't tell you how relieved I was that he didn't get up and come into the house."

"And you saw him when you were taking the leash to the utility room, or on your way out of the house?"

"Definitely on my way out."

Nikki thought for a minute. "So Mars was there then, servicing the fish tanks?"

"No, not then." Alison hesitated. "I left, but then I got to thinking about the video. I pulled over in the van and I sat for a few minutes. Then I went back."

"You went back to the house? Why? To talk to Ryan?"

"No, I went back because of the surveillance videos in the house. They have a bunch of cameras. If Diara saw what happened between me and Ryan that morning, I was afraid she would fire me."

"But *he* propositioned *you*. If you pushed him, she wouldn't have thought you were coming on to him," Nikki argued. "It would have been obvious what was going on."

"Would it have mattered? She'd have fired me anyway. So Ryan wouldn't be *tempted* by me."

"You really think she would have watched the recordings?"

"I was afraid to take the chance. Ryan was smart, but he didn't think things through. I didn't know if he'd think to erase the security recording himself. The thing is, Diara was always reviewing them. She fired two different maids over stuff she saw on the video footage."

"How does she view them?"

"They had the whole system installed when they moved in. There's a laptop in the kitchen pantry. You can watch the recordings from all of the cameras from there."

"And erase them?" Nikki said stiffly. "*You* erased the

surveillance recordings?" *Which meant the cops also had her fingerprints on the laptop.*

She nodded, staring at her hands. "That's when I passed Mars in the hallway. I guess he arrived to work on the fish tanks between the time I dropped Muffin off and went back."

"Weren't you afraid you'd get fired for doing it?"

"If she saw them, I was going to get fired anyway. I was hoping no one would notice." Alison pushed hair out of her eyes. "They got erased all the time."

The back door opened and both turned to see Jeremy walk in.

"Jeremy," Alison said.

He halted in the middle of the kitchen and hooked his thumb in the direction of the living room. He looked a little lost and obviously still pretty upset. "I'm going to get the girls dressed and take them to the park. Then maybe to a movie. I don't know how late we'll be, so you need to pick up Jocelyn at the high school at two."

Alison rose from the table. "Jeremy, I feel awful about this." Her voice quavered. "Can we talk?"

He didn't make eye contact with her. "Not now. I just can't." He glanced at Nikki. "I know you're going to your mom's. I'll call you later." The tone of his voice suggested that he was none too happy with Nikki either.

When Jeremy was gone, Nikki and Alison just sat there for a minute. Alison was the first to speak. "I need to talk to Jocelyn, but are you serious about letting us stay with you?"

"I wouldn't offer if I didn't mean it, Alison. You've known me long enough to know that I mean what I say."

"It's really nice of you. I mean, my own brother . . ." She let her voice fade. "You know, I always wished you and I could be friends. I always admired you so much. You have everything: you're smart, you're beautiful, you've got a great boyfriend, a great career. Your life is so . . . together. I'm not embarrassed to say that I wish I could be more like you."

She was making Nikki uncomfortable. "You wouldn't say that if you knew the truth," she said, only half-joking.

Alison closed her eyes and lowered her head for a minute. "Do you really think we can prove to Jeremy that I didn't do this? Because the more I think about it"—she raised her head to look at Nikki again—"the more I realize that even if Lillie gets the charges dropped, that's not going to mean anything to Jeremy. He really thinks I could have murdered someone. What kind of person does he think I am that I could do that to another human being?"

That took Nikki to a place she didn't really want to go to right then. An image of the man she had killed when she was nineteen flashed in her head. She knew Alison knew about it; everyone did. It had been in the papers and on national TV. But so many years had passed, she knew Alison wasn't thinking about Nikki or the incident. She didn't mean anything by her words. She was talking about herself and about her relationship with her brother.

Nikki patted Alison's hand and got up. "Why don't you go to work, and talk to Jocelyn tonight after you pick her up? I don't know that you need to actually *move*. Maybe . . . just stay with me for a few days and give Jeremy some space. You could present it to Jocelyn that way."

"Give him some space, huh? You think that's all he needs? Space?"

"And a little time," Nikki said, trying to sound as upbeat as possible. "He'll come to his senses. He's a sensible guy."

Alison rose from her chair. "I want to think you're right. I really do."

"I am," Nikki reassured her. She was already contemplating what her next step would be. Whom did she talk to next? "Thanks for talking to me. I'm going to run all this stuff around in my head and see what I can come up with."

Alison groaned. "God help me. I sound guilty to myself when I hear my story."

"Well, thanks for trusting me." Nikki grabbed both cups of their now-cold coffee. "I won't share anything you told me with anyone. Lillie Lambert need never know you spoke to me."

Alison followed her to the sink. "You have any idea who *could* have killed Ryan? I mean, everyone liked him. It just doesn't make sense."

Right now, the only possible suspect Nikki had was Diara, which made no sense. She was shooting on the set of *Casa Capri* the day her husband was murdered. Nikki would have to look into that. She needed to make sure Diara was on the set at the time of the murder, which she was guessing fell in the window between one when Alison dropped the dog off and when Mars arrived. Which couldn't have been much time. She'd have to find out from Mars what time he arrived at the Melton/Elliot residence.

Nikki rinsed out the coffee cups and put them in the sink. "I'm going to go."

"Right. Sure. I'll walk out with you. I should go anyway, and not force my brother into an awkward moment in front of his girls." She followed Nikki out of the house.

"Ms. Sahira!"

"Miss Harper! Nikki Harper, do you have a statement?"

A group of men and women with cameras had gathered outside Jeremy's gate. The minute they saw Nikki and Alison, they started hollering to them and taking photos with cameras with telephoto lenses.

"Great," Nikki muttered, heading for her car.

Alison stood on the front porch, frozen for a moment. "What do I do?" she asked, staring at the men and women outside the gate.

"Any comment on the accusation that you starred in pornographic movies in the nineties, Alison?"

Apparently, someone besides Marshall was reading Miss Tinseltown Tattletale's blog.

Alison covered her face with her hands and turned her back to the paparazzi.

Nikki was glad that while she was dressed casually, she looked okay. Thank goodness she'd taken the time to follow Marshall's advice and put on some makeup. If her photo was going to end up in a tabloid, she didn't need Victoria criticizing what she looked like. Nikki opened her car door, grabbed her sunglasses, and slid them on. "I'll wait for you, if you like," she called back to Alison. "We can make a run for it together."

"I don't want to go," Alison groaned.

"You need to go to work, and you need to show *them* that you haven't done anything wrong."

Alison looked over her shoulder at the paparazzi at the gate and then to Nikki. "I'll be right out."

Nikki backed up her car and turned it around so she could leave first. Jeremy's car had a device to open the gate coming and going, but Nikki and Alison had to operate it manually. He'd just had the fence and electronic gate installed a couple of months ago.

Which was a good thing, apparently. Otherwise, the paparazzi would have been at his door. Nikki had grown up with the press and had experienced this—to some degree—her whole life. But Jeremy and Alison, they lived pretty quietly, despite Jeremy's previous fame. The only time anyone approached Jeremy with a camera was when he occasionally showed up at a cancer research fundraiser or was spotted at a restaurant with someone more famous than he was.

A minute later, Alison came out of the house wearing a baggy fleece jacket and dark sunglasses, and carrying a canvas messenger bag on her shoulder.

"Ready when you are," Nikki called.

Alison got into her van and pulled behind Nikki. Nikki eased up to the gate, ignoring the paparazzi in front of her, put down her window, and hit the button to open the gate. The gate began to slide open and she eased the Prius forward. The crowd parted and Nikki stepped on the gas. She pulled onto the street and looked in her rearview mirror. Alison was right behind her, a death grip on the steering wheel.

They wound through the quiet neighborhood and then pulled onto Rockingham, a street made famous by the location of O.J. Simpson's house. Nikki glanced in her mirror again, waved to Alison, and dialed the number for the Age of Aquarius Aquariums.

"Age of Aquarius Aquariums, this is Mars."

"Mars, hey, this is Nikki Harper."

"You ready to have that fish delivered?"

She chuckled. "Not quite. Listen, what I called about was . . . do you know what time you arrived at Ryan Melton's that day?"

"Uh, a little after one. One-fifteen, maybe."

That meant someone had to have gotten into the house, killed Ryan, and gotten out in under fifteen minutes. That was an awfully tight window. Was it even possible?

"And . . . I'm sorry to be a pain," Nikki said. "But do you know what time you placed the call to 911?"

"Around one-thirty. One-forty at the latest. Hey, that was really cool of you to get those tickets for Moon and her friend to see the Dalai Lama."

"I hope they have a good time. I have to run. Nice to talk to you, Mars."

"You too. Just give me a holler and we'll get that fish tank of yours set up."

"Have a good day," Nikki said. As she hung up, she tried to decide what her next move should be. In the meantime, apparently she'd be cleaning Victoria's attic.

Chapter 16

"Why won't you tell me what she said?" Victoria pursed her lips in annoyance. She was in hair and makeup, preparing to shoot her next scene for *Casa Capri*. Then she had an interview with Ryan Seacrest. Nikki stood beside her mother's chair, watching her in the big mirror. She was as gorgeous as ever. To Nikki's surprise, the long days of filming seemed to energize her, rather than drag her down. Lately, it seemed as if Victoria had more energy in a day than Nikki did.

Saturday, while starting the attic project at Victoria's, Nikki had expressed her desire to snoop around the set a little and learn what she could about Diara, without being too conspicuous. Victoria had invited her daughter along for her Monday shoot. Nikki had had to call out at work, which she could be in trouble for because on Mondays the brokers all got together for Monday Morning Meeting. But she figured that she could get away with it this week since she was certain she was going to be the top broker in the agency again this month.

"I can't tell you because Alison spoke to me in confidence," Nikki told Victoria.

"Could you lift your chin, Ms. Bordeaux?" the makeup artist asked. She was a cute Japanese girl with super-short hair and rosebud lips she had painted with bright red lipstick, staying inside the lines of her mouth so she had kew-pie doll lips. Bizarre for seven-thirty in the morning. She didn't look a day over twelve, although Nikki guessed she was a little older than that since she was here and not in middle school.

Victoria raised her chin regally so the makeup artist could swipe a powder brush down her neck. "But I'm your mother. I won't tell anyone. And Asami won't either, will you, dear?"

"I don't hear anything anyone says," the girl assured her. She dropped one brush onto the counter and grabbed another from a black brush roll that must have had fifty brushes in it.

"I gave my word, Mother." Nikki sat down on a stool Asami had brought for her.

"I suppose you won't tell Jeremy either?" Victoria turned her head left, then right as Asami shaded her cheeks.

Nikki really didn't want to discuss Jeremy with her mother. With anyone. She hadn't talked to him since she saw him at his house Saturday. He'd told her he would call her. He hadn't. She left a message on his cell Sunday, while trying to put some order to her spare rooms for Alison and Jocelyn. So far, he hadn't called back. Nikki tried to tell herself it was just that he was busy with the kids. He liked to spend as much time as he could with them on the week-ends.

But he was avoiding her. She knew that. Maybe he would call her tonight when he didn't see his sister and niece at the dinner table. They were coming to Nikki's today, after school. But then, maybe he wouldn't call her.

"What do you think?" Asami leaned over Victoria's shoulder.

All three of them stared in the mirror. Even clothed in a black cape to protect her clothing, Victoria was gorgeous. Her platinum hair framed her petite face elegantly, and her bright blue eyes shone even brighter than usual, thanks to Asami's tricks with her makeup brushes.

"Maybe bring the blush a little higher?" Victoria suggested.

"Definitely." Asami went back to her brush roll on the counter.

"I haven't seen much of Diara, except when we're shooting," Victoria's tone suggested casual conversation, but her glance at Nikki suggested more, which Nikki found interesting since her mother thought there was a chance Alison might have actually killed Ryan Melton.

"Do you know how the poor dear is doing?" Victoria asked.

Asami raised perfect black eyebrows. "She seems fine, which creeps me out a little. I can't imagine. If my boyfriend was murdered, I'd . . . go crazy. I'd be ripping my hair out, sobbing uncontrollably. There's no way I could work. Ah-ha!" She held up the brush she had, apparently, been looking for and went on. "And what's with the private burial? Just the Fab Four. Gabriela, in props, said she overheard that they all had dinner at Angel and Betsy Gomez's Saturday night. She said Ryan's already been cremated and stuck on a shelf. In the same mausoleum as Norma Talmadge at Hollywood Forever. We're going Friday, my boyfriend and me, to check it out."

Nikki met her mother's gaze.

"You don't know Norma Talmadge?" Victoria asked. "The Talmadge sisters."

Nikki shook her head.

"Then I was remiss in your early film education. Norma was a star in the twenties. She was the first to have her footprints in cement in front of Grauman's Chinese Theatre."

"Ah," Nikki said.

"We should watch one of her films." Victoria turned in her chair. "Asami. Would you like to come to a Movie

Night? We're doing Thursdays now, although I've had to go to every other week with our shooting schedule. Either dinner or cocktails, then a movie. It's quite fun."

Asami's dark eyes, ringed in blue eyeliner, got wide. "Your house, Ms. Bordeaux?"

"Yes, I had a screening room long before it was in vogue, didn't I, Nicolette?"

Nikki knew her mother well enough to know that it was a rhetorical question.

The young woman clutched a makeup brush with two hands as if it were a scepter. "I . . . I'd loved to come."

"Wonderful. I'll have my secretary, my *assistant*," Victoria corrected herself, "put you and your boyfriend on the guest list for sometime soon."

Nikki had been trying to get her mother to use the word *assistant* rather than *secretary* for years. Victoria's assistant, Cora, who only worked part-time, was older than her mother and equally sharp. She reminded Nikki of Granny on the *Beverly Hillbillies* TV show. Until she opened her mouth. Then she was Margaret Thatcher. With extra attitude. Scary woman, Cora. Nikki didn't cross her.

"It's always a small group," Victoria went on. "I like a mix of guests. I'd never invite a whole room full of actors or politicians. Dull." She fiddled with a piece of platinum hair at her temple. "Do you have a cocktail dress, dear?"

Asami nodded.

"Good. That's what you wear. And nice heels. A girl your age and height should stay away from flats."

"Thank you so much, Ms. Bordeaux," Asami gushed.

"Certainly. Are we done here, because if we are, I'll thank you for doing such a nice job with my makeup this morning. Of course, you always do wonderful work." She glanced at Nikki. "Asami is a very conscientious worker. She started out here on the show as an assistant makeup artist, and now she's been promoted to a lead makeup artist."

"Mostly because of Ms. Bordeaux," Asami said. "When Ms. Andrews said she didn't want me near her anymore because I knocked over a water bottle she'd left open on the floor, I was afraid I was going to get canned. Then your mother requested that only I do her makeup"—she raised both hands—"and I ended up being promoted."

"How is dear Beatrice?" Nikki asked her mother. "You haven't mentioned her since she didn't make your garden party."

"Oh, she had some silly excuse. I didn't believe it for a moment. Do you know I heard she actually spoke to the writers about killing off my character?" Victoria grew more indignant by the moment. "When they said no, at least not yet, she requested she not share any scenes with me. How does she think that's supposed to work? How can our characters be enemies if they never speak?"

Again, rhetorical. "Um . . ." Nikki tried to think of a way to steer the conversation back to Diara. "So . . . Asami, what other cast members' makeup do you do?"

"It varies day to day. There are three of us makeup artists and two assistants."

"Ah."

"She does Diara's all the time, though," Victoria put in. "Diara likes Asami."

"What's she like?"

"She's nice. Not as nice as Ms. Bordeaux. Ms. Bordeaux is always giving me cool makeup from the freebies left here for her." Asami began to roll up her makeup brushes. "But Ms. Elliot is nice. She gave me a Coach scarf once. Mr. Melton gave it to her. She said she didn't like it."

"Did . . . Mr. Melton come to the set often?" Nikki asked.

Asami shook her head. "Nah, we hardly ever saw him. I think she liked keeping her private life separate from her work life."

Or she liked keeping him in the dark about what she was doing? Whom she was doing it with?

"Ms. Bordeaux?" Megan, the redhead Nikki had met the previous week, walked into the room. She had a headset on again and was carrying a stack of paperwork in one arm. "They're going to be ready for you in ten." She spotted Nikki. "Ms. Harper, nice to see you again."

Nikki remained on the stool. "You too. We were just talking about Diara and Ryan. Nice couple. Although Asami said he didn't come to the set very often."

Megan thought for a second. "No, I guess he didn't. Which I always thought was a little strange because Angel Gomez and Julian Munro come all the time. And Kameryn's husband, Gil."

"Any other men visit her?" Victoria injected.

"No, not really," Megan answered. She shrugged. "Her agent, that's it."

"Do Angel, Julian, and Gil come together?" Nikki questioned. "Or separately?"

Again, Megan thought. "Both. I guess they still have business together, you know."

"You see one more than the other?" Nikki dared.

"Not really. Julian's pretty nice. He always says hi and calls me by my name. He gave me an autograph the first time I met him. I made the mistake of asking Angel for one once." Megan rolled her eyes. "He was *not* nice."

"Ginger, in food service, told me he threw a muffin at her once," Asami put in, packing up her makeup case that was the size of a small trunk. "She brought the wrong kind to him."

Megan frowned. "Hard to believe he's married to Betsy; she's so nice to everyone when she's on set. She doesn't act like her husband is rich and famous. She acts like a regular person."

Victoria started to stand up and Asami hurried to help

her remove the black cape. "I should go. Don't want to be late for my cue. Coming, Nicolette?"

Nikki rose off the stool and grabbed her Prada. "Be there in a sec."

Victoria glanced in the mirror one last time as she went by. "Thank you again, Asami."

"Nice to meet you, Ms. Harper." Asami headed out of the room, behind Victoria, carrying her massive makeup case.

"Nice to meet you, too." Nikki waited until her mother and the makeup artist were out of the room.

Megan stood at the door and touched her headset at her ear. "I'll be right there," she told someone.

"I'm sorry. I won't keep you." Nikki slung her Prada over her shoulder. She was wearing gray Armani slacks and a pale blue Chanel sweater her mother had bought for her ages ago. "Now, don't feel like you have to answer me, but . . . do you know if Diara was here the whole day, the day her husband was killed?"

"The detective asked me the same question."

"Detective Dombrowski?"

"That's him. Good-looking. He was here Thursday or Friday."

So, Dombrowski had had Alison arrested, but he's still looking into other possibilities. Interesting.

"The police don't think Diara had anything to do with her husband's murder, do they?" Megan breathed.

"I . . . I think everyone is just trying to get a timeline."

"Right. Well, we all left early."

"Because of the argument Diara and Kameryn had?" Nikki said.

"No one knows what it was about." Megan shrugged. "Of course, after Ryan was found dead, Diara and Kameryn were fine. Kameryn's been sticking pretty close to Diara. Being a good friend."

"Do you know what time the argument was?"

Megan shifted the pile of papers from one arm to the other. "One, maybe? We were getting ready to break for lunch. It was crazy because I've never seen them argue."

One. And about the same time Alison said she dropped the dog off with Ryan. But Mars said he placed the 911 call around one-thirty. There was no way Diara could have argued with Kameryn at one in the CBS Television Studio on Beverly Boulevard and gotten to her house on Mulholland in time to kill her husband for Mars to find him at one-thirty.

Which meant Diara couldn't have been at her house to kill her husband.

"Thanks," Nikki said.

"Sure." Megan led the way out of the room. "I'll show you where they're shooting the next scene and get you a chair."

Nikki followed. So she would have to cross Diara off the list of suspects.

But maybe not.

Just because Diara didn't strangle her husband, didn't mean she wasn't a part of the murder. What if she'd staged the fight with Kameryn so she *would* have an alibi?

"Thanks for dinner, Aunt Nikki." Jocelyn got up from the mission-style cherry dining table and pushed in her chair.

Nikki smiled. She didn't know when she'd become *Aunt Nikki,* but she liked it. Of course, Jeremy still hadn't called her, so maybe it wasn't going to last very long. "You're welcome."

"And thanks for letting us stay a few nights." She picked up her dinner plate. "I think Mom and Uncle Jeremy needed to be separated for a little while. It's just like they were little, the way they used to fight, Mom said."

Nikki glanced across the table at Alison, who had mostly picked at the pasta primavera Nikki had thrown together for dinner. "Siblings disagree sometimes," she said, wanting to defend Jeremy, but not sure how. "And this is hard. For everyone."

Alison looked at her daughter. "I hate to see you hurt by this mess."

"It's fine. *I'm* fine. The police made a mistake. It happens all the time, Mom. Your lawyer will take care it. I know she will. It's not a big deal. Kids at school hardly said anything."

"You're kidding," Nikki said.

Alison's phone, sitting on the table, vibrated. She ignored it.

"A lot of their lives are a lot crazier than mine, I guess." Jocelyn shrugged. "This girl in my English class, her father and grandfather were just deported back to Nicaragua. Part of a drug cartel or something. I'm going to go do homework, if that's okay." She turned to her mom. "If you don't need me."

Alison smiled. "I'm fine. You're right. It's just a terrible mistake. This will all work out. I have a good attorney." She glanced at Nikki. "And *Aunt Nikki* is looking out for me." Her cell phone vibrated again.

Nikki glanced at the phone. "You want to get that?"

Alison looked at the phone, hesitated, then picked it up. She looked at the screen, hit a button that would delete the message saying who it was, and set the phone down again. When she realized Nikki was watching her, she said, "Client. I'll get back to them."

"I can take your plate." Jocelyn reached for Nikki's. "But, Mom, I'm not taking yours. You're already too skinny. Eat something. It's delicious."

"Thanks, Jocelyn." Nikki waited until she heard the water running in the kitchen sink before she leaned forward on the dining table and lowered her voice. "Did you speak with your attorney today about the laptop?"

"I called. She's going to call me back."

"Don't drop the ball on this, Alison. She needs that information to prepare your case." She smoothed her placemat. "I tracked down the Melton/Elliot gardener today and the dry-cleaning service who delivers to their house. I came up with nothing."

Alison nodded.

"I was on the set of *Casa Capri*. Diara has a solid alibi."

"Diara didn't kill Ryan." Alison frowned and poked at a mushroom on her plate with her fork. "What would make you think Diara would kill him?"

"Well, *someone* killed him. I have to start somewhere. You always start with the husband or the wife." Nikki sipped water from her glass and watched Alison poke at the pasta on her plate with her fork. "If Diara was cheating on Ryan and Ryan knew . . . maybe she wanted to get rid of him. Permanently."

Alison didn't say anything.

Nikki studied her. "How well do you know Julian and Angel?"

Alison lowered her gaze to her plate again. "Not . . . well . . . I . . ." She stopped and started again. "I walk their dogs, but . . . I rarely see them."

"*They're* your clients, too?" This was the first Nikki had heard of this.

Alison barely nodded. She kept her eyes downcast. "And Kameryn Lowe."

"So you work for the Disney Fab Four? All of them? Why didn't you tell me before?"

"I don't know. I don't give out my client list." Alison looked up. "Does it matter?"

"I don't know." Nikki glanced away, thinking. "I hope not."

Chapter 17

"Thanks for the ride, Marshall." Nikki sat in the back seat of his limo, throwing on some face powder, staring into the little round mirror of her compact. "I meant to get to the dealership earlier; then I could have just waited for my oil change."

"House guests will do that to you."

"They've been great so far. No problems. Alison hasn't been too mopey, and Jocelyn loaded the dishwasher for me last night before doing her homework. Alison was going to work today."

"Of course, it's only been one night."

She cut her eyes at him and dug into her bag for mascara. "You sound like Victoria."

"If there was anyone on earth I could be, it would be Victoria Bordeaux." Marshall grinned.

Nikki uncapped the mascara and began to apply it to her lashes. She had a nine a.m. with a client. She still had paperwork to gather, but Mr. Belka would be late. He always was. He was interested in commercial property, as an investment, and she had several good options to talk to him about. "I actually believe you when you say that, Marshall."

He laughed. "I'm glad Alison and Jocelyn are doing okay at your place." He looked handsome and relaxed this morning in jeans and a tight, yellow polo that showed off his buff body and dark skin tone perfectly. "Dare I ask how Jeremy is doing with the new arrangement?"

"You can ask." She dropped her mascara into her bag and fished out a tube of lipstick. MAC, in spice, from one of Victoria's swag bags.

"Oh, dear."

She exhaled. "He's always been so reasonable. So sensible. I don't know this Jeremy."

"And you've tried to talk to him?"

"Of course."

He gave her a look that demonstrated his lack of confidence in her. "You're not always good about talking things out in relationships, Nik."

"I've tried to talk to him. Sort of. I explained why I feel like I need to defend Alison."

"Maybe he's just had enough of her problems after all these years."

She swiped lipstick over her bottom lip. "But she hasn't done anything wrong." Her top lip.

"What if she's not being truthful with you? Still."

"Alison did not kill Ryan Melton."

"Okay. But what if she knows who did?"

Nikki took her time putting her lipstick and compact away. They had just pulled up in front of the office building that Windsor Real Estate occupied on busy Beverly Boulevard in Beverly Hills. "That's crazy. She's got a child custody case with her ex coming up. She wouldn't risk losing Jocelyn trying to protect someone."

"But maybe to protect herself?"

Nikki was beginning to think she was going to need another cup of coffee. She was trying to limit herself and go back to drinking green tea; she knew it was healthier. But coffee just made her *feel* better. "I hope your interview goes well."

The driver got out and opened Nikki's door for her.

"It'll be fine. They always are." Marshall leaned over to see her as she got out, then spotted someone behind her. "Hey, is that your cop?"

"My cop?" She frowned, knowing very well whom he had to be talking about. She didn't look behind her. "I don't have a cop."

"Well, *someone's* cop is standing at the door with two cups of coffee."

"Talk to you later," she called. "Thanks, Charlie." The driver closed the door and she strode across the sidewalk to the door of the office building where Tom Dombrowski was waiting. "Detective."

"Good morning." He offered one of the paper cups in his hands. It smelled heavenly.

"Thanks." She accepted the coffee and took a sip. "You just happened to be passing by this morning and thought I might need a cup of coffee?"

"Something like that." He glanced away, holding his cup, but not drinking from it. His suit was navy blue today. It had to be tailored; it fit him perfectly. "I paid a visit to Diara Elliot's gardener yesterday. Apparently you talked to him already?"

She didn't answer.

"You know, Nikki, you could hinder my investigation," he said. "You understand that, don't you? You could negatively affect Alison Sahira's case."

"So the investigation is still open?" She looked up at him. "Even though Alison was arrested and charged?"

"You look nice this morning. I like the bangs." He reached out but didn't actually touch her hair. He let his hand fall to his side. "We're still gathering evidence."

She smiled slyly, pleased. "Detective Dombrowski, you believe me, don't you? You know she didn't do it."

"We've got her fingerprints on the murder weapon. Her fingerprints also came back on computer equipment"—he met Nikki's gaze—"used to record the security footage in the house. The security footage that was erased. But I bet you already knew her fingerprints were on the home's security laptop, didn't you? She tell you?"

Nikki didn't answer. The coffee was good. She took another sip.

"Maybe Ms. Sahira would like to come in and talk with *me*. Explain herself."

"What's Lillie Lambert say about that?"

He scowled, then took a sip of coffee.

Someone approached the door and Nikki and Dombrowski stepped to one side.

"I have an appointment," Nikki said. "I should go."

"Ms. Sahira tell you what was on Ryan's laptop we confiscated?"

Nikki hesitated. "She did."

"And you don't think that's awfully suspicious?"

"Too easy." Nikki shook her head. "He tries to blackmail her, so she kills him?"

"She does have that child custody case coming up. Maybe she was afraid her husband would use the porn film against her."

"It happened too long ago," Nikki came back. "It was filmed before she met the husband. Before she had her daughter. She's obviously reformed."

They were both quiet for a second. They sipped their coffee.

"I'd tell you again to back off, but I'm thinking that's going to be a waste of my time and yours." Dombrowski met her gaze. "If you find any real evidence that suggests she didn't do it, will you let me know?"

She stood there thinking for a minute, savoring the warmth of the cup in her hand and the aroma of the coffee beans. "Did you look into any of the Fab Four?" she asked. "Did you question them?"

"Didn't have cause. You know we have limited access to celebrities. And as soon as they hear that the police want to speak with them, they're calling their attorneys."

He didn't say they couldn't be suspects. She was quiet for a moment, then said, "Well, I have that appointment. I should go."

"If you had any information that might suggest I should talk to them," Dombrowski said under his breath, "you'd tell me, right?"

She looked up at him and smiled. "Of course, Detective. Thanks for the coffee. Have a good day."

On the ride up in the elevator, Nikki wondered if it was time *she* talked to the Fab Four. She could probably finagle a way to speak with Kameryn on the set of *Casa Capri*, but Julian and Angel would be trickier. Maybe it would make more sense to talk to their spouses? They'd certainly be easier to get to. It also made sense to her to look into the Fab Four's past. She knew they all met in their teens when they were cast on *School Dayz*. They had to have worked with many, many people. She thought about Asami and Megan. They were the kind of people who knew what kind of person Victoria Bordeaux really was.

Nikki stepped off the elevator. "Good morning, Carolyn," she called to the receptionist.

" 'Morning. An Oda left a message that she'd given the names at the door of the nightclub for Thursday night." She held up a yellow *While You Were Out* notepad. "She said you'd know what she meant."

Nikki grinned. The call she'd made to Oda had panned out. Jessie and Monica would be the happiest girls in L.A. this week.

"And Mr. Belka is waiting for you in the conference room. He didn't want anything to drink."

"He's early?" Nikki hurried down the hall. "Thank you, Carolyn." In her office, she pulled her cell out of her Prada and dropped the bag into a drawer in her desk. She grabbed a file and her laptop and, with a smile, walked into the conference room down the hall. "Mr. Belka, great to see you again."

He stood and pumped her hand enthusiastically. "You looking as pretty always, Nikki." Originally from Poland, his English wasn't always perfect, but she never had a problem understanding him. In fact, she found his accent as charming as his personality.

"I apologize for making you wait. Please, sit down." She took the chair next to him. He was a balding, paunchy man in his early sixties; nothing to look at, but a really nice guy. "Crazy morning. I have house guests, and I had to drop my car off at the dealership for an oil change, and—" She chuckled. "So it goes on a Tuesday morning."

"You should call me, I come later. Tomorrow." He raised his voice at the end of his sentences, as if asking a question.

"You're a busy man, Mr. Belka. I wouldn't do that."

He pulled an envelope from inside his suit jacket and slid it across the table to her. "I have *dese* tickets. Six of *dem*. American baseball, Dodgers. Goods seats. Box seats. For you."

She looked at the envelope in front of her. "That's so nice of you, but I couldn't take them."

"For Saturday. I will not in town. You take *dem*. You go, or"—he shrugged his broad shoulders—"you give *dem* to friend." He laid a hand on the envelope and slid them toward her. "Please. Someone else, *dey* give *dem* me. You make me feel bad, *dey* go to waste, you not take *dem*."

Nikki smiled. Jeremy and Jerry loved baseball. Maybe they could all go together? She smiled. "Thank you so much, Mr. Belka."

"Please. We will do business together you and I. You call me Jakub."

"Okay." She slid the envelope of tickets aside. "Jakub, I think you're going to be happy with the properties I've found for you to take a look at." She flipped open her laptop. "I thought you could see what you might be interested in, and we can meet later this week and go take a look." *Which will give me time today to get back to work on my murder investigation.*

After Jakub Belka left, Nikki took care of some paperwork on her desk. She set up two appraisals and an inspection, and called a bank to look into a snag with one of her client's escrow accounts. Then she called a broker to talk up one of the properties she'd had listed for a while, and ended up in a long conversation about the guy's mother-in-law's illness. Nikki was trying to get off the phone gracefully when her cell rang. It was Jeremy. Seeing his number come up made her smile; then she felt silly. What? Was she still in high school? Of course, Jeremy hadn't called her very often when they were in high school. He was too busy being a teen mega star.

"Sorry, John," she cut in. "I've got a call on another line. Big client. Big," she repeated. "I've got to go." She barely let him say good-bye before picking up her cell from her desk.

"Jeremy!"

"Hey, Nik." He didn't sound like himself, but he didn't sound too down in the dumps either.

"I was going to call you at lunch," she told him. "How's your day going?"

"Fine. Had a cancellation." Phones rang in the background. "Just thought I'd . . . say . . . hi."

Nikki hated the awkwardness she heard in his voice. The awkwardness she felt. What if she was wrong about Alison and she lost Jeremy over this? "I . . . was going to call you," she said, "and see if you and the kids wanted to go see the Dodgers this Saturday. A client gave me box seat tickets." She eyed the ticket envelope on her desk. "I've got six, so I thought we could even ask Jocelyn. If you want." He wasn't saying anything on the other end of the line. "Or not. If you . . . just want to take your kids."

"Saturday? Sorry. Can't."

She felt an immediate sense of disappointment. Her first impulse was to say, "Can't or don't want to?" but she caught herself before the words came out of her mouth.

"We made plans with my mom and dad. LEGOLAND. They're coming up from San Diego to meet us. Staying in the LEGOLAND hotel and everything. Everyone is looking forward to it."

This was the first Nikki had heard about LEGOLAND. She usually knew everything that was going on with Jeremy. "Oh . . . okay. Well . . . that should be fun. It'll be nice for you to get away. You and the kids. See your mom and dad."

"Yeah, definitely. Jocelyn's coming, too."

"But not Alison?" It was out of her mouth before she could catch it.

"No."

They were both quiet for a second.

"Jeremy," she finally said. "I invited Alison and Jocelyn to stay a few nights because I thought it might be easier on you. To give you some space."

"No, it's fine. You're right. Space."

Nikki squeezed her eyes shut. Opened them. "They didn't move out of your house. They just came to mine to . . . stay a few nights. To give everyone some room to breathe." She exhaled. "Jeremy, I don't want this thing with Alison to be a problem between us."

"I don't either," he answered stiffly.

The right reply, of course, would have been: *Of course, not, honey. I would never let my sister's murder charge get between us, even if you were trying to defend her when I think she's guilty.* But when did people ever say what they ought to say?

"Maybe we can get together for dinner this week?" she

asked, knowing she probably sounded totally pathetic. "Or just a glass of wine?"

"Maybe. I've got a crazy week. And we're leaving right after school on Friday. Nik, I have to go. They seated my next patient."

"Sure. I've got to get going, anyway. Busy day."

"Talk to you later."

She didn't know if he noticed he didn't say "love you" before hanging up, but she noticed.

Chapter 18

The Internet was a wonderful thing. Nikki didn't discount the importance of meeting people face-to-face; that was sometimes where she got her best information when she'd investigated the other murders. Whatever it was about her personality that made people think she was easy to talk to was an advantage. But the Internet was a good place to start her questioning. And it was a heck of a lot faster than driving all over L.A.

Not surprisingly, there was a ton of information on the Disney Fab Four: articles, blogs, photos. There were websites devoted to their TV show, *School Dayz*, which she read was now being watched by a new generation of kids. Once the show ended, it went into syndication, not only in the U.S. but in other countries as well. There was a huge fan club in Australia; six months ago, Angel and his band had played to a sold-out audience three nights in a row in Sydney.

There were also websites devoted to the individual stars of the runaway teen hit, which really appealed more to pre-teens, from what Nikki gathered. The first hits on the Internet, surprisingly, were devoted to the now-deceased Ryan Melton, who wasn't even a cast member. No one had anything bad to say about him before his death; now, he was approaching sainthood. There were sites for fans to leave comments, tributes, or even contribute money to some sort of foundation.

After taking a break, drinking a cup of green tea and eating a bag of cashews, and returning a few phone calls, Nikki began to research each of the cast members individually, starting with Diara. She learned what Diara's favorite perfume was, what she ordered at Starbucks, and who her favorite designers were: Prabal Gurung and Altuzarra. There was chatter about her role on *Casa Capri* and significant positive reviews. Nikki found postings of Diara's best hairstyles, information about her childhood, and tons about her marriage, but nothing about her cheating on Ryan; not a hint of impropriety.

Nikki moved on to examining Kameryn Lowe next. She found information on her fashion sense, her exercise regimen, and photos of the last vacation she and Gil spent with her cousins in Greece. Like Diara, there was nothing negative about her. Anywhere. The cattiest thing Nikki found was a fashion critic who thought the lipstick Kameryn was wearing at a movie screening was too bright.

Research on Angel and Julian produced similar results. Lots of girls talking about how hot the men were, how great Angel's voice was, and about how excited they were for the release of the new Calvin Klein ad featuring Julian. It appeared that Angel's solo singing career was about to take off. Critics didn't think he had range, and someone else said he was *weak in melody*, but his pre-teen and teen fans didn't seem to care. Julian had two movies coming out in the next year in which he played supporting roles, but was getting good reviews.

Nikki couldn't find any dirt. On any of them.

She went back to looking up info on *School Dayz*. With her initial research done, she was hoping to find someone who had worked with the Fab Four who she could talk to. She found an assistant producer, now working on *The*

Tonight Show, filming in Universal City. She also found someone named Maurice Pillion who was a cast member for two seasons. Then his character was written off the show. She found an interview that mentioned tension between him and Angel and Julian on the set. After Maurice's character left the show, the actor had guest-starred in various TV comedies and dramas, with no parts that were memorable. He had starred in a family drama that lasted only half a season. In the last two years, he'd only appeared once, and that was on a celebrity game show. Apparently, his career had fizzled out.

Maurice Pillion owned a comic book store in West Hollywood. Bingo! Captain Kinney's Comics. Kinney had been the name of Maurice's character on *School Dayz*. She went to the store's website, read up on what was new in the comic book world, and decided to go pick up a couple of comic books for Jeremy's son, Jerry. She was always buying things for the girls because she knew what they liked, but Jerry was harder. He'd be tickled if she showed up at the house with something other than a T-shirt or a cupcake for him.

At four forty-five, Nikki was on Melrose Avenue looking for a place to park. She'd grabbed a ride from someone in the office to the car dealership and picked up her Prius. She found a spot on North Fuller and walked to the store, which featured comic books and collectibles, according to the website. Nikki walked into Captain Kinney's Comics; a bell rang somewhere in the store.

"Welcome to Kinney's Comics," a young man called from a register at the counter in the middle of the store. He was tall and slender, and wore a Spider-Man T-shirt and khaki shorts. College-age, he was cute and far too hip-looking to be working in a comic-book store. At least he was too hip-looking for Nikki's idea of who worked at/went into a comic-book store. Of course, her opinion had been formed solely from episodes of *The Big Bang Theory,* which was about a bunch of science geeks living in Pasadena.

She glanced at the display table closest to her. Comic books were laid out faceup with a sign advertising NEW RELEASES! AMERICA'S GOT POWER, WINTER SOLDIER, THE PUNISHER. She didn't recognize any of these comics or the characters they featured. She moved to another table, these filed vertically, and picked up one. *Wonder Woman.* Aha! Wonder Woman, she knew. She flipped through a couple of pages and glanced around. There were two customers browsing, in addition to the teenager the clerk was helping at the counter. Nikki was the only female in the store, and the oldest by fifteen years. She replaced *Wonder Woman* and grabbed another. *Aquaman.* Aquaman, she also knew. Jerry liked Aquaman.

She moved to a display shelf of Marvel Comics collectibles: action figures, jewelry, coffee mugs. She picked up a box with a *Nick Fury S.H.I.E.L.D. Pistol* in it. She had no idea what a Nick Fury S.H.I.E.L.D. pistol was, or who Nick Fury was, for that matter. She glanced around the store, trying not to look like she was casing the joint. She watched the teenager from the counter go out the door. She flipped the box in her hand over to read it. She held in her hand a replica of a needle gun prop. She still didn't know what it was. She placed it back on the shelf.

"Can I help you, ma'am?" the guy in the Spider-Man T-shirt called from the register.

She met his gaze. Smiled *the smile.* "I'm just looking around."

He nodded, started to turn away, then turned back. "Aren't you . . . ?" He pointed at her, as if having an *aha* moment. "Nikki Harper, Victoria Bordeaux's daughter?"

"That's me." Again, *the smile.*

"Wow." He leaned on the counter. "I grew up watching

Victoria Bordeaux movies: *The Widow's Daughter, Fifteen Green Street, Tell Me No Lie*."

"Really?" Nikki was genuinely surprised. This young man was not in the age group that still watched Victoria's early movies. She walked over to the counter.

"*Fortune's Wheel* is my all-time favorite," he told her. "It should have won best picture over *Marty*."

She lowered her voice and leaned closer. "My mother thinks so, too." She stood up. "You're young to be a Victoria Bordeaux fan."

He grinned and offered his hand to shake hers. "Sean McFee. I was raised by my grandmother. She said that when she was younger, people used to say she looked like Victoria Bordeaux. And my grandmother's from Idaho." His cheeks brightened. "So she always loved your mother."

"I love hearing stories like that. What's your grandmother's name?"

"Elsie. Elsie McFee. She lives in a nursing home in Glendale now. Alzheimer's. But I see her a couple of times a week. We still watch your mother's movies together. Nana can't remember what she had for breakfast, but she remembers all the plots to all the Victoria Bordeaux movies."

A door in the back opened. "Maury, guess who's here?" Sean called. "Nikki Harper, Victoria Bordeaux's daughter." He turned back to Nikki. "Maury's in show business, too. Was. He starred in *School Dayz* when he was younger."

From his photos on the Internet, Nikki recognized the man who walked out of the back of the store. He wasn't aging as well as his costars were. He looked older than his twenty-nine years. His brown hair was already receding and his skin looked splotchy. He had a bad spray-on tan that made him look glow-in-the-dark orange. His orange polo didn't help.

"Ms. Harper, nice to meet you." Maurice Pillion offered his hand and shook hers. He wore a gold necklace, bracelet, and ring. The ring was on his right hand, not the left; according to Wikipedia, he'd never been married.

"Nice to meet you." *The smile.*

"Hey, man. Can I help you?" Sean spoke to one of the other customers.

The twentysomething guy nodded. "I'm looking for a comic called *Mickey Finn*. For my dad."

"Not sure if we have any. But if we do, they'd be over here in the case." Sean turned back to Nikki. "Really nice to meet you, Ms. Harper. My nana will be thrilled when I tell her you came in today."

"Nice to meet you, too, Sean." She returned her attention to Maurice. "Sean was telling me that you starred in *School Dayz*. I recognize you."

"That was a long time ago. Seems like another life." When he looked at her, his pale blue eyes seemed sad. "Thanks for stopping by. What can I help you with? We just got more copies of the latest *Kotaku* in."

She must have had a weird look on her face because he chuckled. "You're not looking for yourself, are you?"

She laughed with him, repositioning her Prada on her shoulder. "No, I have no idea what *Kotaku* is. I was looking for something for a friend's son. He's in middle school. I wanted to help him start collecting comic books."

"Great age to start. You know what he likes?"

"Hm. Aquaman. I know he reads other comics, but I've heard him talk about Aquaman."

"If you want to help him get started collecting, I'd suggest getting him something vintage, but not too expensive. Until you know he's serious about collecting."

"And that he's going to take care of them."

"Exactly," Maurice agreed, leading her to the back left corner of the store. "Let's see, *Aquaman*." He began to flip through a row of comic books displayed upright, all in plastic sleeves.

"So you were on *School Dayz*. A teen star."

"Yeah," he said.

"Crazy life, I guess. My boyfriend was . . . *is* Jeremy Fitzgerald. Dr. Fitzgerald now."

"Really? I know Jeremy. He's my dentist. Wow." He continued flipping through the comic books. "Now, *he* was a star."

"So . . . I guess you knew the Disney Fab Four pretty well?" she asked, hoping it didn't sound as awkward to him as it did to her.

He frowned. "I was pretty good friends with Julian and Angel, but I was never one of them. They were tight with Kameryn and Diara from day one on the set. It was like everyone, including them, knew they were special." He pulled out a comic book and showed it to her. "I've got a couple of these. 1962, first series. This is number thirty-two."

She took the comic book from him and glanced at the front cover. It had a giant hand clutching Aquaman. "Thundering from the deep . . ." she read. "Tryton the Terrible."

"That's really awful, Diara's husband being murdered in their home," Maurice said.

"Dreadful. I'd met him just a few nights before he died. I met all of them. The Fab Four and their spouses. My mother is working with Diara and Kameryn on *Casa Capri*." She began to flip through the pages of the comic book. "I don't know if you've been reading the paper, but the police made an arrest early on."

"I heard that. Some woman." He was flipping through the comics again.

"Actually, it's Jeremy's sister, Alison."

He frowned as he looked at her. "Jeremy's sister? You're kidding? I don't really keep up with that kind of stuff. Did she really do it?"

"No."

"I've got a *Justice League of America*, 1960. See, Aquaman appeared in other comics before he got his own."

"Maurice, do you mind if I ask you about the Fab Four?"

"What about them?"

"I . . . I guess I want to know something about what they were like, before they became famous."

"You mean before they were the Fab Four? That term wasn't even coined until after I left the show."

"Why *did* you leave the show?" she asked.

"Wasn't my idea. I was making good money and having a blast. I got written off. The show started out with my character, Kinney, being good friends with Angel's and Julian's characters. I had equal billing, in the beginning."

"I didn't know that," she said.

"We started out with the same pay and then, for whatever reason, more stories were written around their characters and less around mine. At the time, my parents and I were told that their characters were more popular, but I always wondered if the fact that more stories were written for them made them more popular." His last words were spoken with an emotional catch in his voice. "I'm sorry, I don't mean to seem harsh. Or jealous, or anything. I have a good life. It didn't turn out like I thought it was going to, but I . . . I'm happy. My girlfriend and I, we just got engaged." He smiled. "She's got a little boy from a previous marriage. Cute as can be."

"Good for you. Can you tell me what the four of them were like?"

He hesitated. "I don't mean to be a jerk or anything, but why are you asking?"

"Because my friend Alison didn't do it. I'm checking around. Trying to get some information on other possible suspects."

He looked around. They were alone now in the shop:

no customers. Sean had disappeared into the back. "You think it could have been one of the Fab Four?" he asked, incredulously.

"No . . ." She hesitated. "I don't know. I just . . . to tell you the truth, I'm suspicious . . ."

"Of Diara," he finished for her.

"What makes you say that?"

He shrugged. "Because she married a nobody. Maybe she was tired of him."

"But they all married nobodies," she countered.

He thought for a minute. "I guess they did, didn't they? Maybe none of them wanted to be overshadowed by their partners?"

She didn't know how much she should reveal to him, so she didn't respond to his statement. "They were all good friends, right? Did . . . were any of them a couple at some point?"

"Did they date each other? No. Well, Angel and Kameryn had a thing for a little while, but then she started dating some musician that was quite a bit older than we were."

As Nikki listened to Maurice, she found herself pleasantly surprised by his demeanor. From what she had read on the Internet, she had expected a has-been star who was bitter about the Fab Four's careers taking off when his didn't. But he wasn't that guy.

"Of course, they dated plenty. We all did. We were just supposed to be discreet about it."

"And they were, I guess?"

"Publicly?" He thought for a minute, then nodded. "Yeah, they were. But on the set? They all had a bit of a reputation. Particularly Julian."

"Really?" Nikki asked.

"The weird thing was," again, he lowered his voice, "they . . . shared."

"I think I'll take both of these comics." She handed them back to Maurice. "*Shared,* like would kiss and tell?"

"No, shared like Julian would have a girl from makeup in his trailer one week and Angel would have her in his trailer the next. Then she might be with Julian the following week again." He walked back toward the register and she followed him. "I knew they were good friends," he continued, "but I always thought, even then, it was weird."

"That *is* weird," Nikki agreed, wondering why their promiscuity hadn't come out on the Internet.

"A camera guy once told me they took the same girl home for a weekend and really *shared* her." He made a face. "But that guy was a known gossip, so who knows?" He stepped behind the counter.

"And Diara and Kameryn? What did they think about the *boys'* behavior?"

"*Think* about it? Shoot." He rang her up. "Diara and Kameryn were as promiscuous as Angel and Julian."

Chapter 19

Victoria gazed down. "I wasn't expecting to see you this evening, dear. What a pleasant surprise."

Nikki sat on the floor of her mother's legendary pink boudoir, a sealed, cardboard box in front of her. She'd brought it down from the attic Saturday but hadn't opened it yet.

Victoria was on the couch, wearing a fluffy white robe, her hair twisted up in a white turban. She had scrubbed her face clean and covered it with a film of moisturizer. Without makeup, Nikki thought her mother actually looked younger. Softer. She liked Victoria this way, slightly exposed. Here, safely in her room, Nikki had found that her mother could be herself. Or, at least, she could be less guarded.

They were sitting in the lounge area of the bedroom suite of pink walls and pink and white draperies. The flat-screen TV was on, turned to an entertainment news show, but the volume was down. Nikki had brought her spaniels and both relaxed beside her on the plush Turkish wool carpet. Stanley rested his muzzle on Nikki's leg.

Seeing the attention his friend was getting, Oliver inched forward until his head was in Nikki's lap. She stroked his soft, spotted red and white coat. Oliver was a Blenheim. Stanley, a cousin twice removed to Oliver and two years older, was a black, white, and tan tri. Nikki had brought them with her tonight because she felt guilty leaving them home for the evening, when she'd already been gone all day. Besides, she missed them.

Nikki had left Alison and Jocelyn with takeout Thai and a rented DVD, giving them a little time to be alone; talk in private, if they wanted. Nikki didn't know who Alison's arrest was harder on, mother or her teen daughter. What Nikki did know, from observation, was that they had an excellent relationship. Certainly better than Nikki had had with Victoria when *she* was Jocelyn's age.

Nikki stared at the cardboard box in front of her. The word *John* was written in bold black Sharpie in Victoria's handwriting. John Harper was Nikki's father, dead almost ten years now. He'd been murdered during an armed robbery of his East Side apartment in New York City. The cops had botched the investigation, then the DA the prosecution. The perpetrator ended up being released on a technicality, only to kill again in a robbery with a similar MO. Because of her own run-ins with the law when she was in her late teens, Nikki wasn't fond of police in general, but her father's case had made her trust them less.

Overworked, underpaid, she knew that most police did their best, but her father's murder was proof that their best wasn't always good enough. That was how Nikki got involved in the Rex March and the Eddie Bernard murder investigations. In both cases, she hadn't trusted the justice system with the lives of her loved ones who were.

Nikki hadn't really thought about it, but that was one of the reasons she had to see her questioning through with Alison's case. She knew Tom Dombrowski was a good guy, that he wouldn't intentionally make a mistake or falsely accuse the wrong person. But he had nothing personal at stake. Nikki did. And now that she was knee-deep into her own investigation with no real leads, she felt as if she was fighting not only for Alison's freedom, but for her relationship with Jeremy.

"You going to open that box or just stare at it?" Victoria asked. She was sorting a stack of old photos on her lap. She'd been approached about writing an autobiography and was seriously considering taking on the project. If she did, she wanted to use previously unpublished pictures of herself . . . but only good ones.

Nikki ran her fingertips over her father's name, then stroked Oliver. "I went to a comic-book store today."

"Did you? I didn't even know there was such a thing." Victoria reached for her electronic cigarette on the table beside her.

She was trying to stop smoking. Again. She'd smoked on and off her whole life, but never, ever in public. She could go days without a cigarette, which made Nikki think it was more a habit than a dependence on nicotine. She was pleased her mother was giving the smoking cessation aid a try.

"Taken an interest in reading comic books, have you?" Victoria asked, one eyebrow arched.

"I went to talk with the owner of the store. He starred with Diara and the others in the TV show that made them famous."

"A kids' show, wasn't it?"

"Arguably the most popular teen drama *ever* on TV. It's still making a ton of money between residuals and merchandising."

"I never saw it. Oh my, whatever made me think that dress was attractive?" Victoria rejected a photo. "What was this TV show called?"

"*School Dayz.* I bet we could find it on On Demand." She reached for the remote control on the white coffee table between her and her mother. "This guy I talked to, Maurice, he started out as one of the stars on the show, just like Diara, Kameryn, Angel, and Julian. But as their parts got bigger, his got smaller until he was written off the show. He never did anything else big again. He owns a store now and sells comic books for a living."

Victoria drew the ceramic cigarette to her lips. "Did this comic book gentleman have anything helpful to say?"

"I don't know." Nikki flipped through screens on the TV. "Possibly." She glanced at her mother. "He suggested that the four of them, while working on the show, were pretty promiscuous."

"How old were they?"

Nikki thought for a minute. "I think they were all around seventeen, eighteen when they were hired. They always played characters younger than themselves. But the show ran for five seasons, I think. So they were *old enough*. I'm just surprised. You know, because it was Disney backing them."

"Not all that surprising. You don't want to have that conversation, do you? Young people today . . ."

Nikki chuckled. "I do *not*." She continued to flip through screens on the TV, in search of *School Dayz* reruns. "He hinted at an even racier suggestion than simple promiscuity."

"Maybe he wasn't telling the truth."

"Maybe. Aha!" Nikki found a listing for episodes of *School Dayz*.

"What did he tell you they were doing?"

Nikki glanced over her shoulder at her mother. "That not only did Angel and Julian date a lot, but they dated the same girls at the same time. And Diara and Kameryn were doing the same thing."

"When you say *dated,* I assume—"

"The word has a broader meaning than it once did." Nikki turned back to the TV and selected the first episode available. It was from the third season, after Maurice was gone.

"Hmmm," Victoria mused. "And you feel this comic store gentleman is reliable?"

"He didn't seem vindictive. Or eager to trash their reputations." She thought for a minute. "I do believe him." She hit PLAY and the episode began.

The two of them watched in silence for ten minutes. The episode revolved around a misunderstanding between three girls, which included Diara's and Kameryn's characters. Several boys, including Julian's and Angel's characters, got involved. As well as the goofy female biology professor. Confusion and laughter ensued.

"What kind of school is this supposed to be?" Victoria finally asked. Obviously, she wasn't enjoying the show.

"It's supposed to be a boarding school for rich kids, but Kameryn's and Angel's characters are kids from *da hood,* there on scholarship."

"Well, who on earth would pay a salary to *that* woman?" Victoria said, indicating the biology teacher on the show. "She shouldn't be teaching kindergarteners."

Nikki chuckled and paused the show. She'd watched enough, too. It was interesting seeing the Fab Four younger, but the comedy, aimed at middle-schoolers, was pretty silly. She turned to her mother, peeling the tape off the cardboard box in front of her, as she spoke. "I spent hours on the Internet today looking for negative gossip on the Fab Four and there was nothing. Not a hint of impropriety."

"What kind of impropriety are you looking for? Whose?"

"My first thought was Ryan Melton's. If he was cheating on his wife—"

"Maybe she killed him," Victoria said dryly. "Or had someone do it for her. Regrettably, an age-old story."

"Right. It was, at least, worth looking into. Only no one I spoke to knew anything about Ryan ever cheating on Diara. What I did hear, from two separate sources, was that Diara may have been cheating on him." Nikki hesitated. "Have you heard any gossip like that on the set?"

"I haven't." She laid a black and white photo of herself in a one-piece bathing suit, standing on a beach, on a separate pile on the table beside her. It looked to be from the 1960s. "But that doesn't surprise me."

"That she might have been cheating on Ryan?"

"That I haven't heard anything," Victoria sniffed.

Nikki slid Ollie off her leg and rose on her knees to open the box. "Why does that not surprise you?"

"Because Diara is a Disney sweetheart. She always will be and she knows how to behave herself, at least publicly. That's probably why there's nothing on the Internet about their inappropriate behavior when they were working for Disney. Their images were being protected."

"By whom?"

She dismissed the TV with a wave of her hand. "By everyone associated with that inane show."

Nikki rested her hands on the box, letting her mother go on.

"That's the way the studios used to do things. Back in the days when stars were made. Actors and actresses didn't just change their names and allow the studios to give them personas, they agreed to behave in a certain way, to give the public a certain impression. We signed morality clauses. We agreed not to leave the house without being dressed like a star, hair done, makeup on."

Nikki listened as her mother continued.

"And when we did step out of line, the studio executives and public relations staffs were there to cover it up. To hide it from the public. I knew stars who dabbled in drugs, did away with pregnancies, and committed adultery. The public never heard about that nonsense. We were shuffled around in the middle of the night in limos. Bribes were paid to keep witnesses' mouths shut."

"But things are different now," Nikki countered. "Studios don't own actors and actresses the way they once did."

"I understand that. That doesn't mean in this instance that the reputation of the young actors and actresses wasn't protected."

"So . . . just because there's nothing on the Internet about the Fab Four being wild, doesn't mean it didn't happen," Nikki said, thinking out loud.

"True. Though what does that have to do with Ryan's murder?"

"I don't know." Nikki sighed. "Does what Maurice said suggest that they're at least capable of less than G-rated behavior?"

Victoria set the remaining pictures on the couch beside her. "I know one thing. Nowadays, inappropriate behavior is harder to hide, what with tweeting and such."

Nikki smiled, shocked her mother even knew what Twitter was. After all, she was just getting the hang of using a cell phone. "Tweeting?"

"Well, I don't *tweet*, of course, but I know what it is!" She frowned and reached for her glass of tonic water with lime. It was a weeknight and she had to work the next morning, so she had passed on the evening cocktail Amondo had offered her.

Nikki stared at the cardboard box in front of her.

"Oh, for goodness sake, open it, Nicolette."

Nikki didn't know if she was up to it tonight. It had been a long day. She should be getting home and letting her mother get to bed. And . . . she just didn't know that she needed to stir up all those feelings, looking at her father's possessions. "What's in here?"

Victoria sighed. "I don't remember. Pictures, I suppose. Of us. A paperweight you made him for Father's Day. Things."

Nikki pushed the box away from her and stood up. "I think I'll go."

"Nicolette, what on earth has gotten into you?"

"What do you mean? I'm tired. You're tired. You have to be on the set in the morning. I should go home and let you get some sleep. The box can wait."

"I'm not talking about just the box. I'm talking about

this whole thing with Jeremy's sister. Ina said that Maria said that you and Jeremy are barely speaking. Why do you feel compelled to dig into other people's personal business for her sake?"

"Because I know she didn't do it," Nikki said firmly. "And Jeremy . . . he's afraid she might have." She went on faster. "And . . . and someone should believe Alison. Someone should be there for her the same way you were there for me when people didn't believe me."

"Ah . . ." Victoria held up her finger. "I knew there was something going on with you. You're talking about *the incident.*"

"Mother, that's silly."

"Do you want to talk about it? It's been a long time since we have. Maybe not since your father's death."

Nikki picked up her Prada and snapped her fingers. Both dogs popped up off the carpet and ran for the door. "This is not about me. And, no, I don't want to talk about it."

"Dear, an incident like that—"

"It wasn't an *incident,* Mother. I killed someone. I pulled the trigger and I killed someone!" The last words came out louder than Nikki intended and she immediately felt guilty. She tucked her hair behind her ear. "I'm going to go," she said softly. "Good night. I'll talk with you tomorrow."

Victoria said something under her breath, but Nikki ignored her. She didn't know what her mother said. She didn't want to know.

The next day, Nikki was checking on the staging of a house in the West Flats when Marshall called. "Maybe a stack of old books to give this corner an Old World look?" she asked the woman there doing the staging.

"Great idea, Ms. Harper."

Hey," she said into the phone. "I thought you were still shooting that commercial."

"Wrapped up this morning. Lunch? I might have something for you."

"Something for me?"

The woman held up two vases, questioning which one to set on a side table. Nikki pointed at the white Lenox.

"What kind of something for me?" Nikki asked, walking out to the terrace, noting the pool had leaves in it.

"On Diara," Marshall whispered with obvious delight. "Meet me at The Ivy. One-fifteen?"

Nikki hesitated. She and Jeremy often met for lunch on Wednesdays, but she hadn't heard from him. So it was pretty safe to say she and Jeremy weren't having lunch together today. "Sure."

"I'll have Eli make the reservation."

"How's he working out?" Eli was Marshall's new assistant.

"Perfect. He's a good worker and he has lots of drama in his personal life. A love triangle," Marshall bubbled.

Nikki had to smile. "Thanks for calling. See you at one-fifteen."

"See you then, sweetie."

Nikki hung up and considered calling Jeremy. Just leaving a message. Instead, she walked back into the house and went back to work.

Chapter 20

The Ivy was a darling open-air restaurant on Robertson Boulevard that featured a white picket fence, English bric-a-brac, climbing roses, and, of course, ivy. Nikki walked up the sidewalk as Marshall was just arriving. He stepped out of his limo, followed by Eli, the new assistant.

Paparazzi camped out on the opposite side of the street stepped to the curb as soon as the limo pulled up. They called to Marshall as he acknowledged them with a wave and a handsome smile.

"Mr. Thunder!"

"Marshall!"

"How's your day going?"

"Great, Martin. Yours?"

There was a round of chuckles. The press didn't just like Marshall Thunder; they *adored* him.

"Having lunch with Nikki? Is this business or pleasure?"

"Always a pleasure with Nikki Harper." Marshall smiled as he adjusted his Dolce and Gabbana aviator sunglasses.

The cameras across the street were whirring and snapping like insects. Nikki ignored the cameras and the men and women who wielded them. It was always this way when she was out with Marshall. Fortunately, growing up in the shadow of Victoria Bordeaux, she knew the ground rules. Never appear flustered or annoyed by the presence of the press, and never, *ever* step out of a car without lipstick and proper undergarments beneath your clothes. The press could be bothersome, Victoria had counseled many times, but without them, there would be no stars.

"Good afternoon, Ms. Harper." Eli practically beamed.

"Hey, Eli."

He led the way from the limo, through the picket fence gate to the open porch of the restaurant. Eli was nice looking, well-dressed, and appeared to be the epitome of efficiency; he held an iPhone in one hand, a BlackBerry in the other.

A slender, cute blonde greeted them. "I'm Amy and if there's anything I can do for you, Mr. Thunder, or Ms. Harper, just let me know. Your table is this way. You requested outside?"

"That okay with you?" Marshall asked Nikki as they followed the hostess. "It's shady. I thought we both could use a breath of fresh air."

"Perfect," she answered.

Marshall pulled Nikki's chair out for her. Eli said his good-byes, and Nikki and Marshall waited to speak until after the hostess had left glasses of water and menus with them.

"So?" Nikki said excitedly. She unfolded her pink napkin on her lap.

"Sooo . . ." Marshall studied the menu. "I *should* have the grilled vegetable salad, but I'd love the India's burger, or . . . the fish and chips."

"You know I love fish and chips." Nikki sipped her water. "But I should have the salad."

Marshall groaned in obvious indecision, ignoring the stares from other patrons. Fortunately, their table was in the corner, so it was somewhat private. Sun umbrellas, hanging plants, and potted flowers pretty much blocked the view of the paparazzi across the street.

"I know," he said, sitting back. He was wearing tan slacks and a Gucci oxford shirt, opened two buttons, to show his sun-glowed, broad chest. "Why don't we order both and we'll share?"

"Works for me." She set down her menu and glanced at the gorgeous white gardenias in a clay pot on the table. "Then maybe we can split a dessert."

"Just what I was thinking! Ooh. Maybe an apple croissant, or a red velvet cupcake?"

Nikki met his gaze through their sunglasses. "Both, if you like." She slapped the table. "Okay, you're killing me here, Marshall. You called saying you had information. What did you want to tell me?"

"Well . . ." He lowered his voice conspiratorially. "I took a meeting with James Cameron yesterday. You know him?"

She rolled her eyes. "Of course, I know who James Cameron is. 'But this ship can't sink' " she quoted from the movie *Titanic*.

"Decent British accent you have there," Marshall quipped.

"Thank you."

"So, anyway, my agent and I met James Cameron at Patina to discuss a new movie he's writing. I had a fabulous black cod confit. Have you tried it?"

"Marshall."

"You don't like cod?"

"I swear, you get more like my mother every day. I don't care what you ate. Tell me why I should care that you *took a meeting* with James Cameron. Besides because it's pretty cool, even for Marshall Thunder," she teased.

"*Because* . . . Diara Elliot and her agent, Lex Bronson, joined us," he said triumphantly.

Nikki scooted forward. The tables were far enough apart that she doubted the three young women in super-short, super-expensive dresses could hear her and Marshall, but she didn't want to take any chances. Especially since the paparazzi had crossed the street and were now attempting to take pictures from the sidewalk, through the potted plants. "Diara took a business meeting? Already?"

"It's James Cameron, sweetie. James Cameron calls, you take the meeting."

"So . . . James Cameron is interested in having you star in a film."

"Diara and me. The male lead is a bigger part, but she'd be billed as female lead." He fluttered his hand. "But that wasn't what was so interesting. The script isn't even done yet."

The waiter appeared at the table; he was wearing a pink shirt and a bright blue tie. "Could I take your order, Mr. Thunder, or would you like a few more minutes?" He smiled at Nikki. "Good to see you, Ms. Harper."

"Nice to see you, Teddy." Victoria had taught Nikki to always learn the names of maître d's and the wait staff of the restaurants she frequented. "How's your sister?" Nikki recalled that his sister had been ill last time she and her friend Ellen had lunch here. She had been undergoing radiation treatments for cancer.

"She's doing great." Teddy smiled from ear to ear. "Thanks so much for asking. I can't believe you remembered!"

Marshall placed their order. Both of them declined anything to drink beyond water and the minute the waiter walked away from the table, Nikki leaned forward again. "So?"

"So, do you know Lex Bronson?"

Nikki wracked her brain, squinting behind her sunglasses. "Vaguely. Nice looking, dark, curly hair, expensive suits, and a bit of a head twitch when he's nervous?"

"That's him. Recently divorced."

"I think I saw him on some kind of list of up-and-coming talent agents."

"He's got quite a few A-list clients," Marshall agreed, "and signing more every year."

"Wasn't he trying to romance you a year or so ago?"

Marshall sipped his water. A young woman two tables over tried to, inconspicuously, take a picture of him with her cell phone. She wasn't all that inconspicuous. He smiled, but went on talking to Nikki. "Funny you should use that word. I think Diara and Lex were playing footsie under the table at Patina."

"Playing footsie?"

"Subversive flirting," he told her, lifting both dark eyebrows.

She took off her sunglasses. "Are you serious?" Glancing away, she thought for a second. She looked at him again. "You think there could be something going on between Diara and Lex Bronson?"

"I'd bet my mansion on Beverly Drive." He slapped the table triumphantly. "And my new property in Oahu."

Nikki sat back in her chair. "Did this seem like something new or . . ."

"Come on. Who starts a new relationship two weeks after her husband is murdered?"

"Wow." She sipped her water. "Wow," she repeated. "You know, I met an assistant on the set of *Casa Capri* who told me that Diara didn't have a lot of male visitors. Just Julian, Angel, Gil, and . . . her agent. So, maybe it's been going on for a while."

"I definitely thought it was interesting, but I don't know how that information helps Alison. So Diara cheated on her husband with her agent. So what? You already know she didn't kill him."

"But I don't know *he* didn't."

They were both quiet for a moment, lost in their thoughts.

Marshall broke the silence. "So, now what?"

"I don't know. Guess I'll see what I can find out about Lex."

"My agent and he are pretty good friends. You want me to see if Alex can find out where Lex was that day? I mean, if he had an alibi, he didn't do it, right?"

"That would be wonderful."

"I'll look into it. But if there's anything else I can do. Anything, anything at all, just tell me." He reached across the table and squeezed her hand. "You know I would do it."

"I know. You're a good friend." She slipped her hand out from under his and reached for her water. "I'm thinking I need to talk to Alison and see if she can think of anyone who came and went in the house who I haven't thought of. Other than the pool boy, the fish guy, the dry cleaners. And I'd still love to speak with Alison's attorney. Just to get a feel for where she stands on the case. I know she won't tell me anything, but I'd like to know if she thinks they'll get as far as a trial."

"You want to talk to Lillie Lambert? Good luck with that. You can't get anything out of Alison?"

"Not much," she admitted. "I told her she had to be honest with me from now on, and I think she is, but she's still being pretty close-mouthed about the whole thing. She answers direct questions, but never volunteers anything."

"Well, if she admitted to making the skin flick, maybe she is being honest."

Nikki cut her eyes at him. "It's not like she had a choice. She knew I knew. Of course, maybe if she had come clean sooner, Jeremy—"

"*Wouldn't* have kicked her out of his house?"

"He didn't *kick her out*. He just . . . didn't ask her to stay." She put her sunglasses back on. Someone else was taking a picture of Marshall with her cell phone, this time from the front gate. "It's all going to blow over with Jeremy. Alison and Jocelyn are just staying a few days with me. That's all."

Marshall listened without arguing. Both of them were quiet while the waiter placed the fish and chips and the salad in the middle of the table and gave them both pretty white plates with ivy painted all over them.

"Tartar sauce, cocktail sauce, malt vinegar, and fresh lemon wedges," Teddy said brightly, setting down a small tray. "And I'll be right back with water refills. Anything else I can get you?"

"Nope, this is perfect. Thanks."

When he was gone, Marshall placed a piece of fried fish on Nikki's plate and added some French fries. "So how's that going, having Alison and her daughter in your house?" He took some fish and chips for himself.

"Fine."

"Alison working?"

"Yeah, I think so. She seems to be doing okay, considering. Salad?"

He let her put some on his plate. "And how about you, love? How are you doing?"

"I don't know. Frustrated. I know she didn't do this, but I don't feel like I'm getting any closer to figuring out who did. I need to talk to Ryan's wife, Ryan's friends; to Gil, Kameryn, Julian, and Angel. And Betsy and Hazel, too. But I don't know how to get to them. It's not like we're friends or anything."

Marshall chewed on a fry. "Hmm. How about—" He looked up suddenly. "How about if I have a little party. A little cocktail thing to . . . to celebrate the meeting with Cameron and Diara. I invite her and her friends."

"You think they'd come? Her husband's only been dead two weeks."

"Diara was *very* eager to do this project with me. She'll come. And she'll make her friends come. I'll just make it a little informal, spur-of-the moment thing. My publicist will be thrilled. And, of course, Lex Bronson will be there. Just think, you'll have them all together at once. You can grill them to your heart's content."

"That would be perfect."

"It would, wouldn't it? It actually sounds like fun, now that I think about it. What if the killer is actually there?" He grabbed another fry. "Saturday night. I'll do it Saturday night."

"You can do it that quickly?"

"I can do anything I want." He grinned. "I'm a star. Remember?"

She chuckled and took a bite of her salad.

"Okay. So that's taken care of. Now tell me, how are things with Jeremy? Or shouldn't I ask?"

"You shouldn't ask." She chewed what was in her mouth and went on. "Not great. After the porn film *reveal* Saturday, he left the house with the kids. I haven't seen him since."

"And it's Wednesday." Marshall didn't say it in an accusing way; he was just stating a fact.

"It's Wednesday," she agreed. "I have these tickets for the Dodgers this weekend. Box seats. I thought maybe we could go together. Take the kids. But he's going away for the weekend with the kids. Meeting his parents. *LEGOLAND.*"

Marshall grimaced. "Gads. And he didn't invite you?"

She shook her head and picked up a fry. "I was thinking that maybe I'd go over to his house after work. See if he wants to talk. What do you think?"

Marshall frowned. "I think Jeremy would be a fool to let this thing with his sister come between the two of you. Whether she did it or not."

"She *didn't do it*," Nikki said.

The question was, if she said that often enough, could she make it come true?

In the end, Nikki chickened out and didn't go by Jeremy's that night. Instead, she called his cell when he should have been on his way home. He didn't pick up. She left a message.

She stopped at the market on the way home and arrived at her Craftsman bungalow to find Jocelyn at the dining room table doing her homework.

"Hey, Aunt Nikki." Jocelyn pulled ear buds out of her ears and Nikki heard the faint pound of music from the ear buds. "Need help?"

"Nah, I just have these two bags." Nikki heard Alison talking to someone on the phone in the kitchen. She could see her through the doorway, standing with her back to them. "Geometry?" she asked Jocelyn.

"Yeah."

Both dogs began to bark and run around the dining table as if it were a dog track.

"I hated geometry when I was in school," Nikki told Jocelyn.

"Of course I haven't!" Alison said from the kitchen.

Nikki tried to pretend not to be listening to Alison as she continued to talk to Jocelyn. "That was the closest I think I ever came to failing a class."

"I would never say anything," Alison insisted.

Nikki glanced in the direction of the kitchen. "Who's your mom talking to?"

Jocelyn shrugged. "I don't know." She reached for her ear buds.

"You get back to work. I better put these groceries away." Nikki walked through the dining room and into the kitchen.

"Because it could hurt me, too," Alison said into her

cell. She spun around as Nikki entered the kitchen. "So you're cancelling for tomorrow. Got it. No problem. I'll talk to you later."

Nikki dropped the bags on the counter. "Who was that?"

"Just a client." Alison set her phone on the counter next to the stove and grabbed a pair of tongs. Chicken breasts sizzled in a pan.

Didn't sound like *just a client*.

"You're making dinner? Great." Stan and Ollie flew into the kitchen, around the two women and back out to the dining room. "Enough, you two!" she called after them. She eyed Alison's cell phone. Obviously Jeremy's sister had tried to hide the true nature of that phone call.

"You're letting us stay here." Alison flipped the chicken breasts in the pan. "It's the least I can do."

Nikki began putting the groceries away. "I had lunch with Marshall today."

"Did you?" Alison blushed. "He's so good-looking."

"He is that," she agreed, putting half-and-half in the refrigerator. She glanced at Jocelyn, who sat at the dining table with her back to them. Ear bud wires hung from her ears. She was listening to her iPod again. "He told me something interesting about Diara."

Alison looked nervous at once. "Did he?" She dumped baby spinach from a bag into a wooden salad bowl.

Nikki put a box of crackers in a cabinet. "He and his agent had dinner with Diara and her agent last night. They were talking with a director." She hesitated. "Alison . . . do you think it's possible that Diara might be having an affair with her agent?"

"An affair? I don't know. How would I know that?"

"Because you said that Ryan said something to you suggesting his wife might be cheating on him. I didn't know if maybe he said who—"

She shook her head and turned away. "He never said."

Nikki dug into her grocery bag. "Okay. Do you know who had access to Ryan and Diara's house? Other than the people you already told me about?"

She thought for a minute. "Like . . . who?"

"I don't know. That's what I'm asking you. Family. Friends. Who could have walked into Ryan's house, killed him, and walked out again without causing any concern in that neighborhood?"

"I never heard about any family. I don't think either of them had family nearby." Alison dumped the chopped carrots into the salad bowl. She reached for a cucumber. "Julian and Hazel live down the street. They came over sometimes. Angel and Betsy live only a few houses down from Diara and Ryan."

"Where do Kameryn and Gil live?"

"Coldwater Canyon."

"Do they all come and go in Ryan and Diara's house?"

"I guess. Yeah, I think so. But Angel and Betsy and Julian and Hazel more often. You know, because they live nearby. Angel stops by when he runs in the neighborhood."

Nikki leaned against the counter, two avocados in her hand. There was something about Alison's tone of voice that . . . bothered her. It was on the tip of her tongue to say, "Alison, what are you not telling me?" She glanced at Alison's cell phone on the counter. Had she been talking to Diara? She turned around and sniffed the air. "You smell something?"

Alison began to chop up some dried tomatoes. She inhaled. "No."

"Aha." Nikki opened the cupboard beneath the sink. "Yuck." She pulled out the garbage can and removed the bag, spinning it before tying it up. "You mind taking this out?"

"Sure." Alison grabbed the trash bag.

The minute Alison went out the back door, Nikki

glanced in Jocelyn's direction and picked up Alison's cell phone. It took her a second to find the recent calls screen. She only prayed the caller had called Alison and not the other way around, because she had no idea how to find a list of outgoing calls on an iPhone.

There had been an incoming call seven minutes ago.

Nikki heard Alison turn the doorknob, on her way back in. The trashcan was only a few feet from the back door. Nikki rolled it out front on Fridays.

Nikki stared at Alison's phone. The call had come from *BG*.

Who the heck was *BG*?

By the time Alison stepped into the kitchen, her phone was on the counter and Nikki was on her way upstairs. *BG . . .*

Chapter 21

BG was *Betsy Gomez,* Angel's wife. It took Nikki only twenty minutes to figure it out. What she still didn't know was why Alison was talking to Betsy. What was Alison talking about when she told Betsy she hadn't said anything? And why had Alison mentioned that Angel sometimes stopped at Ryan's house when he was out for a run? Was it just an off-hand comment, or was Alison trying to tell Nikki something?

The following day, Nikki was still mulling it over. The elevator beeped as it moved from floor to floor. The law offices of Lambert, Poore, and Johansson were conveniently located on Wilshire Boulevard, only a few blocks from Windsor Real Estate. Nikki ate a granola bar for lunch as she walked over.

When the elevator doors opened into the lobby of the attorneys' offices, Nikki stepped off. She didn't have much of a plan . . . but it was better than no plan.

Instead of going to the reception desk, which was a huge, curved slab of teak, with the name of the firm on the wall behind it, she took a seat in a leather chair in the waiting area.

The receptionist looked up. Nikki smiled at him and pulled her iPhone from her bag. She was going with the *act as if you belong there* and people will assume you do. She listened as the receptionist answered the phone. He was the same young man she'd spoken to two weeks ago when she tried to get an appointment with Lillie Lambert; she recognized his voice.

Nikki checked her e-mails. Responded to several. All the while, she kept an eye on what was going on around her. Several clients came and went. Two male attorneys, talking over a case, returned from lunch. But there was no sign of Lillie. Half an hour passed before the young man behind the front desk stood, cleared his throat, and spoke to Nikki. "Can I help you?"

Nikki looked up. Smiled *the smile*. "I'm waiting for someone. Thank you."

He smiled back and answered the chirping phone again. She held her phone in her hand and continued to glance in the direction of the glass wall, behind which she could see a hall and doors, some open, some closed.

Only fifteen minutes passed before the receptionist spoke again. Apparently, she was beginning to make him nervous. "May I ask whom you're waiting for?"

She crossed her legs, taking her time in responding. She was wearing black and white Armani pants and a cool knit jacket. And black boots, of course. She preferred boots to high-heeled shoes for work. "I'd rather not say," she told him.

"Client or attorney?"

"Pardon?"

"Are you waiting for a client or an attorney, ma'am?"

Again, *the smile*. "A client." She stood. "Could I use your restroom?"

He hesitated.

"Down the hall, isn't it?" she guessed.

He pointed to the hall behind the glass wall that she'd been watching.

Nikki took her time walking down the hall. She had no idea what she was doing here, or what she hoped to accomplish. She was just . . . checking out the place. A middle-aged guy with graying hair nodded and smiled as he walked past her, going in the opposite direction. An attorney, she was sure.

A man in his early twenties trotted past her, his arms weighed down with a pile of briefs. Law clerk?

At the end of the hall, just before the restroom, Nikki spotted Lillie Lambert's name on a closed door. The wall between the hallway and her office was all glass and she could see into the dark room. Lillie was out. On impulse, Nikki rested her hand on the doorknob. Locked. Which was probably good because she might have gone in if it hadn't been.

She went into the restroom, which was designated for both males and females. Very progressive of Lambert, Poore, and Johansson. She washed her hands and walked back to the waiting room. The receptionist caught her eye. Was he on to her?

He was accepting a manila envelope from a courier wearing a bike helmet—something you didn't see often in Beverly Hills. A bike messenger. Then he gave the messenger an identical envelope. It was one of those with the round tab and string, the kind you could reuse.

"Thanks. Have a good day," the messenger said, giving the counter a pat. He was early twenties with a shock of orange hair. He was probably only five-two or five-three, but very muscular in his tight bike shorts and yellow T-shirt that advertised *Diamond Courier Service* and a phone number.

"Thanks, Rash," the receptionist called after him as he walked away.

Nikki glided past the reception desk, sighing. "She's not coming. My girlfriend. Apparently she's not going through with it."

The receptionist stared at her, obviously not sure what to do. "Is . . . there an appointment I can cancel for you?"

"Nope, her problem." A stiff smile this time. "Thank you. Have a good day."

The messenger boy held the elevator door for her as he stuck the envelope into his backpack and swung it onto his back.

"Thanks," she said as she stepped in.

"No problem. Lobby?"

"Yes, thanks."

As he reached for the button, he did a double take. "Hey," he said. "Aren't you Nikki Harper?"

The doors closed.

"Guilty."

"I swear! I meet *everyone* in this elevator." He stamped his foot excitedly. "Victoria Bordeaux's daughter, right? Man, she was hot in her day."

Nikki chuckled. She heard plenty of people remark on Victoria's beauty, but they were rarely the kind of people who used the term *hot*. "I guess she was, wasn't she?"

The elevator stopped on the next floor.

"Would you mind . . . signing my autograph book?" He reached over his head and pulled, from his backpack, what looked like a bound journal. "I've got a pen."

Nikki had given up years ago arguing with fans that she wasn't a celebrity and that her autograph wasn't worth the ink it was written in. "Sure." She accepted the book and pen.

"You can just sign it. I'll add the date." He leaned toward her to watch. "I like to keep the dates."

Two women in business suits stepped onto the elevator, both engrossed in their smartphones.

"There's a paperclip marking where you can sign. I keep them in chronological order." The messenger slipped his finger between the pages for Nikki and opened it up. "I'm Rash. Well, that's what everyone calls me. I fell off my bike the first day I worked for the Kincaids—they're my bosses. Husband and wife. Super-nice people." He was blushing now, which was actually kind of sweet. "Anyway, I got a road rash and everyone started calling me—"

"Rash. Right." Nikki chuckled. The elevator door closed. "Got it." She clicked the gel pen and scribbled her name at the bottom of the right-hand page. As she was closing the book, her gaze wandered farther up the page. She recognized some signatures, but her gaze locked on one in particular.

Rash reached for the autograph book, but Nikki held on to it. "You always date these?"

"Yeah, I don't know why." He shrugged. "Just started doing it when I took this job nine months ago. Been doing it ever since. I'm not going to sell the signatures or anything. But I've got some good ones. See"—he pointed to the page opposite to the one Nikki had just signed—"Cameron Diaz. She was super nice. I ran into her at the coffee shop."

Nikki nodded, but she wasn't interested in Cameron Diaz's signature. "Is that Julian Munro's signature?"

He leaned over to look as the elevator arrived on the ground floor. "Sure is."

The doors opened.

"And he signed it on September nineteenth?"

The two women stepped off the elevator. Nikki followed, with Rash taking up the rear. Nikki walked away from the elevator bank, stopping beside a huge potted palm, and handed him back his autograph book and pen. "You're sure it was Friday, September nineteenth?" *The day Alison was arrested. The day Lillie Lambert was hired to defend her.*

"Yep, says so right there."

She got a tingly feeling. This might be the break she was looking for. "Do you remember where you ran into him?"

He hesitated.

"You like fish, Rash? Fish in tanks? Like a big tank?"

Now he was looking at her with more than a little suspicion.

"Someone gave me a fish tank, setup, fish, everything." She wondered if her nose was growing. "You can have it if you want. I really don't have room for it at my place."

He frowned. "I live with my girlfriend. I don't know how she'd feel about a fish tank."

Nikki tried to think fast. What did she have in her bag? Why hadn't she thought to grab something from her mother's stash of swag bag goodies? In the past, she'd been successful gaining information with a little... *bribery* was too harsh a word.

Then she remembered the tickets. The baseball game tickets Mr. Belka had given her. "How about tickets to see the Dodgers Saturday night?" She rifled through her Prada. "Box seats."

"Box seats? Jeez!"

Her fingers closed around the envelope and she pulled it from her bag. "Six tickets. I just need to know where you were when Julian Munro signed your autograph book."

"And you'll give me the tickets?"

"Yup. Here, take them." She handed him the envelope. "I can't go anyway."

He looked in the envelope. "Oh gosh, Ms. Harper. These really are box seats to see the Dodgers!" He looked up at her. "He signed it in an elevator, that can't be a breach of confidentiality, right? Because it wasn't in someone's office or anything."

She waited.

"Right here."

"You're kidding?" Nikki stared at him. So her hunch had been right. "Here." She pointed at the tile floor. "In this building?"

Rash nodded. "He was with Angel Gomez. They're like best friends, I guess. Have been ever since they were on *School Dayz* together."

"And where did you get on the elevator?" Nikki held her breath.

"Upstairs. At Lambert, Poore, and what's his name's."

"Johansson's."

"Yep," Rash agreed. "Like I said. I meet all kinds of people here. Of course, there's a talent agency on the fourth floor, so . . . you run into people. If you're here once or twice a day, like me."

Was he telling the truth? Why wouldn't he be? "Wait, you said that Angel Gomez was with him?"

"Yep, they got on the elevator together right after me on the lawyers' floor."

"But only Julian signed your book?"

Rash scowled. "Yeah, Julian was nice. He didn't act like I was bugging him or anything. He even asked me what kind of bike I rode, but Angel Gomez? He was totally pissy. Famous people are like that sometimes. But I think he was already pissed when he got into the elevator."

Nikki glanced away, thinking for a second. So had Julian and Angel hired Lillie Lambert to defend Alison? If so, why? Who were they protecting? Diara? Themselves? And why was Angel angry?

"Thank you so much, Rash."

"No, thank you." He had pulled his backpack off his back and was sliding the tickets and the autograph book into it. "Have a good day." He waved.

After an appointment Friday morning at eleven at a house in the Bird Streets, Nikki headed for Mulholland for a *drive-by* of Julian and Hazel Munro's and Angel and Betsy Gomez's houses. She found the addresses through sales records on the Internet. The Munros lived on Mulholland, three quarters of a mile from Ryan and Diara, but Betsy and Angel lived on Sumatra Drive. An easy walk . . . or jog from where Ryan Melton was killed. Nikki got lucky on her second pass when she spotted a familiar lawn-care truck next door to the Gomez home.

Nikki parked on the street and walked past the *Jorge & Son* truck, toward the sound of a hedge trimmer. It wasn't her childhood friend, Jorge, but she recognized his employee, Harley. He often did yard work at Victoria's house.

He smiled when he spotted her and cut the engine on the trimmer in his gloved hands. He had misaligned teeth that could have used some serious orthodontia when he was a kid. "Missth Nikki." He slid his safety goggles onto his forehead and set the trimmer on the ground.

She'd told him several times to call her Nikki, but old habits died hard. Harley was from South Carolina and had been raised by his grandmother. To quote Harley, if he didn't show proper respect to a woman, his grandmother would "whip histh heinie with a sthwitch."

"How are you, Harley?"

He adjusted his *Jorge & Son* ball cap and nodded. "I'm good. What bringsth you to thisth neck of the woodsth?"

"Just checking on a house down the street." She shifted her bag on her shoulder. "And . . . I saw you and I . . . I remembered I had these coupons for some free fries at Carney's." Harley loved fast food. "And I thought maybe you'd want them." She dug in her bag, remembering that she'd just seen them this morning when she was looking for a pen.

"That'sth really nice of you. You're always so niceth, Missth Nikki."

She produced the coupons Jessica had given to her, glad she had thought of them. "You do this house regularly?" she asked, glancing at the home. She recognized the modern lines; it had to have been designed by architect Jeff Allsbrook.

"Sure do."

"Always on Fridays?"

He blushed. Grinned sheepishly. "You caught me there, Missth Nikki. I shthould have been here Tuesthday. I took a few daysth off. Went fishin'. Little Rock Reservoir."

Nikki tried not to get excited. *What are the chances?*

"Tuesday? Really? Were you . . . around the day the murder took place around the corner? Ryan Melton's murder?"

"Sthcared the sthnot out of me. All thoseth police carsth and ambulancesth. I high-tailed it out of here, I can tell you that."

"So you were here?"

"Wasth justh finishthin' up. Had been here for hoursth thinnin' that hedge." He pointed to a natural barrier along the edge of the property.

"Did you . . ." She glanced in the direction of the Gomez house, which she could just make out through the trees. "See anything or anyone unusual? Before the police and ambulances?"

He narrowed his pale blue eyes. "You playin' detective again, Missth Nikki?"

She gave him a little smile but didn't answer.

"Nope." He slipped the coupons into his back pocket. "Didn't sthee nothin' unusual. Didn't sthee anyone." He thought for a minute. "Not a sthoul, excthept Mr. Angel. He jogged by same as he does most Tuesthdays."

"Angel? Angel Gomez?"

Harley nodded. "Livths next door."

"And you were sure it was that Tuesday that Ryan Melton died?"

"Crossth my heart, hope to die." He crossed his chest with his hand for good measure.

And Nikki had to refrain from giving him a big kiss on the mouth.

Chapter 22

A nd her day got even better. After talking to Harley and determining that he had seen Angel jog by at one-fifteen (he was sure of the time because he'd stopped working to have the second half of his bologna *sthandwhich*), Nikki headed home. She was getting into her car when, lo and behold, she saw Hazel Munro drive by in a light blue Mercedes convertible. Nikki recognized her red hair.

Hazel pulled into the driveway and five minutes later, she left with the blonde, Betsy. Nikki didn't hesitate. She followed the women into Beverly Hills, using all of her tailing skills. Which were nil. But how hard could it be? Don't be seen. It didn't matter. Betsy and Hazel were busy talking all the way into town; they wouldn't have noticed if an elephant had been tracking them.

Nikki followed them to Grove Drive, which featured a large outdoor shopping mall, The Grove. "A little shopping, ladies?" she said aloud.

They pulled into a cobblestone circular drive with a gorgeous magnolia tree in the middle. A parking valet hurried to open Betsy's door. Where else but in L.A. could you get valet parking at a shopping mall?

Nikki pulled in two cars behind them and stepped out of her car, keeping an eye on the two women while she waited for a valet.

"Thanks so much," Nikki said as the valet approached. "The key's on the console." She flashed *the smile.*

"Enjoy your day," the young woman called after Nikki.

Nikki followed Betsy and Hazel. They boarded a green trolley, which took shoppers to various points at the mall. It was a big draw; women in their spiky high heels could shop the day away without blisters.

Nikki debated whether or not to try and hoof it, for fear of being seen, but in the end, she hopped on the trolley and sat behind Hazel and Betsy. Again, the women didn't notice her.

So where are we going, ladies? Nikki wondered. *Coach? MAC Cosmetics?*

The two women got off and Nikki followed them, staying behind a gaggle of blondes, obviously all together. Instead of entering a store, Betsy and Hazel went into a restaurant.

"Lunch? Okay, why not?" Nikki murmured. She waited outside two or three minutes and then followed. It was a pub-like restaurant with dark wood and signs advertising not just Guinness, but Harp Irish Lager and Carlow O'Hara's Irish Red. Her stomach grumbled at the delicious smell of fried potatoes. She was starving.

Nikki took a guess and walked into the bar area. Betsy and Hazel were just sitting down.

Nikki slipped into a small booth so she could watch them without easily being spotted. A young woman with hair the color of Nikki's approached.

"Good afternoon," she said with a melodic Irish accent. "I'm Bryda. Can I get you something to drink? We've got a thirty-two-ounce draught that's half price for happy hour."

Nikki glanced in the direction of the bar. Hazel and Betsy were seated at one end. There were two men in conversation at the other end. Only two other booths were occupied. "I'm waiting for my boyfriend, but I guess he's running late. I'll take a Harp while I wait. But just a small one." She chuckled. "I have to get back to work."

The redhead smiled. "Be right back."

Nikki sat back and watched Hazel and Betsy. Hazel was wearing a blue and green dress that went perfectly with her red hair. Sky-high heels, of course. Betsy was dressed all in white: white flowing pants, white silk top. Her four-inch heels were teal, as was her Rebecca Minkoff handbag. A little too matchy-matchy for Nikki.

Nikki wiggled her feet in her comfy Cole Haan, knee-high boots, which had sensible two-inch, stacked heels. Betsy's and Hazel's heels were cute, but Nikki's feet never hurt at the end of the day and she hadn't *had* to take the trolley. She could have walked.

Bryda brought Nikki her ale in a pilsner glass. Nikki wasn't going to order anything to eat; she'd packed a salad, which she could have at her desk later. But she caved and asked for an appetizer-sized order of chips. When they came, they were better than even she'd anticipated. The freshly fried, hand-cut potatoes were amazing with malt vinegar.

As Nikki ate, she continued to keep her eye on the women. Harley had said that he'd seen Angel jogging the day Ryan was killed. Around the time of day he was killed. Had Angel done it? Why would he? Did his wife know?

After finishing off the fries and half the beer, Nikki licked her fingers, trying to decide what to do. She wanted to talk to the two women, but obviously she didn't want to get caught *spying*.

Betsy and Hazel were having glasses of white wine and salads. They were laughing and talking a mile a minute; Nikki could tell they were good friends. Were they outsiders among the Fab Four? The same way Ryan had been? Nothing really to do but look nice? Shop? Take long lunches at the mall?

After a moment of indecision, Nikki grabbed her bag and strode toward the ladies' room. She was almost past Betsy and Hazel when she stopped. Smiled. "Betsy! Hazel." She pressed her hand to her chest. "Nikki Harper. We met at my mother's, Victoria Bordeaux's, a few weeks ago. At the garden party."

"Oh my gosh!" Hazel bubbled. "Of course!"

Betsy smiled. "Good to see you, Nikki." She glanced around. "You here shopping with friends?"

Nikki sighed. "I was supposed to meet my boyfriend for lunch, but he cancelled at the last second. Running late with a patient or something." She made a "What can you do?" gesture. "I was already here. Thought I'd run into . . . Ugg," she said. (What? For sheepskin boots?) "Before I head back to the office." She segued as seamlessly as possible. "Hey, I was really sorry to hear about Ryan. I . . . I can't imagine how hard this must be. I know you were all such good friends."

The two women exchanged glances.

Nikki was immediately suspicious, then realized she had no reason to be. What was wrong with two friends who had lost a friend looking at each other?

"Would you like to join us?" Betsy asked. She was polite, but not overly enthusiastic. She was definitely the more reserved of the two women.

"Oh, please," Hazel begged. "Just sit for a minute." She patted the bar stool beside her. "Here, next to me."

Nikki pretended to hesitate, then gave in. "Just for a minute." She stepped up onto the barstool.

"Can I get you a drink?" a male bartender, about Nikki's age, asked. He had dark hair, but an Irish brogue as well.

She suspected that everyone working in the restaurant had one. "No, thanks. But I do need to pay my tab. Bryda was my waitress."

"Just put it on ours, Seamus," Betsy declared with a wave.

"Oh, that's not necessary," Nikki insisted. She crossed her legs, feeling a little uncomfortable perched on a stool at a bar in the middle of the day. Not that she spent much time on bar stools at night either. "I've never been here. Do . . . you two come often?"

"Every once in a while." Betsy pushed her unfinished salad away and reached for her wine.

"Every once in a while," Hazel repeated. "We like to shop here. The trolley's so much fun."

"Oh, it is." Nikki laid her palm on the bar. "So, how's Diara doing? My mother says she's been a champ on the set. Has she moved back into her house?"

"Oh, I don't know that she ever will. She's staying at the Beverly Wilshire." Hazel shook her head, her red hair brushing her shoulders. "I know I could never go back into our house, not if Julian . . . died there."

"Right," Nikki agreed.

Hazel nibbled on her lower lip. "But this must be awful for you, too. You're boyfriend's sister being arrested for Ryan's murder. And she seemed like such a nice girl. She walked our Duchess and Duke. Yorkies."

"And your dogs, too?" Nikki asked Betsy.

Betsy didn't meet Nikki's gaze. She drank the last of her wine. "I'm afraid so. I suppose we're not as good a judge of character as we thought."

"Oh!" Hazel patted Nikki's hand. "Julian got the invite to the cocktail party Saturday night at Marshall Thunder's house. I'm *so* excited."

"So you're coming?"

"We wouldn't miss it for the world. You'll be there, won't you? Julian said you're best friends with Marshall."

"We've been friends for years. He's a great guy."

"And *so* good-looking."

"Marshall was concerned it would be too soon, you know, after Ryan's death. But apparently there's a good chance he and Diara will be doing a movie together with James Cameron. I guess he wanted to celebrate." As the words came out of Nikki's mouth, she wondered if she was dooming her soul with such lies. But they weren't hurting anyone, right? And the Fab Four and their spouses would be treated to good caviar and champagne at Marshall's.

"Are you and Angel going to be able to make it?" Nikki asked. *So I can question him about your friend's murder?*

Betsy gave a quick smile that seemed a little forced. "We wouldn't miss it."

"It's going to be a very small group," Nikki said. "I'm looking forward to it."

"We should go, Hazel, if we're going to go shopping." Betsy slid off the bar stool. "I think I'll run to the ladies' room. Hazel?"

Hazel stood.

"We'll be back for the check in a few minutes, Seamus," Hazel called to the bartender.

"No problem, Mrs. Munro. I'll get yours, too, ma'am," he told Nikki as he turned to the cash register.

"So we'll see you Saturday night at Marshall's?" Hazel bubbled.

"Looking forward to it."

"Have a good day," Betsy said as the two women walked away.

Nikki sat where she was and waited for her check. "Nice ladies," she remarked when the bartender brought her a slip of paper and left one on the bar for Betsy and Hazel.

He began to stack up their salad plates and collect their silverware. "Mrs. Gomez and Mrs. Munro? Nice enough. They always tip well."

"So . . . they come often?"

He glanced in the direction of the ladies' room. "First Friday of every month. Wondered if they'd be here today, what with their friend being gone, God rest his soul."

Nikki wasn't quite following what he meant. "You mean, Ryan Melton?"

"Aye." He slid the dirty dishes into a tub under the bar. "Because they always met him here. First Friday of the month."

Nikki looked at him as she pulled her wallet from her handbag. "Always?"

He nodded. "For . . . the last six, seven months."

"But it was just the three of them, not Gil, Kameryn Lowe's husband?"

He thought for a minute. "No, just Mr. Melton and those two. Always sat at the bar, right here."

"So they all had lunch together, the first Friday of every month?"

"He never ate. He came in, had a beer," Seamus said. "One of the ladies handed him a big envelope and he left. They stayed for lunch. Cobb salad for the ginger, chicken Caesar for the blonde. No croutons."

"An envelope?"

"Big one." He demonstrated the size of a manila envelope.

Nikki slid some bills across the counter. "You know what was in the envelope?"

"No, but they always tried to hide it. Either Hazel or Betsy would take it out of her bag and slip it to him when she thought no one was looking." He gave her a crooked smile. "But a bartender sees everything."

"You said one of the women. Not the same one every month?"

He thought for a second, then shook his head. "Just one of them."

She slid off the barstool. *An envelope? Sometimes Betsy*

gave it to him, sometimes Hazel. What did that mean?
"Thank you. Have a good day."

"You, as well."

What on earth could Betsy and Hazel have been giving Ryan at the beginning of each month, in an envelope? Money? Was the answer that easy? But if it was money, what for? Was he blackmailing them? Their spouses?

Nikki walked out into the warm sunshine and back to her car. No trolley, no Ugg shopping for her.

Back at the office, Nikki retrieved her salad from the refrigerator in the break room and went back to her office. Sitting down, she glanced at the empty desk across from her. It had belonged to her partner, Jessica. Even though Jessica had been gone for a year, the powers that be at Windsor Real Estate hadn't given her desk to another broker yet.

She took a bite of romaine and avocado, and debated making a phone call. She wondered what Jess would do. Of course, she already knew the answer. "Go for it" had always been Jess's motto.

Nikki opened her drawer and pulled out a business card; it had been in the drawer for six months. His office phone number was printed on the front, but he'd penned his cell number on the back. Not all that subtle, now that she thought about it.

She punched in the numbers on her cell and the call clicked through. The phone rang on the other end.

"Lieutenant Dombrowski."

Nikki had an urge to hang up. How juvenile was that? "Tom? Nikki Harper."

"Hello, Nikki Harper."

She could hear his handsome smile in the tone of his voice. "I have a question for you," she said.

"What makes me think I'm not going to like this?"

Nikki heard phones ringing in the background. People

talking. She guessed he was at the police station, in some sort of bullpen. "Did you check Ryan Melton's bank statements?"

He didn't answer right away. Then, "You want to tell me why I should?"

"Nah."

"Well, it so happens that I have."

"And," Nikki said, "you found out that he's been making a deposit the first week of every month. A large one," she dared. It was just speculation, of course. "I'd even go so far as to guess the first Friday of every month."

Again, quiet.

"I'd also guess that if you were to subpoena Alison Sahira's bank accounts records, which I'm sure you already have, you would not find withdrawals of the same amount around the same date each month."

"You saying that Ryan Melton was blackmailing someone, but not Alison?"

She could tell by the tone of his voice that everything she had said was correct. He already knew Ryan was getting money from somewhere. He did not, however, know where it was coming from. But he knew it wasn't from Alison.

"You want to get together and talk about this?" Dombrowski asked.

Nikki thought about Hazel and Betsy. Had one of them killed him? It was certainly possible, but the fact that Angel had been out jogging the same time poor Ryan was getting himself killed nagged at her. It couldn't just be coincidence that he was out jogging when his supposed friend was being murdered, could it? "Nah," she said to Dombrowski. "Not yet."

"Nikki—"

"Sorry. Gotta run, Detective. Have a nice weekend."

Chapter 23

The following morning, Saturday, Nikki gathered her dogs' leashes and a travel water bowl for them. Jocelyn had gone with Jeremy and his kids to LEGOLAND. Alison had left earlier to meet with a potential client. She'd lost several jobs due to her arrest, but interestingly enough, the idea that she could possibly have committed a murder intrigued some people. Alison said she was getting enough calls that she could choose which jobs to take.

As Nikki walked the dogs to the car, her cell rang. She juggled the dogs' leashes, a small bag, her phone, and a bottle of water. "Hello."

"Nicolette."

"Good morning, Mother."

"How are you?" Victoria asked.

Nikki unlocked her car door. "Fine." There was something in Victoria's tone that worried her. "Why?"

"Because, frankly, I'm worried about you. I've been thinking about this. And . . . if you won't talk to me . . . I think you should consider *seeing someone*."

Nikki opened the back of her Prius. "See someone? Mother, what are we talking about?" She lifted Stan, then Ollie, into the kennel they shared.

Victoria exhaled impatiently. "A shrink, a therapist. Whatever you call them these days. As you know, Nicolette, I've always thought that things that are private should remain so. I don't believe in airing unmentionables in an office any more than in public, but—"

"Go back." Nikki dropped the bag that contained the dogs' water bowl and water for them. "*Why* should I see a psychiatrist?"

"This is not the kind of thing we should speak of over the phone, Daughter. Where are you?"

"At my house. The boys and I are going for a walk in Runyon Canyon Park." Nikki's plan was to see if there was anyone there who knew Alison. Alison took her clients' pets there all the time. There was a certain camaraderie between dog owners; maybe Nikki could learn something about Jeremy's sister she didn't already know. If not, at least she'd have a nice morning with the dogs before meeting her friend Ellen for lunch. Maybe a walk in the sunshine would help her work through the information she'd gathered yesterday.

"Ah. Fresh air and exercise will be good for you," Victoria declared. "I could use a nice walk. Come get me and we'll go together. We can talk."

"Mother—"

The phone clicked.

Nikki groaned. Then headed to Roxbury to pick up Victoria.

"We should have taken the Bentley," Victoria complained as they got out of Nikki's Prius. "There's more room. It's a very nice car."

"It *is* a nice car," Nikki agreed, letting the dogs out of the kennel. "But not really the kind of car one takes to the park."

Nikki led Stanley and Oliver through the secondary gates to the area of the park where she would be able to let them run off-leash.

If she was alone, she might have taken the trail up to Indian Rock. Hero Trail was the toughest hike in the park, with a slope that led to the spine of the ridge, where there were amazing views to the west and to the south. But no hike to the ridge today, not with two dogs and a mother.

"Isn't this lovely," Victoria remarked. She was dressed in a pale blue jogging suit, pristine white athletic shoes, and, of course, her pearls. Big sunglasses rounded out her ensemble.

Nikki leaned down to release the spaniels. "There aren't many public places dogs can run off-leash. I think it's great that the city allows it here."

The dogs took off, but only ran ten feet before looping back to circle Nikki and Victoria.

"So what were you talking about this morning when you suggested I see a psychiatrist?" They walked side by side. Nikki was wearing black yoga capris and a worn blue T-shirt.

Victoria glanced at her. "I think this business with Jeremy's sister has brought up . . . feelings in you. About what happened."

"I'm fine."

There were at least a dozen other dogs running around: two pugs, a French bulldog, three Labs, a Bernese mountain dog, and several mutts.

"It was a terrible thing, Nicolette. You did what you had to do to protect yourself, and your friend. But that doesn't mean—"

"I don't think about it. Ever. Alison's arrest has nothing to do with me," Nikki said, feeling as uncomfortable as her mother sounded.

Victoria had been there that night for Nikki after Nikki killed Albert Tinsley with his own handgun. But she and her mother didn't talk about it. They *never* talked about it.

"No, actually, it does," Nikki admitted. She glanced at her mother, then at the dogs running ahead of them. Stanley had stopped to sniff the black Bernese mountain dog.

"But only because you taught me how important it is to stand by someone you think is being falsely accused."

Victoria adjusted her sunglasses. "I would have stood by you, had you been guilty."

The tears that stung her eyes surprised Nikki. She was glad she was wearing sunglasses; otherwise, she would have been embarrassed. She looked up to check on the dogs. Ollie had already plopped himself down in the grass, but Stan was still checking out the Bernese that was apparently part of an entourage. A pug sat beside the Bernese, and a Golden Lab circled them both. "Come on, Stan," she called. "He's a lot bigger than you are. He'll eat you for an appetizer."

The woman with the Bernese laughed. She was a slender blonde wearing a bandanna and hiking shorts. Early thirties. Three dog leashes hung from a carabiner hooked to a loop on her shorts. "Don't worry," she called. "He's a big sweetie."

"Stanley!" Nikki called, slapping her thigh. He ignored Nikki. "Sorry," she said, approaching them. Victoria kept walking along the path.

"No problem. Stanley and Bingo are buddies. Aren't you, guys?" The blonde leaned down to scratch Stan's head. Bingo just stood there, looking like a big, black bear, tongue lolling contentedly.

"Oh?" Nikki said. "You know Stan and Ollie?" She pointed to Oliver, who was rolling in the grass, probably in something disgusting.

"We're friends, aren't we, Bingo?" the blonde said.

"What a cute name." Nikki put out her hand. "Okay if I pet him?"

"Bingo's cool."

As was Bingo's owner. She was wearing amber aviator glasses with her bandanna tied like a cap. Sort of a chic, hippie look.

"Nikki Harper." She gave a little wave.

"Prudence." She slapped her forehead playfully. "I know, what were my parents thinking? And that's Roko." She pointed to the pug seated in the grass. "And that crazy gal"—she indicated the Lab that was still running in big circles around them—"is Cindy."

Stanley began to lick Bingo's paw, which was bigger than his little, fluffy Cavalier King Charles head.

"Nice to meet you, Prudence, Bingo, Roko, and Cindy."

"We used to run into your dog walker all the time," Prudence said. "That's how we know Stan and Ollie."

"Alison?" Nikki looked up with interest, then glanced around to locate her mother.

Victoria had stopped to speak to an elderly woman.

Nikki returned her attention to Prudence. "You know Alison?"

"Yeah. Actually, we used to hang out once in a while after we left here. I'm a dog walker, too," she explained.

Nikki nodded. She got the impression that Prudence didn't know anything about Alison's arrest.

"We'd go for coffee or a sandwich," Prudence continued, "but then she got into party planning and she didn't have as much free time. You know, trying to juggle both businesses."

Party planning? Nikki thought. Alison didn't have a party planning business. She used to own a party *store,* but that was a while ago. It went bankrupt *before* she started the dog-walking business.

"When was the last time you saw Alison?" Nikki asked.

"Oh, I see her all the time. I saw her here last week. We say hi. Chat while we walk the dogs, but we haven't gone for coffee in . . . gosh, since Christmas. She doing okay?" Prudence asked.

"She's doing well. Actually, she's my boyfriend's sister, so I see her all the time."

"Cool. Well, she's nice. Shy, but nice. I like her."

"She is nice. And a hard worker. I . . . didn't realize she

was getting back into party planning," Nikki said, trying to sound casual. "She say who she was planning parties for?"

Prudence shook her head. "Nah, we didn't really talk about that. We talked mostly about the dogs."

Losing interest in the Bernese, Stanley trotted away, turned his head, barked at Nikki, and headed off in the direction of Oliver and Victoria.

"Looks like you're moving on," Prudence said, watching Stanley go.

"I guess we are." Nikki walked away. "Nice to meet you."

"You, too," Prudence called after her. "Have a nice walk. Tell Alison I said hi."

Nikki turned and waved. "I will. Enjoy the sunshine."

When Nikki caught up to Victoria, her mother looked back at Prudence. "A friend?"

"No, Stanley just stopped to say hi. Come on, boys." Her dogs trotted to catch up. "She said she knew Alison. That they used to get coffee after walking their dogs. She's a dog walker, too."

"That's interesting, dear."

"What's interesting is that she said she and Alison used to go for coffee, but then Alison got too busy with her *party planning business*."

"What party planning business?"

Nikki frowned. "That's what I was wondering."

"How do you feel about tamales?" Ellen asked as Nikki got into her new, white, Audi convertible.

"How do I *feel* about them? I feel good."

Ellen put on her sunglasses. "I mean, do you like them? Homemade tamales?"

"Is there any food I *don't* like?"

They both laughed as Nikki buckled in and Ellen pulled away from the curb in front of Nikki's house. The two had met under unfortunate circumstances the previous year when Victoria's neighbor had been murdered, but since then, they'd become good friends.

"I want to try out a tamale place on Pasadena Avenue. Mom's Tamales. Guy told me about it."

"Guy?" Nikki asked, pulling a scarf from her handbag to tie over her head. If they were going to hit the freeway, she'd need it. Otherwise, she'd be sporting a tangled mess for Marshall's cocktail party that evening. "As in Guy *Fieri*?"

Ellen had the most beautiful smile. She could have been a model. Instead, she became a chef. "You know him?"

"Only from watching The Food Network," Nikki chuckled. *"Triple D: Diners, Drive-Ins and Dives."*

"That's him. We've run into each other a couple of times over the last few months. Network parties and stuff. Anyway, he heard how much I love tamales, so he recommended I try these."

"So . . . you going to end up making cupcakes that look like tamales, or vice versa, for your show?" Nikki teased.

Ellen adjusted her white ball cap. "You never know." She signaled and turned. "So how was your morning? Have a nice walk with the doggies?"

"And Mother."

"Your mother?" Ellen laughed. It was Victoria who had first suggested that Nikki and Ellen become friends. Ellen knew exactly what she was like. "You took Victoria hiking in Runyon Canyon?"

"We didn't hike. We went for a walk." Nikki relaxed in the smooth leather seat. Ellen had the top down. It was warm and sunny and the breeze felt good on her face. "It was actually nice. She was on her good behavior."

"That's always a plus."

Nikki watched the houses, then businesses fly by as they drove out of her neighborhood and turned onto Santa Monica Boulevard. "I ran into someone who knows Alison. Another dog walker. She told me that she and Alison used to go for coffee after walking their dogs."

"You mean before she was arrested?" Ellen knew that Alison was Jeremy's sister, and knew Nikki was looking into the circumstances of her part in Ryan's murder.

"No," Nikki said, thinking back to her conversation with Prudence. "That's what was weird. This woman said they used to go out for coffee before Alison opened her party planning business and got too busy."

"Why's that weird?"

Nikki looked at Ellen. "Because Alison doesn't have a party planning business. She has a dog walking business."

Ellen frowned and adjusted her big, white, Gucci sunglasses. "I thought she had both." She braked as the light ahead turned red.

"No, she had a party store in West Hollywood, but when the economy went south, she lost a lot of business. She ended up closing it two years ago. Then about a year ago, she started walking dogs."

They sat at the light.

Ellen removed her sunglasses and looked at Nikki. "Nik . . . are you sure . . ." She stopped and started again. "Alison doesn't have *any* kind of party business?"

"Hasn't in years."

Ellen thought for a minute. The light turned green and a second later, someone blew their horn behind them. She put on her sunglasses and hit the gas. "Hmm. I just assumed . . . because she asked me for a recommendation."

"For what? When?" Nikki asked.

"Gosh, now *I* feel weird." She glanced at Nikki, then back at the road. "Like I'm tattling on Jeremy's little sister or something."

"Look, I'm trying to help Alison, and I know for a fact that she's not being totally honest with me. Which means she's not being totally honest with Jeremy. I'm afraid this could be the end of their relationship."

Ellen sighed. "We were at Jeremy's last fall. November, maybe. He had that backyard barbeque."

"Right. His annual *Turkey Day Is Almost Here* party."

"Alison and I were just chatting in the kitchen while she tossed a salad. She asked me if I could recommend a discreet caterer. She said something about losing hers."

Nikki made a face. "A discreet caterer? What for? Alison didn't have a party last fall. Certainly not one she needed a caterer for."

Ellen shrugged. "I'm not sure what she meant. But I'm sure that's what she said. She needed a *discreet caterer.*"

A discreet caterer. Nikki was still mulling that over when she arrived at Marshall's that evening.

Chapter 24

Nikki arrived at Marshall's early, in her Prius, and parked beside a Maserati she didn't recognize. The Fab Four and their spouses, she was sure, would come in limos. As she walked up the driveway to the house, she took in its massive elegance. It was a 12,000 square foot Neoclassical with a dramatic two-story marble entry. The monument to Marshall's box-office stardom was lit up by spotlights and featured multiple fountains that were arranged all over the finely trimmed front lawn (thanks to Jorge & Son). The statuary was life-size: Roman and Greek replicas.

The house had seven bedrooms and ten baths, a library, a formal dining room that seated twenty-four, a gourmet kitchen, and a master suite that included a marble bath with a sauna. Outside, there was a pool, a spa, an outdoor kitchen, two open cabanas, a tennis court, and a bocce court, among additional amenities. Marshall's partner, Rob, thought it was ridiculous that one man should own such a house. He'd grown up with a mother and father and six siblings in a single-story, three-bedroom house. He thought Marshall's place was more like a mausoleum than a home. And Marshall didn't like it any better. He bought it as an investment, and to satisfy his agent and his publicist. It was all part of his movie-star, heterosexual image.

He didn't like the house, said he was lonely there, and only stayed overnight when he had to. Most nights he slept in the cozy two-bedroom bungalow next door to Nikki, with Rob.

Before Nikki could ring the doorbell, which sounded more like a door gong, the front door opened. A gentleman in a tux greeted her. "Good evening, Ms. Harper. Shall I have your car parked?"

"Parked it myself, Elgin." She walked into the cavernous open hall; her voice seemed to echo off the Carrara marble floor. "You look nice this evening."

He smoothed his finely pressed white shirt. "Thank you." Elgin ran the monstrosity of a house for Marshall and did a superb job, but more importantly, he was devoted to keeping his boss's secret. Nikki would have trusted the guy with her life; Marshall did.

"Would you care for a cocktail? We're serving in the library."

"Nikki!"

She looked up to see Marshall coming down the white marble staircase that was broad enough to drive a Roman chariot down. He was dressed in a black Armani tux and was fiddling with a diamond cuff link.

"Hey." She smiled, tickled to see him. She had so much to tell him.

"You look gorgeous," he called. "I love you in that dress."

She cut her eyes at him. She was wearing a fifties vintage teal Ceil Chapman dress. It had a scooped neckline and teal bugle beads in swirled patterns. Her favorite part of the sheath dress was the godet at the hem in back; she'd bought the dress for the flirty little kick pleat. "Are you making fun of me? You know I like to get my money out of a dress."

"They don't call you Victoria Bordeaux's daughter for nuthin'," he teased with a wink.

Both Victoria and Nikki were known, in the celebrity world, for their habitual reuse of gowns, something rarely done in Hollywood. Victoria thought nothing of appearing in public in the same dress three times in the same year; she thought it was a waste to wear a dress once and then donate it, sell it, or let it sit in a closet. And while Nikki had more money than she knew what to do with because her father had left her a fortune, she was as *thrifty* as her mother. Besides, when she bought a dress or a gown that she loved, she wanted to wear it again.

"Let me see." He took her hand and she twirled for him on her three-inch silk heels. "Gorgeous," he repeated. "I love the French twist. And the new bangs."

"*Fringe*." Nikki patted her updo, which she had, of course, done herself. "Thanks."

"You ready?" He offered his elbow. "You know who you're going to ask what?"

She looked at him. "Are you suggesting I'm going to interrogate your guests?" She pretended to be shocked.

"Well, I certainly hope you're going to. That was the point of this party, wasn't it?" He led her down the hall toward the library.

He'd just had a new Crestron system installed in the house. It featured security, phone, lighting, and audio control throughout the house by the means of monitor screens and touch pads. Classical music—Bach—played softly in all the rooms.

"I don't," she hemmed. "Mostly I think I just want to watch them. See how they all behave."

"So you're sure one of the Fab Four killed Ryan?"

"No, I'm not *sure*. I just have a feeling. But it could be one of the spouses."

"Ooh. I like that idea. Do tell."

"Later. They'll be here any second. Lex Bronson coming, too?"

"Oh, he'll be here. I think he thinks I'm looking for a new agent." They walked into the library.

Nikki was surprised to see that she wasn't the first guest to arrive. Lieutenant Detective Tom Dombrowski turned to them, a book in his hand.

"Good evening." He was dressed in a tuxedo; tailored, not off the rack. Brunello Cucinelli.

Nikki couldn't help herself. She laughed out loud. "You invited *him*?" she asked, looking at Marshall. "You plan on having the kind of cocktail party that requires police protection?"

Marshall's mouth twitched with a smile. "For your information, I actually know Tom outside of the police world."

"Good to see you, too, Nikki." Dombrowski returned the book to its place. "You've got a great collection here, Marshall. Eclectic. The *Iliad* of Homer and *Odyssey* of Homer, first edition, folio issues, London, 1715, Thomas Hardy's works bound by Rivière & Son. *And,* signed, limited first editions of Stephen King's *Dark Tower* books, one to seven."

Marshall looked at Nikki, then back at Dombrowski and laughed. "I have to confess, I'm not much of a reader. When I bought the house, Nikki said I had to fill the library with books. Apparently, I bought books."

Dombrowski turned to Nikki. "Flying solo tonight?"

"Jeremy's out of town. A weekend with the kids."

"So, the gossip blog I read this morning is not to be believed? You and Dr. Fitzpatrick haven't broken up over the fact that his sister is a murderess?"

"What blog?" she asked, not sure if he was serious or not.

"Ooh, I read that, too," Marshall said.

Nikki rolled her eyes.

The doorbell rang . . . gonged. All three of them looked in the direction of the front of the house.

"If you'll excuse me." Marshall gave his best movie-star smile. "I have guests to greet. Have some champagne, kids." He indicated a waiter standing unobtrusively in the corner of the room. "Enjoy yourselves!"

Nikki shook her head as Marshall walked away, laughing to himself, she was sure. She waited until he was gone to speak to Dombrowski. "So how *did* you get an invitation?" she whispered. "And what are you doing here?"

"As Marshall said, we know each other outside law enforcement."

She frowned. "Right. And you don't think your presence here isn't going to be a little *conspicuous*? Like some kind of Agatha Christie scene?"

"I don't know what you're talking about. Marshall and I are friends. He invited me to his home."

There was something in his tone of voice . . . She studied him for a second. "Wait. You're saying you're here as a friend, but . . . You know she didn't do it, don't you?"

"Would you like a glass of champagne?" he asked.

He did know Alison didn't do it! A part of her wanted to jump in the air (something difficult to do in three-inch heels) and give a little yippee. She was right and he knew she was right. Did he also suspect Ryan's group of friends? But a part of her wanted to snap at him—because he didn't think Alison did it. Yet, the charges hadn't been dropped.

"You want to tell me what you know?" she whispered.

"You want to tell me what *you* know?"

She crossed her arms. "You going to have the charges dropped against Alison?"

"No reason to do that. She's still our prime suspect."

There were voices now coming from the front hall. Feminine laugher. Nikki recognized Betsy's voice. Diara's. She moved to face the door, standing beside Dombrowski. Waiting, apprehensively. "Feel a little like James Bond tonight?" she whispered.

He smiled.

And suddenly, there were twenty people in the library, all talking at once. The Disney Fab Four were there, and their spouses, minus Ryan, of course. Lex Bronson was there, Marshall's agent, Angel's agent, and their dates or spouses. Marshall's publicist. Introductions were being made. Dombrowski jumped right in, as if he spent every evening rubbing elbows with celebrities.

Watching him, Nikki was intrigued. *Who are you?* she wondered. Maybe she should take him up on that drink he once offered. Then she felt guilty. She cared for Jeremy. She maybe even loved him. She didn't know. And she certainly didn't know where they stood right now.

But she didn't have time for personal reflection right now.

Nikki put on *the smile* and approached her first victims. Betsy and Hazel were standing together chatting. "Betsy, Hazel. So nice to see you."

This time, Hazel's smile was wary. Something had changed since Nikki saw them the previous day at that pub.

"Nice to see you," Hazel said, sounding as awkward as she was acting. She was wearing her hair down, in a forties style with a side part, tucked behind one ear. A cute, black dress and towering black Christian Louboutin heels.

"Marshall's house is lovely," Betsy said. White cocktail dress, silver Christian Louboutin heels.

Had there been a sale somewhere?

"Did you help him buy it?" Betsy asked.

"I did. It had been on the market for a while. I think it's turning out to be a good investment."

"Ladies, I think you know Tom." Marshall stepped between Betsy and Hazel with Tom in tow.

"How are you, Mrs. Munro? Mrs. Gomez? It's nice to see you in more pleasant circumstances."

Betsy turned to Nikki. "The detective interviewed us. You know, after Ryan . . . died."

"If you'll excuse me," Marshall said. "My publicist is waving me down." He walked away.

Nikki met Dombrowski's gaze. "So, Hazel," she said, shifting her attention. "How was your shopping trip?" Again, she looked at the detective. "We ran into each other at The Grove yesterday, Hazel and Betsy and I."

"Ah," Dombrowski said. He had a lowball glass in his hand.

Single malt Scotch? Nikki wondered. Did that surprise her? It didn't.

"We had a great time. We always do," Hazel said, glancing over her shoulder at someone.

"And the pub was nice."

"Yeah, too bad your boyfriend couldn't join you." Again, Hazel.

"Too bad," Dombrowski echoed.

"Champagne?" Angel Gomez joined the group, a flute in each hand.

"Ooh, thanks." Hazel accepted a glass.

"Thanks," his wife said.

"Is this house over the top or what?" Angel asked. His words were slightly slurred.

Had he been drinking before he arrived?

"Bordering on obnoxious," Angel went on, grabbing another glass of champagne as a waiter went by. "One for you, Nikki?"

"No, thanks."

"I guess this is what happens when you have too much money," Angel went on.

He'd definitely been drinking.

"Seems rather unkind to criticize your host while you're drinking his champagne, doesn't it?" Dombrowski said.

Angel looked at him. "What the hell are you doing here?"

Hazel, at least, had the good sense to squirm a little. Betsy just looked at Dombrowski with distaste.

"An invited guest, the same as you." Dombrowski smiled, but there was something behind his smile. Nikki liked it. Not a threat, just . . . a warning.

"You don't belong here," Angel went on, taking a step closer to the detective, who was taller and broader shouldered than the singer. "You don't belong with people like us. In places like this."

"Angel," Betsy said softly. She rested her hand on her husband's arm, but he pushed her away. Hard.

Is this a man who could wrap a dog leash around his friend's neck and strangle him? Nikki wondered. *Possibly.*

"Angel." Marshall was back again. He smiled at his drunken guest. "I know you know Tom as the detective who investigated Ryan's death, but did you know his mother is a Tisch?"

Nikki knew her eyes got big. She met Dombrowski's gaze. His blue eyes were twinkling. His suits *were* tailored. And if she was a guessing girl, she'd guess that the Maserati in the driveway was his.

"Tisch?" Angel scoffed.

"I'm really sorry," Betsy murmured. "He's . . . had a long week."

"Loews Corporation," Marshall said. "You know, CBS, Loews theaters."

Angel stared at Dombrowski. "You mean he's rich?"

"Something like that." Marshall smiled. "Tom, I have a book I want to show you. Some kind of rare edition."

"Excuse me." Dombrowski met Nikki's gaze for a split second, then walked away.

Betsy led Hazel away to find an hors d'oeuvre. Which left Nikki standing alone with Angel. She wondered if Dombrowski was jealous. Was he watching them?

Nikki looked at Angel.

"What do you want?" he asked quietly, surprising her

with his vicious tone. When she didn't answer, he went on. "Leave *us* alone."

"I don't know what you're talking about." She held his gaze, wondering if it was the gaze of a killer. Mostly, right now, it looked like the gaze of a drunk. "Where were you when Ryan was killed?" she dared.

"Why do you care? The police already arrested the dog walker." He smirked. "But if you must know, I was having lunch. At Pizzeria Mozza. Check, if you like." Again, the smirk. Then he went on. "So, listen, I don't want you bothering my wife. Or Julian's. I don't want you talking to Diara, or Kameryn or Gil, either."

"Why?" She kept her voice down, but she felt like steam might be coming out of her ears. "Are you afraid that people are going to find out that the Fab Four aren't the sweethearts your publicity wants us to believe?"

He took a step toward her. "I'm warning you, back off. You don't know what we're capable of."

Nikki stared into his eyes for a moment. Was he threatening her? Or revealing a clue as to what had happened to Ryan? Either way, there was something in his green eyes that would have frightened her if she were more easily frightened.

"Nikki, good to see you again."

Nikki looked over to see Diara, arms linked with Kameryn. Had they come to diffuse the situation?

Nikki smiled. "Diara, I'm so sorry about Ryan."

"Thank you." She looked away and a few tears glistened in her eyes. She was dressed in a gorgeous white cocktail dress and sparkly white heels. Every hair on her long, blond head was perfect.

"Your mother's a delight to work with," Kameryn said. "We have a few days off from shooting. I hope she enjoys them."

Nikki watched Angel walk away. "I'm sure she will."

"Gil, honey, come say hi to Nikki." Kameryn waved her husband over. Like the other men in the room, he was dressed in a nice tux. Again, Nikki was struck by how similar in looks he was to Angel.

"Hey, Nikki." Gil flashed a handsome smile. He hadn't shaved in a couple of days, but it looked good on him. He could have done a menswear ad in *GQ* with his jawline. "It's good to see you again. It was nice of Marshall to invite us. Nice for all of us to get out. You know, after the tragedy." He slipped his arm around Diara, then his wife.

He was smooth; Nikki would give him that.

"It's nice to see you, too, Gil."

After that, they fell into conversation about *Casa Capri* and what was going on with the characters. It was awhile before Nikki could break away from the group. She tried several times to get to Lex Bronson, but he seemed to be purposely avoiding her. And watching Diara. Seeing him in the same room with her, Nikki could tell he was definitely enamored. He excused himself within an hour.

Nikki must have had a look of disappointment on her face because Marshall came over with a canapé for both of them. "I didn't get a chance to talk to him," she said quietly.

"Doesn't matter. He *is* having an affair with Diara. He thinks he's in love with her, but he didn't kill her husband."

She popped the lemongrass cured salmon canapé into her mouth. "No?"

He passed her his cocktail napkin so she could wipe her mouth. "Nope, in Brussels the week it happened."

"Guess I can cross him off my list." She turned to him. "Hey, why didn't you tell me Tom was a Tisch?"

A shrug. "Never came up, I guess."

"So he's a multimillionaire . . . and a cop?"

"I don't know his personal finances, but he grew up

well, yes. So," he lowered his voice, "you find out anything?"

She glanced in the direction of the Fab Four and their three remaining spouses, all standing together, alone, heads together. It reminded her of the first night she met them, at Victoria's garden party. That evening Ryan hadn't been with them either . . .

"Possibly," she whispered. "Very possibly."

Chapter 25

Sunday morning, Nikki's phone rang as she was making coffee. She wore boxer shorts, a T-shirt, and a robe. It was early for a call. She picked up her cell from the counter.

Victoria didn't wait for Nikki to speak. "How was the party at Marshall's? I don't know why I wasn't invited. I could have questioned the suspects."

Nikki frowned. If she kept it up, she was going to need Botox. "I thought you thought Alison did it," she said, keeping her voice down. Alison was still upstairs, but she could hear her moving around.

"I never said that."

"Mother, you most certainly—"

"So do you want to hear what I found out or not?"

Nikki poured boiling water over the fresh ground coffee in a French press. "Found out from where?"

"A party rental company in West Hollywood."

Nikki fitted the lid on the French press. "How did you—"

"I made phone calls, of course. Yesterday. I said my planner dropped the ball when she was arrested for murder and she wasn't returning my calls."

"Mother, whose name did you give?"

"I didn't *give a name*, Nicolette."

"And you talked to someone who knew Alison?"

"Ah, so *now* you want to hear what I know."

Nikki groaned.

"Have you thought any more about what we talked about, darling? About seeing a shrink?"

"That's an awful word. I don't need a psychiatrist." *What I need is caffeine before I talk to my mother.* She thought it, but knew better than to say it. "Back to what you found out?"

"Fine. Alison was buying some sort of party favors, renting costumes—"

"*Costumes?*"

"Let me finish," Victoria said. "She was renting costumes and props twice a month. She always rented them on a Friday or a Saturday and returned them on Monday. She refused delivery." She added, "Even though it's free."

Nikki leaned against the counter, utterly impressed. And a little in awe. "How do you *know* all this?"

"Joshua."

"Joshua who?"

"Heavens, I don't know. The young man who answered the phone at the seventh place I called. I told him I knew Victoria Bordeaux and offered to send him a signed glossy."

Nikki laughed. "I can't believe you, Mother."

"I can't believe myself sometimes," she chuckled.

"What made you decide to call party rental stores?"

"I saw no reason for that nice girl in the park to lie to you. Which meant maybe Alison was doing some sort of party work again. Maybe she doesn't like dogs as much as she thought she did. I, myself, don't understand how one can make a living *walking dogs.*"

"Back to the parties, Mother."

"From what I gather, Alison was throwing some sort of themed parties: knights, pirates, and so forth."

"Unbelievable," Nikki whispered to herself. "And you're absolutely sure it was Alison?"

"Well, I wouldn't have been calling to tell you if it wasn't Alison, now would I?"

She had a fair point.

"Did this Joshua know who she was giving parties for?"

"He did not. But he said it was a small group."

Nikki felt a buzzing in her head. It wasn't caffeine because she hadn't had any yet. "Did you ask how small?"

"Well, of course. Honestly, Nicolette."

Nikki waited. Victoria did know how to create drama.

"Eight," she finally said. "Always for eight. Four men. Four women. So four princes, four princesses, four pirates, four tavern wenches."

Nikki couldn't help herself. She laughed when her mother said "wenches."

"What on earth is so funny?" Victoria inquired.

"Nothing." Nikki grabbed a mug from the cupboard. "Thank you, Mother. I really appreciate this."

"Well, do you know what it all means?"

"No." Nikki poured her coffee. She heard Alison coming down the steps. "But I'm going to find out. I'll call you later."

"You do that."

Click.

Alison walked into the kitchen as Nikki poured half-and-half into her coffee. She didn't give Alison time to speak. "We need to talk."

"O . . . kay . . ." She drew out the word.

"Grab your coffee. Come on outside. It's beautiful out."

Alison stared at Nikki. "Is Jocelyn all right?"

"I'm sure she's fine." She grabbed an orange from a bowl of fruit on the counter and called to Stan and Ollie, who raced to the back door.

Her backyard was fenced in and overgrown with gorgeous flowering plants and bushes. Marshall was always telling her she needed to clean it up, but she liked it this way. It reminded her of an old English garden. She even had a little patch of herbs she could snip from for cooking.

There was a table for two under an arbor covered in clematis and honeysuckle. Nikki tied her robe around her waist before sitting down with her coffee. Stan and Ollie trotted down a stone path that wound around toward Rob's house. "Stay here, guys," she called after them. "No visiting this morning."

Five minutes passed before Alison came outside, looking pale and scared.

"Jocelyn's okay?" she asked again.

"I haven't heard from Jeremy, which means she's fine. Sit down."

The air smelled divine under the arbor. Nikki took a sip of coffee, letting Alison get settled in the teak chair across from her.

"At my mother's garden party, you told Marshall that Diara and Ryan didn't spend much time at clubs or out partying. You said they dined privately with their friends."

Alison kept her gaze downcast, concentrating on the coffee in her cup.

"You were talking about the Fab Four and their spouses."

Alison said nothing, but her pale face was looking paler by the second.

"I need to know what you were doing for them, Alison. Besides walking their dogs. Costumes? Twice a month?"

Alison was quiet for a moment; then her voice was shaky when she spoke. "Do you think it has anything to do with Ryan's murder?"

"I don't know," Nikki answered evenly. "Because I don't know what *it* is."

Alison pressed her lips together. She looked like she was going to cry, but she was fighting it. "The whole point was confidentiality. I signed something saying I'd never tell."

"And go to jail for murder if you had to?" Nikki challenged. "To keep their secrets?"

"If this gets out, if Farid finds out . . ." Alison's voice quickly took on a desperate tone. "No judge will let me keep Jocelyn. Making a skin flick fifteen years ago, before I was a wife or a mother, when I was young and foolish, that's one thing, but this—" Tears finally filled her eyes and she looked away.

"So tell me, tell me everything and maybe we can keep it from getting out." Nikki slid her hand across the teak table. "I'll do everything I can to keep the information private."

"It's too crazy. You won't believe me," Alison murmured.

"Try me."

Alison slowly dragged her gaze up to meet Nikki's. "Please find out who killed Ryan. I can't go to trial. I can't risk it."

"So tell me," Nikki insisted softly.

Then Alison launched into a tale that Nikki had to admit was far-fetched, but the longer Jeremy's sister talked, the more the puzzle pieces fell into place.

"I don't know how it even came about that they asked me," Alison began. "That . . . Angel asked me." She took a sip of her coffee. "I didn't just walk their dogs. I planned private parties for them. Very private parties."

Nikki kept her face blank. She didn't want to appear judgmental. She wasn't judgmental.

"They wanted private, themed parties at their houses. I was to provide the food, decorations, costumes, props, whatever. It was at different houses, but only the four houses."

"The houses of the Fab Four," Nikki said.

Alison nodded and went on. "It was always the same. I went in on a Friday or Saturday afternoon and set up. Just me. No help. I even went to the caterer and took the food to the houses myself. I carried the stuff in my van."

"So it looked like you were there to take care of a client's dog," Nikki said, "but actually . . ."

"Oh, I took care of their dogs, too." Alison nodded her head up and down. "This was just a way . . . to make extra money. You know what real estate costs these days. I'll show you my bank accounts. I can prove to you that I've been saving every penny I could. I wanted to get a nice place for us. For Jocelyn and me."

"So . . . you set up for the party on a designated day . . ." Nikki nudged. "And then what?"

"And then I left. And I went back the next morning and cleaned up the house. I removed all the costumes, props, caterer's equipment, whatever. And erased any video recorded on their security systems for the previous twenty-four hours. They said I wasn't to look and I never did. I didn't want to see what they were doing."

Nikki almost smiled at Alison's seeming innocence, which was interesting, considering the film she had once made. "That's why you knew how to erase the security footage at Diara and Ryan's house the day he was murdered?"

She nodded. "No one ever said what the parties were. What the eight of them were doing." Her voice trembled. "But I had a pretty good guess."

Nikki waited.

"I read about it in a magazine. It's called swinging. They . . . you know, share partners. Have sex with other people's husbands and wives."

Share partners . . . that was exactly what Maurice had suggested. It was what the men had been doing years ago when they were still filming *School Dayz*. And he'd said the girls were worse than the men.

"I didn't ask," Alison said. "They paid me well. To be discreet. It wasn't my business what they were doing."

And Alison had been discreet, hadn't she? The Fab Four had gotten away with it. There had never been a word about their *private parties* in print, blogged, or spoken. Their reputations had been protected.

"I'm sorry," Alison whispered. "I knew it was wrong, but I wasn't making enough money with the dogs. And this seemed like a quick, easy way to buy a home to take Jocelyn to." She gripped her coffee cup. "So do you think their parties have anything to do with Ryan's murder?"

Nikki sat back in her chair to think. She reached for the orange she had brought out and began to peel it. Her dogs had returned from whatever adventure they'd found in the garden and now lay under the table. Stan rested his head on her bare foot.

Her thoughts were flying in a hundred directions. They had paid Alison well to keep their secret. So what would they have done to protect it if it had been threatened from another source? Would they have paid to keep someone else's mouth shut? Even if *the someone* was one of them? That would explain Betsy and Hazel's meetings once a month with Ryan and the envelope. What if he was blackmailing the Fab Four? What if he was threatening to disclose their secret sex lives and destroy their squeaky-clean images?

Ryan had wanted money to open a club. An expensive club. It all made sense, in a crazy way.

So what happened? Why kill him? Had he demanded more money? Is that why he was murdered?

Which led to the next question. Who had done it? Not Diara or Kameryn. They had been at the studio.

Nikki looked at Alison, who sat in the chair looking like she just wanted to disappear. To fade away. "Can you tell me again what happened the day Ryan was murdered?"

"I've told you everything. I swear I have."

"I believe you. I just want to hear it again. In case . . . there's some detail you missed. I missed."

Alison exhaled. "Okay." She exhaled again. "I went to Ryan and Diara's house to pick up Muffin. Ryan was in a towel in the living room. He came on to me. He said he liked what he'd seen on the film he found on the Internet. He said he was tired of Diara getting away with whatever she wanted. He was going to do what he wanted to do." She stopped.

As Alison spoke, Nikki tried to picture it all in her mind. She'd been to the house. She remembered the white living room. "It's okay. Go on when you're ready."

"When I went into the living room to get Muffin, Ryan touched me. I pushed him away, and I left the house. I took the dogs to Runyon Canyon Park. When I took Muffin back to Ryan and Diara's house, he waved to me from the pool deck."

"But he was seated in the lounge chair, right?"

"I hung up the leash in the back and left by the front door. He waved from Diara's chair on my way out. I left the house, but I pulled over on Mulholland because I got to thinking about the security recordings and how paranoid Diara was about them. When they had the parties at their house, she always erased them herself. I was supposed to check, but they were already always erased."

"Wait. Go back. You said Ryan waved to you from Diara's lounge chair?"

She nodded. "Hers is the white one. Everything she had was white. You should have seen her bedroom." Alison took a deep breath. "So then I went back to the house, and I went to the pantry and erased the security recording for the day so Diara wouldn't know that Ryan and I had . . . had an altercation. I was on my way out of the house when I saw the fish guy. I went to my van. Then he came out and said Ryan was dead."

"Mars," Nikki said.

"Yeah. And you know the rest."

Both of them were quiet.

"So?" Alison finally said. "Do you know who did it?"

"No," Nikki said. She closed her eyes for a second. "But it's there. It's *right* there."

Chapter 26

A t noon, Nikki walked out onto her mother's stone terrace, which extended around the pool. The dogs ran past her and out onto the freshly cut grass.

Victoria was sitting in a lounge chair in a black bathing suit, wearing a big white hat. Nikki noted that she looked darned good for a woman her age.

Victoria had been reading. There was a pile of magazines on the glass table between two chaise longues: *Ladies' Home Journal*, *The Economist*, and *Variety*. Victoria Bordeaux had eclectic taste in reading.

Which was even more evident when Nikki saw the paperback book open in her mother's lap that featured a young woman in a bonnet on the cover. Nikki pulled off her T-shirt and tossed it on the vacant lounge chair. "What on earth are you reading?"

"An Amish romance. It's quite good."

Nikki laughed and stepped out of her gym shorts. Her bikini was bright blue.

After Alison left the house to walk clients' dogs, Nikki had felt restless. She'd had to get out of the house. She had so much going on in her head. Alison's story was so unbelievable that she believed her. Completely. She felt as if she had all the puzzle pieces that would lead her to Ryan's killer; she just had to put the pieces together.

Nikki's best guess right now was that Angel had killed Ryan. He'd jogged over to the house, killed him, and jogged home. Harley had seen him jogging home. But the previous night Angel had made a point of telling her he'd been at lunch when Ryan was killed. Had Harley been mistaken as to what time of day he'd seen Angel? Had Angel been lying about being at the restaurant?

"Since when are you reading Amish romances?" Nikki spread out a pink towel that Victoria had left on the chaise longue for her.

"Since I started reading this one. I bought it at the drugstore. It's very sweet. Renews my faith in mankind."

Nikki sat on the chaise and then laid back. "So what are you doing laying out in the sun?" She removed her Persol sunglasses and closed her eyes. "You never lay out."

"Vitamin D."

"I'm sorry?"

"I'm laying out to absorb vitamin D. And because it feels good."

"Ah."

"There's tonic water and I sliced a lemon. Would you like a drink?"

"You sliced a lemon?" Nikki asked. "You didn't have Ina do it?"

"No, I didn't have Ina do it." She slipped a bookmark into the paperback. "It's Sunday. Ina has the day off."

"Ah, that explains it."

Victoria was quiet for a moment. "Nicolette, that was unkind. I know you and I have this . . . repartee. It's part of who we both are, but . . ." She hesitated. "But I'm worried about you. It's not like you to be unkind."

Nikki groaned. "You're not going to use the word *shrink* again, are you? I didn't come here to talk about this."

"I think you did. I think you've needed to talk about it

for some time. For some reason, this nonsense with Alison has brought it all back."

Nikki reached for her sunglasses, then slid them on.

"You shouldn't feel badly that you did what you did to that monster. He was going to kill you."

"Mother."

"Say it. For me, if not for yourself. Say it."

Nikki pressed her lips together. "I killed Albert Tinsley to save myself and Erica."

"He would have raped and murdered and left you both buried in the desert like he did those other girls."

"But I didn't know that," Nikki whispered. "No one knew he was doing that." It had all come out later when the police investigated him.

"You knew your life was in danger," Victoria insisted.

Nikki felt her eyes sting with tears. What was wrong with her? She'd fought with Albert Tinsley in that parking lot over twenty years ago. Where were these feelings coming from? "I shouldn't have gotten in his car with him. I shouldn't have been drinking. I shouldn't have told Erica we should go."

"No, you shouldn't have."

Nikki pressed her lips together and looked out over the pool. The water was so blue and looked so inviting. Oliver lay under the diving board, in the shade. Stanley was standing on the edge of the pool, watching something. His shadow? A water bug?

"You shouldn't have been in that bar. You shouldn't have had too much alcohol to drink," Victoria went on. "And you *certainly* should not have gotten in his van with him."

"But I did," Nikki whispered.

"You did."

"He could have killed me." Tears slipped down Nikki's cheeks and she wiped them away, self-conscious. "He could have killed Erica."

"He would have," Victoria agreed. "But you didn't let him. You protected her when she couldn't protect herself."

Nikki squeezed her eyes shut. She remembered laughing and dancing with Erica and Albert Tinsley at the club where they met. He had been nicely dressed. Said he was in finance. She and Erica had agreed to go back to his apartment for a glass of wine after last call. On the way, Erica passed out in the back seat. It wasn't until he pulled into the abandoned parking lot that Nikki realized something was wrong. Something was *very* wrong with Albert Tinsley.

Nikki exhaled, fighting the flashes of memory. Usually she could keep them at bay.

She remembered how light from a streetlamp reflected off the steel barrel as he pulled the 9mm handgun out from under his seat. She remembered the smell of his cologne. The feel of her heart as it pounded in her chest. It was raining.

Everything happened so fast.

He told her to get out of the van. Erica was out of it on the back seat. Nikki remembered that when she glanced at her friend, she noticed that Erica only had one heel on. Blue. Where was her other shoe?

Albert told Nikki to get out of the van, then pointed the gun at her face when she refused.

Seeing the 9mm had sobered her.

Nikki couldn't leave Erica in the van, not with a man with a gun. She hollered to Erica, called her name. But Erica wouldn't wake up. Albert got mad. He said he'd shoot Nikki; then he'd take Erica with him, *do what he wanted,* and then he said he'd kill her, too. He told her he'd done it before. She had believed him.

The parking lot was empty. It was three-thirty in the morning. Nikki had remembered thinking that no one would hear her scream. No one would hear the gunshot when he killed her.

"Nicolette?" Victoria murmured.

Nikki shuddered. She didn't remember making any plan. She just knew she couldn't get out of the van. Not leave Erica with him.

He got out of the van and walked around it to Nikki's door, holding the gun on her. When he started to open it, she pushed as hard as she could, startling him. He fell back, dropping the handgun. Nikki fell out of the van, onto the wet pavement, and scrambled to get to the gun.

He came at her with a knife from a sheath on his ankle. A hunting knife, with a serrated edge. She remembered thinking to herself that financiers didn't carry hunting knives.

Nikki felt her mother's hand on her arm. Victoria was sitting on the chaise longue beside her. Nikki didn't see her mother move over.

Nikki cringed as, in her mind's eye, she saw Albert lunge at her with the knife. He said terrible, awful things about what he was going to do to her with the knife.

So Nikki pulled the trigger.

"If you hadn't come . . ." Nikki realized she was sobbing. "If you hadn't come . . ."

"If I hadn't come, you'd have dealt with it yourself just fine."

Nikki shook her head. "No, I couldn't have . . ."

Nikki had called Victoria that night. From Albert's cell phone. Amondo had put Victoria on the phone. Victoria had been calm. She had told Nikki to get in the van and lock herself inside with Erica. She had told her to say nothing to the police, to anyone until she arrived. Then she had disconnected. First, Victoria had called her attorney, then the police.

Even when the police arrived, the ambulances, the EMTs, Nikki had said nothing until her mother and the attorney had arrived. At first glance, it looked like Nikki had simply shot a man. It was Victoria who held Nikki's hand, who kept telling her everything was going to be all right.

"It's all right," Victoria soothed, putting her arms around Nikki.

Nikki sat up and clung to her mother.

"It's going to be all right, darling," Victoria assured her. "It's just a nasty old nightmare. You're going to be fine."

"But I wouldn't have been," Nikki managed, her tears falling on her mother's bare shoulder.

In the weeks and months that had followed Albert Tinsley's death, Victoria had helped Nikki put the pieces of her life back together. The pieces of herself. It was after that that Nikki began to find herself, her true self. That was when she started working for her father, first in his restaurant, later managing apartments. That job had led her to become a real-estate broker.

"Shhh," Victoria soothed, stroking Nikki's hair.

"I'm sorry." Nikki let go of her mother and pulled off her sunglasses to wipe her face with a towel from the table. "I don't know what's wrong with me," she sniffled.

Victoria, who had removed her sunglasses, gazed into Nikki's eyes. In Victoria's Bordeaux blues, Nikki saw herself.

"Sometimes a girl needs a good cry." Victoria brushed her hand across Nikki's cheek. "How about a little tonic water?"

Nikki sniffed. "Sure. I could use something to drink. I'll get it." She started to get up.

"Nonsense." Her mother rose. "I'll get it, and then we'll just sit here for a while and enjoy the peace and quiet. And when you're ready, you can tell me all about your conversation with Alison this morning."

By the time Victoria returned with the drink, Nikki had wiped away her tears and actually *did* feel better. She didn't understand what had been going on in her head, but just allowing herself to relive killing Albert Tinsley, just for a moment, had been cathartic. She didn't think about the incident often, so maybe she needed to allow herself a few tears over it once in a while.

Victoria poured her daughter a drink and added a slice of lemon. "Put some sunblock on, dear," she instructed as she sat in her chaise longue and adjusted her hat. "Use mine."

Nikki took a drink of the tonic water and then, while applying sunblock, relayed to her mother everything Alison had told her. When she got to the sex party part, she warned her mother she could never speak of it, not to anyone, including Alison. Or Jeremy.

"Good heavens," Victoria remarked. "I know what gossip to repeat and what gossip not to repeat. How do you think I've made it this long in this town?"

Nikki laughed and went on with her story. Victoria was fully onboard until Nikki got to the timeline.

"So, you think Angel went into the house, after Alison dropped off the dog, killed him, and was gone before the fish tank guy arrived?" Victoria made a face. "That could have been only minutes."

"Yeah, I know. That's one of the flaws in my thinking."

"And Alison was certain he waved to her and he wasn't already dead in the chair?"

"She included that detail from the beginning, even when she wasn't telling the whole truth. I don't think she made it up. Why would she? If she knew he was dead, she wouldn't have said he waved to her."

"What do you think after seeing the Fab Four and their spouses last night? Did Angel seem guilty?"

"He was a total jerk. But did he seem like he'd killed his friend?" Nikki rose and pulled on her shorts. "I don't know. Maybe." She thought for a second. "The thing is, they were all acting weird. Tense."

Victoria watched her dress. "You certain you won't stay and have an early dinner with me?"

"No, I want to go home and relax for a little while, while the house is quiet. Alison thought Jeremy would be dropping Jocelyn off around six. She said she'd be home by then and make dinner."

"You think they'll be staying with you all week, or going back to Jeremy's?"

She exhaled and pulled her T-shirt over her head. "I don't know. We'll see. Stanley! Oliver! Let's go, boys!" The dogs sprinted past her and around the house. Nikki stood for a moment, wanting to say something, not sure what. "Mother . . ."

Victoria smiled. "You're welcome, darling."

Nikki walked away. Victoria waved from her chair; Nikki only saw her hand.

"Ring me later," Victoria called.

Chapter 27

At home, Nikki opened the gate and set the dogs free in the backyard. Then she went through the front door, into the house, cradling her phone on her shoulder. She was on hold with Pizzeria Mozza, waiting for the sommelier, David, to come to the phone. David was one of Jeremy's patients and always made a fuss when she and Jeremy had dinner there.

As Nikki walked into the living room, she heard the dogs barking. She wondered if Marshall was home and they could see him through one of the gaps in the fence. Sometimes, when he was there, if they barked, he'd let them come over and play.

While she waited, she pulled off her T-shirt, stepped out of her flip-flops, and slipped off her shorts. She left them by the door; they smelled of sunblock and she wanted to toss them in the washer.

"Pizzeria Mozza, this is David," Nikki heard in her ear.

"David, hi. This is Nikki Harper, Dr. Fitzpatrick's—"

"Nikki, of course. Need a quick reservation?"

"No." She chuckled. "Actually, I have a question and it's going to sound crazy, but . . . do you remember if Angel Gomez was in for lunch on a Tuesday three weeks ago?"

"He was."

Nikki was completely taken aback by David's quick answer. "He was? You're sure?"

"Absolutely. It was the same day Ryan Melton was murdered. I'll never forget it as long as I live. Such a sad day." David's voice was full of emotion. "I think Angel may have actually gotten the call that Ryan was dead while he was still here. I was in the back, but everyone said he got a phone call and then he got up and left. Tragic. *Just tragic.* I can't imagine having your friend murdered. Strangled with a dog leash." She heard him shudder. "And poor Dr. Fitzpatrick. Having his sister arrested."

"Thanks so much, David," Nikki said, lost in thought. So, was Harley mistaken about the day he saw Angel jogging? About the time?

"You're welcome. I hope I see you and Dr. Fitzgerald soon."

"Have a good day," Nikki said. As she hung up, she realized the dogs were still barking out back. But now it was an odd bark. It was their *there's a stranger at the door* bark.

Nikki went to the back door, slid the dead bolt, and opened the door to find Betsy Gomez. She was wearing a pink, flirty dress, high heels, and white dress gloves. And holding a gun.

Nikki took a step back, feeling like the whole scenario was a little bizarre. She was barefoot, in a teeny bikini. Angel Gomez's wife looked like she was dressed for *Breakfast at Tiffany's.* Nikki stared at the pistol, not fully comprehending what was happening.

Betsy walked in the door, followed by Hazel, who was also in a dress, four-inch heels, and white elbow-length gloves. Hazel was carrying a Fendi shopping bag on her elbow. They left the back door standing open.

"You want me to go back out and break in the door with that concrete block so it looks like—"

"We'll do that later!" Betsy snapped at Hazel.

"What do you want?" Nikki stared at the gun barrel pointed at her. With a silencer. She thought about Albert Tinsley, but wasn't any more afraid than she was a second ago, even though maybe she should have been. The silencer suggested these women meant business. "What are you doing?"

"Turn around," Betsy ordered. Her voice trembled, but her hands were steady.

Nikki calculated that, at this distance, if Betsy pulled the trigger, she wouldn't miss. The gun looked to be a .38. A shot in the back would likely kill her. Two or three would do her in, for sure.

And now Betsy was trying to corner her in the galley kitchen. Nikki knew she didn't have a chance if they backed her up against a wall. Or the cabinets.

So Nikki turned her body slightly so that as Betsy backed her up, she stepped into the hall that connected to the living room, rather than deeper into the kitchen.

"You killed him?" Nikki asked, still slowly backing up, hoping her words would distract the women from what she was doing. "You killed Ryan?"

"No, I didn't kill him!"

Nikki glanced over Betsy's shoulder to meet Hazel's gaze. "You did it?"

"No, thank God I didn't draw the straw." She pressed her hand to her chest. "I don't know if I could have done it."

"*Drew the straw?*" Nikki asked.

"Turn around!" Betsy stretched her arms out a little farther, the black gun with its long silencer pointed right at Nikki's chest.

"You're going to kill me? How do you think you're going to get away with it?" Nikki tried to sound derisive. Intimidating. "You'll never get away with it. Dombrowski will be on you within hours."

"It's going to look like a robbery," Hazel explained. She

held up the Fendi bag. "We're going to take your jewelry. Your wallet and credit cards. Bury them."

Nikki drew one hand over her chest. All she could think of was that she needed to stall them. Stall for time. Time would give her . . . time to think of something . . . or maybe even give Alison the opportunity to arrive. "Could . . . could I put on my shirt? I . . . I feel . . . *naked.*"

"Just turn around!" Betsy shouted. "You don't want to see me do it, do you?"

"God, Betsy, let her put her shirt on." Hazel looked at her friend. "Would you want to be found dead in *your* bikini?"

Nikki had backed her way far enough that now she was in front of the door where she had left her clothes. Watching Betsy, she squatted and grabbed her blue T-shirt.

The dogs flew into the house and came down the hall, barking. They startled Hazel and she did a little sidestep, wobbling on her four-inch heels.

"What are you talking about, drawing straws?" Nikki came to her feet slowly and pulled her shirt over her head. "If you're going to kill me, you should at least tell me *why* you're killing me."

"We're killing you because you wouldn't mind your own business. *We* hired the lawyer. She would have gotten the dog walker off. But you couldn't let it be, could you?" Betsy demanded.

The dogs were still barking.

"Shut them up," Betsy warned. "Or I'll shoot them first."

That scared Nikki more than standing at the end of Betsy's gun barrel. "Stanley! Oliver! Hush."

Oliver jumped up on the couch. Stanley trotted around the two women and stood between Nikki and Betsy. He growled deep in his throat. It was a pretty big growl for such a little guy.

"So you hired Lillie Lambert?" Nikki asked Hazel.

"We did it together. All of us."

"Hazel!" Betsy said. "Let's just do this and get out of here. Turn around!" she shouted at Nikki.

"Please." Nikki held up her hand. "I just . . . I want to understand what happened."

Hazel looked at Betsy. "No one will ever know," she said quietly. "And she was nice to us. No one's ever very nice to us, unless they're sucking up."

Nikki took another step back. They were now in the rectangular living room. The fireplace was behind her; the couch, where Oliver perched, was to her left, under the windows. Unfortunately, the drapes were closed, to keep out the afternoon sun. No one driving or walking by would see that she was being held at gunpoint.

"We drew straws," Hazel said. "Ryan had to die. Diara couldn't just divorce him. He was going to tell people about our private parties. He was going to ruin everyone's career. Ruin our lives."

"Private parties?" Nikki asked.

"Hazel," Betsy warned.

Hazel looked at Betsy, then back at Nikki. "He was blackmailing us so he could open his stupid club, which would fail, just like his stupid restaurant failed. And we were fine giving him the money for a while, even Diara pitched in. Julian said he wasn't even asking that much, the idiot. Twenty-five thousand a month."

"But then he asked for more," Nikki said.

"How'd you guess?" Hazel asked.

"So you decided to kill him?" Nikki tried to figure out if there was anything in the living room she could use as a weapon. The fireplace tools were too far behind her. There was a vase made of green carnival glass on the end table, but it was so lightweight it wouldn't be much help. "You said you *drew straws*. What did you mean?"

"That's just what they call it," Hazel explained. "It was toothpicks. At your mother's party. Seven toothpicks.

Angel broke the tip off one of them and held them out for us to choose. We each had to take one and whoever had the broken one had to kill Ryan."

Nikki thought about that evening at the garden party, how the Fab Four and their spouses had all been standing together when Nikki was talking to Ryan. When she and Ryan approached the group, Diara had slipped something into her handbag. A toothpick. They had just decided who was going to kill Ryan, with him standing twenty feet away.

"And *Gil* got the broken toothpick," Nikki said, as much to herself as to the women. Harley had seen *Gil* jog by the day Ryan was murdered, not *Angel*. They looked so similar that Harley had mistaken one man for the other. She thought about her mother, waving good-bye to her from the chaise longue this afternoon. And it was *not* Ryan who had waved to Alison. It was Gil. He had been there when she brought Muffin back. When he heard Alison, he sat in Diara's chaise. Ryan had been found dead in his chair, not Diara's.

"Gil did it? Oh, God, poor Gil," Hazel said. She looked at Nikki. "We didn't know which one of us got it. We weren't supposed to say. That way, if we were questioned—"

"You wouldn't know anything," Nikki finished for her.

Hazel pointed at Nikki, the Fendi bag on her arm. "Right. That was Angel's idea."

"That doesn't surprise me." Nikki looked right at Betsy. "So that's how you got here today? You drew straws again?"

"Last night, after the cocktail party. When Angel sobered up." Again, it was Hazel who provided the explanation.

"That's enough," Betsy warned. We should just do this, Hazel, and get out of here."

"We went to Kameryn and Gil's last night," Hazel went on, seeming as if she needed to confess to someone. Nikki was the perfect person because she could take the Fab

Four's secrets to her grave. "And Angel said we had to do something to protect ourselves. He said we would all go to jail. Maybe death row." Her eyes began to tear up. "I didn't want to draw straws again. I didn't want to be the one to have to kill you, but Julian said I had to draw. He said it was only fair."

"Cocktail straws," Betsy murmured.

"Betsy got the straw Angel had cut. She was crying in the bathroom. I felt so bad for her," Hazel admitted, "that I told her I would come with her. You know, for moral support. That's when we came up with the idea of the robbery. That's why we're wearing the gloves. No fingerprints." She held up her hands.

"Okay, enough," Betsy snapped. "Nikki, either turn around or I'm just going to pull the trigger, and if you watch me, my aim might be bad. I . . . I might not kill you with the first shot. And . . . and I think it's going to hurt." She took a step toward Nikki and Stanley began to growl again.

"Wait, wait! One more thing, please." Now Nikki's voice was trembling. If these two women had participated in that elaborate scheme to protect their husbands and their friends, there was no reason to believe they weren't going to do this. She couldn't see how Tom wouldn't figure out who did it eventually. But she'd still be dead.

"Alison," she said. "Was the plan to make it look like she did it?"

Hazel shook her head. "There was no plan. If you got the short toothpick, you had to figure out a way to do it yourself. I guess Alison was just at the wrong place at the wrong time. Betsy and I felt bad for her. That's why we decided to hire Lillie Lambert. Because we knew she'd get Alison off. Alison was always nice to me," she added.

Betsy raised the gun.

Nikki's breath caught in her throat.

Stanley growled. Oliver whined. Stanley growled louder.

"Call him off!" Betsy warned, "Or I swear to God I'll shoot him." She turned slightly, moving the pistol in the direction of the dog.

Nikki saw a flash of black and white and brown out of the corner of her eye. At the same time that Betsy turned toward Stanley, Oliver flew off the couch, hitting Betsy in the back. Oliver howled. Stanley growled and went after Betsy as she fell forward on her knees.

The pistol hit the hardwood floor and spun. Slid. Nikki dove for the gun.

Hazel screamed.

Betsy screamed and flailed as she scrambled to get to her feet and get the dogs off her.

Stan and Ollie shot out of the living room, through the dining room, and headed for the back door.

By the time Betsy looked up, Nikki was holding the pistol on her. Hazel began to cry.

"Get in the kitchen," Nikki ordered. She had no intention of giving them any chance to get away. "Or I swear I'll shoot you," she threatened.

Hazel helped Betsy to her feet. In the fall, the heel had broken off one of her white Jimmy Choo shoes; she had to hobble to the kitchen.

"I'm sorry. I'm so sorry," Hazel blubbered. "I didn't want to kill you. I didn't want to kill Ryan. I swear I didn't."

Nikki escorted both women to the galley kitchen where she picked her cell phone up off the counter. She scrolled through her contacts and hit Send.

He answered on the second ring. "Nikki."

"Tom." Nikki's voice quivered. "Could you come to my house?" She gave the address. "And send a patrol car. Now. You're going to need to take someone into custody."

He swore. "You okay?"

She managed a smile. "Going to be."

"What happened?" Dombrowski asked.

"I'll let Betsy and Hazel tell you when you get here."

Chapter 28

"This is an awfully expensive gift, Nicolette," Victoria declared, standing back to look at the fish tank, while Nikki fiddled with the timer on the light. "But it *is* beautiful."

"I'm glad you like it." Nikki hit the button once and nothing happened, then again and the light glowed, but didn't come on.

She'd been surprised when her mother accepted the gift. She was even more surprised when Victoria said she wanted it in her boudoir. A 150-gallon fish tank wasn't exactly *old Hollywood*.

"I just love the pink sand," Victoria declared, clasping her hands. She was wearing her usual Saturday afternoon attire: white jogging suit, pristine tennis shoes, and her pearls.

Nikki squinted to read the miniscule directions on the top of the timer.

"Here, use my readers." Victoria lifted her glasses from her head and handed them to Nikki.

Nikki slid them on.

"Now, what kind of fish do I have again? I want to know if someone asks."

Nikki could see the directions on the timer now, but they were complicated. "You plan to bring a lot of guests into your bedroom?"

"You think I'm too old to have guests?" Victoria sniffed.

Nikki smiled. "I got you the freshwater tank instead of saltwater. You've got rosy barbs and pink kissing gourami."

"Silly names for fish."

"Okay, I'm pushing the button six times, like the directions say, but nothing is happening. It was working fine yesterday when I left here." Nikki removed her mother's reading glasses. "What did you do to the light?"

"I just turned it on."

"You're not supposed to *turn it on*," Nikki explained patiently. "It's on a timer. So the fish have day and night."

Victoria gave a wave. "Just leave it. That nice young man Saturn said he'd come by tomorrow and check on me. He can fix it."

"Mars?" Nikki handed her the glasses. "At least it's on now, so you can see the fish." She reseated the lamp and stepped back to look at the very pink tank. Her mother had even picked out pink artificial plants and fake coral.

"Beautiful." Victoria clasped her hands. "Now come sit and tell me how you are. I feel like I haven't talked to you in weeks."

Nikki followed her to the couch. Victoria had had Amondo move her TV over so she could sit on her couch and also look at the fish tank.

"I'm fine." Nikki sat down. "I'm great. I can't stay. Jeremy and I are going out to dinner tonight. Just the two of us. He got a babysitter."

"Very nice, dear. So that means things are better between you?"

"We're good." She smiled, thinking about Jeremy. "We're great. He was relieved to get Alison and Jocelyn settled into their new house in San Diego."

"And they're doing well?"

"Very well. Jocelyn is volunteering as a counselor at a

kids' summer camp and is loving it. And Alison has a new job, which does not involve dogs or party planning."

"Well, I'm sure Lillie Lambert was disappointed to lose her client."

"Probably not," Nikki said wryly. "She gained seven. One with a murder one charge, and six with a conspiracy to murder charge. That should keep her busy for a while."

Victoria laughed. "And your detective managed to keep the whole sex party thing out of the papers. Alison's ex never heard a word about it. I'm still amazed."

"He's not my detective."

"No, I suppose not." Victoria looked at her. "But he could have been."

Nikki patted her mother's knee. "I should go. I promised Stan and Ollie a run before I go out."

"Fine. Hurry off, if you must. Leave your poor mother here alone to watch TV and eat soup from a tin."

Nikki shook her head as she got up and headed for the door. "Ina left you salmon and capers. I saw the plate in the fridge. But you can come to dinner with Jeremy and me if you like."

"Certainly not." Victoria followed her out of the bedroom and down the hall. "Tell Jeremy I said hello and that I expect him to come to Movie Night next week."

"Oh, you're having Movie Night next week?" Nikki glanced over her shoulder. "I wasn't sure what your shooting schedule would be."

"I'm only shooting two days next week. The writers are working on the tragic death of Diara's and Kameryn's characters. I think they went down in the Pacific in a hot air balloon."

The doorbell rang as Nikki went down the grand staircase. "Expecting anyone?"

"No."

In the black and white tiled front hall, Nikki opened the

door to find Elvis Presley. "E?" she murmured. And smiled.

"Little lady."

He was wearing a tuxedo she'd never seen. "*The Steve Allen Show*," she said. "Nineteen fifty-six."

He nodded and then gave her his best lopsided grin. "I was wondering . . . is Mother home?"